ROTTEN WITH HONOUR

also by Derek Robinson: *Goshawk Squadron*

ROTTEN WITH HONOUR

derek robinson

The Viking Press   New York

Published in 1973 by The Viking Press, Inc.
625 Madison Avenue, New York, N.Y. 10022
Published simultaneously in Canada by
The Macmillan Company of Canada Limited
SBN 670-60858-0
Library of Congress catalog card number: 73-2337
Printed in U.S.A.

Acknowledgment is made to Chappell & Co. Inc.,
for lines from *I Wish I Were in Love Again*,
Copyright © 1937 by Chappell & Co. Inc.
Copyright renewed.
Used by permission of Chappell & Co. Inc.

for Mike and Ann

ROTTEN WITH HONOUR

THE RUSSIAN AMBASSADOR WATCHED

Starin trot down the steps of the Trade Mission, and felt an odd mixture of envy and distaste. The man was certainly very fit for his age; but all the same, wasn't there something of a *posture* about such alertness, a sort of advertisement that he was still totally in command of his squalid job? Yes, there was. The Ambassador took a deep breath and prepared to be pleasant.

The Ambassador's driver held the door and Starin got in, without breaking step. The door closed. The driver walked away and stood in the sunshine.

"I was just passing," the Ambassador said. "So I thought I'd call."

"You could have come inside, Mr. Ambassador. We're not burning anybody with cigarette ends today. I know how the smell sets off your asthma." Starin sounded pleased with himself.

"No doubt," the Ambassador said, "but I make it a rule never to go inside departments such as yours. I suppose some people might consider that cowardly, but I've found it eliminates a great many problems, and problems are never in short supply, are they?"

"Ah," Starin said. "I have a feeling that we are about to come to the point."

"Yes, we are. You've probably heard that the British are becoming restless once more, and if you haven't heard then I'm telling you now, officially."

"What d'you mean, 'restless'?"

"You know what I mean, Starin. They see too many people like you in London. Also too many Czechs, Poles, Hungarians, East Germans, Bulgarians, and Romanians, all of them quote diplomats unquote. They are terribly polite, the British. They keep sending us little Notes about the parking problem and how much worse it becomes when we leave our cars in the wrong place. What they mean is kindly stop parking your big Communist noses in our secrets."

"That's their problem, not your problem."

"It'll be my problem if they decide to purge our embassies. Again."

Starin spread his hands. "If I can help in any way, Mr. Ambassador," he said, "you have only to ask."

The Ambassador looked out of the window. He was tired of this interview already; he had known that it wouldn't work, and now it wasn't working, so why keep trying? "My accounts department say they advanced a lot of money to you," he said. "And they still don't know where it went or what we got for it."

"*We* got?"

"All right, then, *you* got." The Ambassador rapped on the window.

"Information is what I got. That's what I'm here for."

"And *they're* here to balance the books. And *I'm* here to carry the can."

His driver opened the door. Starin got out. He stood for a moment in the sunshine, snapping his fingers to a Latin beat, and then turned away. He spoke as he went. "All accountants live in the past, Mr. Ambassador," he said. "They're actually half dead. If I had my way I think I'd finish the job."

"Thank you, Stanley," Major Divine said. He took the six green files and propped them on the edge of his desk and the bottom of his waistcoat. Hubbard went away to the middle of the room and stood looking intelligent but not clever.

Divine read each file, grunting meaninglessly for Hubbard's benefit as he closed one and opened the next. At the end he said, "And who would you choose?"

Hubbard took off his glasses and polished them with the end of his tie. "Eady or Boyle," he said. He put his glasses on to see how well he had done.

"Splendid fellows both," Divine said. "Smart and experienced agents. In this case, I think we need somebody a bit more second-rate. I think we'll have . . . Hale."

"David Hale? He's not very experienced—"

"But enough, Stanley, enough." Divine opened the file. "Twenty-six, Oxbridge, degree in languages. Cover job in merchant banking—Flekker Handyside, just down the road. No particular politics or religion. No wife, no kids, both parents dead and his next of kin is about seventeen times removed and lives in Buenos Aires. He's as free as the wind, and nobody will give a damn if he dies tomorrow. Perfect." He turned the pages, glancing at the paragraph headings. "You don't agree," he murmured.

"I'm sure you're right, Major. It's just that . . . at twenty-six and not *terribly* experienced, this would seem to be a rather challenging task."

Divine grunted; he was still stock-taking. "Hale had a love affair last year," he said. "His first grand passion, apparently. He spent several months in the furnace and came out looking like a piece of wrought iron."

Hubbard clicked his tongue.

"He'll have got over all that by now, though," Divine said. "He'll be all wound up and ready to go. Get him in, as soon as you can."

———————————

David Hale slid a sheet of paper from his document wallet and pushed it across the desk. "That's the outline of the Lavagarde deal," he said. "He and I hashed it out between us."

Brandon, his boss, looked slightly startled. "Already?" he

said. He scanned the paper. "I thought Lavagarde was in Montreal."

"Yes, he is; staying at the Saint Pierre. That's where I phoned him."

"Did you, by God? Whose idea was that?"

"Mine. I got him at breakfast. I heard he's usually at his best at breakfast."

"Yes, so it seems. . . . Well, that's not a bad start, certainly." He gave the paper back. "Lavagarde thinks the project's worth nine million, does he? I'd have settled for eight, myself, but . . ."

"As a matter of fact, he reckons it's worth ten and a half," Hale said, "and we can go to eleven if necessary."

Brandon raised his eyebrows. "More strength to your collective elbows," he said.

Hale went back to his office. He looked at his appointment book, at his watch, and at the man waiting for him. "I can only give you ten minutes, Jeremy," he said.

"Right. I'll stick to genuine scandal and leave out the wild rumours." He opened his briefcase.

Hale watched him and wondered where he got his information. Jeremy Sanders was a free-lance financial consultant who was said to know more about the international rackets in exchange currencies than anybody still at large. Once a month he visited Flekker Handyside and briefed the account executives. He was an interesting little man, a few years older than Hale, with a face like a collapsed rubber ball: not impressive, but not without appeal, either.

"Ready?" Sanders said. Hale nodded. The telephone rang as Sanders opened his mouth. Hale answered it.

"Hubbard here," a man said.

For a second the name meant nothing; and then it meant everything. "Yes indeed," Hale said. "I'll come over straight-away." Already he was half-standing.

"What a pity," Sanders said. "Just when something strange

is about to happen to the Australian dollar." Hale waved good-bye from the door.

Hale felt the first flicker of excitement as he passed through the security check on the fourth floor of the office block in Tottenham Court Road. Divine's room was on the sixth floor, which was as high as Hale had ever been; he knew that K2 had two more floors above that, but he didn't know what went on up there.

One woman and four men were waiting to see Divine. Hubbard steered Hale past them, knuckled the door once, delicately, to remove any flies which might have been resting on the other side, and showed him in.

Divine shook his hand and at the same time gave him a glossy eight-by-six print. "Mikhail Starin," he said. "Taken at London Airport a couple of weeks ago while he wasn't looking."

Hale looked at the picture. It showed a short, strong man, about five-eight or -nine, with a trim figure and a pleasant face. His mouth seemed willing to smile, there was plenty of brow, and his eyes were alert. He wore his hair short, with a modest wave at the front, and his slightly snub nose gave him a boyish air. The camera had caught a few lines at the corners of the eyes and some creases in the neck. Hale guessed he was in his fifties. The way he was standing—feet slightly apart and weight equally divided, hands clasped behind him—he might have been a games master at an up-and-coming boys' school. "Mikhail Starin," Hale repeated.

"A most dependable man is Starin," Divine said. "He never knocks anybody down unless he plans to kick them in the teeth. We know of a minimum twenty-four people he's killed, not counting immediate family. He had his mother shot in 1937. She was Irish, she'd married a Russian merchant seaman and settled there. They raised Starin to be bilingual. Perhaps that's why he hates the British so much." He gave Hale another photograph.

"Tell me what you make of *him.*"

It was a portrait shot, full face, and the first thing Hale noticed were the eyes: pitiful and hard-done-by, the eyes of a man who has just mopped a thousand floors and watched ten thousand dirty feet march over them. The eyes were guarded by steep, suspicious brows above and dark concentric rings below, ripples pushing outwards to contact a hostile shore. But what the eyes began the rest of the face could not maintain. The nose was too long and twisted one way, the mouth was too narrow and twisted the other. The chin began a controlled retreat in the general direction of the Adam's apple, and the retreat became a rout. It was a face that could obey but would never trust; scepticism was its last surviving privilege.

"He looks like the man who cleans out the lavatories at Euston Station, sir," Hale said.

"His name's Kamarenski. Georg Kamarenski." They sat down, Divine at his desk, Hale on a sofa. "Couple of weeks ago Starin turned up in London and set up shop in a brand-new Trade Mission which the Russians opened in Islington, of all places. It raised a few eyebrows, because we all thought Starin was getting pensioned off, or at least busy throwing snowballs back home in deepest Disneyland."

Divine found a telegram lying on the floor and began making an aeroplane out of it.

"Now, one reason we're so good at making the Russians behave themselves in this country is that we know a lot of people they send here before they ever arrive. In this case we have no idea what Starin's up to." Divine squinted at Hale down the half-finished aeroplane. "But we do have a man inside their Mission. He's Georg Kamarenski, and I've had a message to say that he's on to something. I want you to find out what." Divine spoke these words flatly and finally, like a man informing his mistress that he has been unfaithful. Hale blinked.

"How on earth did you get Kamarenski inside, sir?" he asked. "I thought they always brought everybody with them."

"So they do. They brought Kamarenski. You're probably too

young to remember, but the R.A.F. had a couple of airfields in Russia during the last war. Kamarenski worked at one of them. He picked up quite a bit of English, which is why they've brought him here now."

"Why is he risking his neck for us?"

Divine shrugged. "There's a good reason—something typically agonizing in the way of psychological thumbscrews, which we can apply any time we want to. That's the main reason. We also give him fifty quid a week, for the sake of appearances."

Hale looked at Kamarenski's photograph. "He doesn't look very bright," he said.

"Quite true. Kamarenski is indeed stupid, but he's not foolish, and he has a remarkable memory. That's how he learned his English." Divine studied his aeroplane, and did some more work on the wings. "What's more, they've made him general handyman at the Mission, so he potters about and fixes things, like door handles and light bulbs and sticky windows. We've given him some special tools, all very battered and used looking, with cameras hidden in the handles. He points his screwdriver one way and takes a picture the other."

"And you think he's done it? He must have nerves like anchor chain, sir."

"Well, most men can be brave when they have no alternative. Kamarenski has something to help him: he stammers like the very devil. What good d'you think a bad stammer would be, David?" Divine began experimenting with the tail section.

Hale said, "The only thing I can think of is camouflage. It must be hard to know whether a man with a stammer is panicking or just stammering."

"Right. A stammer is an excellent mask—which of course is the reason why stammerers do it. What other reward does your stammerer get from his affliction?"

Hale looked across at Divine. The man shaved his face right up to the cheekbones, he noticed, giving it a polished, wooden look. It was a strong, unblinking face; if you could hit it hard enough you might break it, but it would never crack or warp, never mellow. Its structure was too rectilinear: the brows ran parallel to the mouth, the angle of the nose matched the angle of the chin, the jaws and the cheeks met in flat, exact planes. His eyes were as dispassionate as a child's; they offered nothing and concealed nothing. "Pity," Hale said with more force than he meant.

"Right again. Stammers, stutters, cleft palates, hare-lips, clubfeet, amputees—I've used them all. They're not only cheap, they're foolproof. They never forget themselves. Kamarenski is a truly pathetic person. He could get past anybody's guard." Divine straightened the aircraft's nose. "Except, perhaps, Starin's."

Hale stared. "But that's exactly where he is, sir."

"Yes, that's exactly where he is." Divine gave his model a final squeeze and launched it towards the light. It fell on its nose, hard, half-way across the room. "You've to meet him on Sunday in the gallery of Saint Nicholas's Church, off Fleet Street, during Evensong. Don't look so thrilled, I don't suppose he's got anything. Good-bye. Send the next customer in."

Hale went to a party that night. It was given by a man who worked for Pan Am, and there were many girls there, mainly stewardesses resting between flights. By midnight Hale was sick of telling girls who had just flown from Canberra via Tahiti, Atlantis, and Shangri-La that he had a job in merchant banking. He got himself a fresh drink and saw the girl in the yellow dress.

She was little rather than slim; her sunburnt arms in the sleeveless dress looked sleek with a kind of fluid grace which suggested strength rather than weakness. The dress was a cool-looking faded-daffodil yellow in a linen weave, beautifully fitted so that hints of the body beneath it came and went in faint, oblique lines as she moved. Her hair was blond and long to the chin; too blond to be true but glossy with weight, until she pushed it away from her face and broke the gloss. Her face was small and simple; it had the delicacy and toughness of a child disguised in adulthood. She was talking and smiling to a man in a dinner jacket. She looked happy.

Hale was deeply disturbed by the girl. She was so vulnerable, she invited protection; yet she was so untouchable, what could you say to her? He spent a quarter of an hour sidling about the room so that he could study her from all angles. She still looked happy. The dinner jacket danced with her. She had other friends.

Eventually Hale gave up. It was absurdly lop-sided, a waste of time, he might as well forget it. He turned away and found himself in front of a girl with a see-through dress and a radiant smile. "If this is Thursday you must be Francesca," he said. She dazzled, and said nothing.

"Can I get you a drink, or vice versa?" he asked.

"Oh, no." She dazzled some more.

"I just strangled my grandmother." The girl gave a little laugh. Her ear-rings tinkled.

"I'll swop you two dead frogs for a Russian destroyer," he offered. She looked down, modestly. "Oh, Christ," he said, and walked away. It was time to go home. Tomorrow was a working day.

He found the Pan Am man and said good night. His coat was in the bedroom. So was the girl in the yellow dress. It seemed an amazing coincidence.

"Are you leaving?" he asked. She put her head on one side and considered his question, and him. He was very intense. Her eyes were wide. "I don't know," she said. "Are you?"

"I am."

"Then so am I."

He helped her on with her coat. As they went down in the lift, he said, "You were the only interesting girl there."

"And you were the only interesting man. Why didn't you come and talk to me?"

They went out into the street. It had been raining, and the cabs made a high, clear, sheening sound on the soaking tarmac.

"I'm David Hale."

"Carol Blazey."

"We should meet again."

"Yes, please." She was calm and completely enjoyable. "We haven't really met at all, yet."

"Tomorrow?"

"Yes again. You could call me. I work for the airline." She told him the number. He put her in a cab and watched it cruise away. He felt astonished; light-hearted. The day had ended with something of a small triumph.

The cultural attaché was tipsy. "I'll tell you what gets on my left tit, Mikhail, old son," he said. "Goddam cocktail party last night." He beat himself weakly on the chest to dissipate his heartburn.

"I know what gets on your left tit," Starin said.

"No, no." The cultural attaché gestured negatively and ash flew from his overloaded cigarette. "Not the cocktail parties. *Caviare.* Tubs of the bloody stuff. Best quality. Know where they get it?" He drained his already empty glass.

"Yes," Starin said. "From us."

"They get it from *us*. We sell it to them! Now, I'm going home tomorrow. Think I'll be able to get caviare like that at home? Think I will?" He drained his empty glass again.

"For God's sake," Starin said, "pour your own." He put the bottle beside the cultural attaché and walked away. The cultural attaché irritated him because he got drunk too easily and then his broken-down, overweight body looked even worse. They'd taken half his stomach out and still he ate too much. Now that the alcohol had reddened his swollen face he looked like a pig, one that felt sorry for itself because it had a terrible shaving rash which it absent-mindedly picked at while it stared at nothing and thought about going home to second-rate caviare.

Starin should have been pleased that the cultural attaché was being retired; he'd known him for thirty years, on and off, and any calibre of caviare was too good for him. What angered Starin now was the fact that the cultural attaché had come to say good-bye because Starin was only a year or so younger, and he thought Starin might appreciate his views on life as they both shuffled towards retirement. That made Starin very angry.

"Not bad stuff, this," the cultural attaché said. "French, eh? What did we give them for it?"

"Machine tools."

"There you are again. Machine tools! All that labour, all that sacrifice, all those five-year plans, and where does it get us? Swopping first-class Russian machinery for a few barrels of French grape-squeezings. It gets right on my left tit, Mikhail, old son."

"There's a reason for it," Starin said. "These things are worked out." He walked around the room, straightening files, tearing up old envelopes, squaring books.

"No, no, no." The cultural attaché drank deep. "Time to face up to it, old son. You and I—relics of the past. Remember the good old days, eh? Remember when it was a clean, straight fight, and any dirty trick was O.K. as long as it worked? Remember?" He tried to smile bravely, but that blight of a shaving rash moved with the smile and deleted it. "No room for old-fashioned warriors like us any more, Mikhail."

"Speak for yourself."

The cultural attaché was deaf with nostalgia. "A man knew who his friends were in those days. Not any more. Know what my job is now? I mean, was now? Trying to stop bloody silly ballet dancers from bloody defecting. I ask you."

"You sound as if you're *ready* to retire."

"Mikhail, old son—I am. More than ready. Frankly, I don't know what's going on any more. I don't know whether we're supposed to be kicking them in the crotch or kissing them on the ass. Do you?"

Starin looked at his fuddled, sincere stare with distaste. "No," he said curtly.

"Course you don't. And I'll tell you why." He pointed his

glass at Starin; wine slopped onto the carpet. "'Cause we're over the hill. Pair of old farts like us. Don't know which way is up any more."

"Speak for yourself," Starin muttered. He looked away. It sickened him to see a Russian representative so dilapidated and defeatist.

Unexpectedly, the cultural attaché chuckled. "Come on, be your age. We're in a dying industry, you and I. They don't need us any more, it's all done with transistors these days. Obsolescent craftsmen, that's what we are."

"I wish you'd damn well go."

"Tomorrow's plane, old son. Plenty of time. Besides, you don't want to waste the rest of this bottle. No, I saw it coming long ago. I shall be all right. Pottery . . . always been interested in pottery."

"Look, I have work to do."

"It occurred to me . . . since we're neither of us married . . . you might like to split the cost of a cottage. I mean, I could start looking around for a place. . . ."

"Good Christ, no *thanks*."

The cultural attaché was surprised. "Well, none of us goes on forever, you know. If I were you I'd start making some plans. Honestly I would." He sucked at his wine, frowning. "It's not like it used to be. If I were you—"

Starin grabbed an ashtray and hurled it at the cultural attaché's head. He missed by a yard. The ashtray bounced off the wall and skidded across the waxed floorboards.

The cultural attaché gaped. Then he burst out laughing. "See what I mean?" he said. "You've lost your touch, old son. Can't afford to miss, you know." Still laughing, he got up and waddled away. Starin stood and listened to him cackling all the way along the corridor to the front door.

Hale waited for Carol outside her office block. He was restless with expectation and at the same time surprised by the force of his emotion: it was almost as if he were seventeen again, and that had been a very uncomfortable age. When she came out of the revolving doors he felt his eyebrows twitch. She stood out like a solitary crocus in a grubby lawn. It was remarkable that he could breathe normally and talk sensibly.

"Hallo, David Hale." She took his arm and they walked. He concentrated on relaxing. "Thank God it's Friday," she said. "No, I shouldn't have said that, it reminded me. New York. That was my favourite bar for a while. T.G.I. Friday's."

"You mean there really is a bar called . . . ?"

"Yes, Santa, there really is a T.G.I. Friday's."

"New York, New York, it's a wonderful town."

"The Bronx has blown up and the Battery's run down." She stopped at an art gallery and looked in the window. "That's not original; they used to sing it in the office. How rich are you?"

"Not very. Credit-card rich, that's all. But I wouldn't buy *that*, even if I could afford it." The painting showed a rustic inn beside a river, with cattle fording, anglers fishing, and drinkers quaffing; it would have made a fine jigsaw puzzle.

"No, I agree, let's not buy it. But I'd like to go there. Or to somewhere like it. Can we?"

"I don't know. I suppose so. I think I'm rich enough for that."

"Have you got a car?"

"Yes, just around the corner."

They set off in the car. "This may take a little time," he said. "Rush-hour, and all that."

"I don't mind."

"Have you had a hard week?"

"Drive, David. You don't really want to know about my week, and I don't want to talk about it, so let's not talk until we get there."

Hale wanted to know everything about Carol Blazey's life, down to her size in socks; but he did her will and drove, refreshing himself occasionally with a quick glance at her splendid face, her small, slim hands in her lucky lap, and her sleekly muscled legs.

They drove for nearly two hours. By that time Hale could have drawn her profile from memory. He stopped the car at the end of the bridge so that she could see the inn on the other side of the river, and then drove across and into the car park. She got out and walked through the garden until she stood on the bank directly above the old millrace. The setting sun spilled gold leaf down the tumbling water. Rose bushes threw out soft explosions of colour along the stone balcony which opened out from the inn, and the inn itself was so mossed and lichened and ivied that it seemed to be rooted rather than founded. "Is this what you had in mind?" Hale asked.

"*Exactly*. How clever of you. Is it tremendously old?"

"I think they put it up last Tuesday. It was all done with a kit of parts, you know. Made in Hong Kong, most of it."

She liked the place even more after they'd had a drink, and towards the end of dinner Hale realized that the evening was going remarkably well. He talked about himself a good deal, because she wanted to know a good deal about him: who brought him up after his parents died, where he was educated, what he did at college, why he went into merchant banking. The facts were ordinary, so he spiced them up in places. His parents had died in a road accident when he was four; he killed them off in a plane crash when he was eighteen months. His guardian had retired and gone abroad; Hale sent him to jail for embezzlement; and so on. Carol enjoyed it all, until he came to Flekker Handyside, where there was little he could do but tell the truth. "I'm good at it, and I enjoy it," he told her. "I enjoy making big things happen."

She studied his face for a moment, and then added more cream to her last two strawberries. "No," she said. "I can't see you in a merchant bank. All they do is move enormous, boring fortunes around between people who already *have* enormous, boring fortunes. It's like shifting slag heaps from one field to the next."

"Certainly not. That's like saying that airlines keep flying the same people from one country to the next."

"Well, so they do, it's quite absurd."

"Ah, but some of them are merchant bankers, on errands of mercy."

"Carrying briefcases full of slag."

"Only for self-defence, in case they get attacked by foreign competitors. Then they beat them off with their slaggy briefcases. You've no idea what a savage, ruthless world it is."

"Is that why you're so stern?"

The question surprised him. "Stern? Am I stern?"

"Oh, *fiercely* stern. You have a way of looking at people as if they're about to let the side down."

Hale frowned, and shook his head. "No, no," he said. "I can't accept that." The waiter arrived and poured their coffee. Hale watched him so closely that the man became nervous, and spilled some. When he had gone, Carol said, "There you are, you see."

"What? Where?"

"You absolutely terrified him."

"Nonsense. The fellow was a shambling incompetent. If I hadn't kept an eye on him, he'd have tipped the stuff straight into the ashtrays."

"Well, what's wrong with a bit of incompetence? There are only about three things in the world that *I'm* any good at."

Hale looked interested. "Really?"

Carol started to reply, then decided against it. She stirred her coffee. "Perhaps when we know each other better," she said.

He tried to look crushed. "How stern you can be. How terrifyingly, brutally stern."

"David, you're a rotten actor. Terrible, frightful. You're absolutely muscle-bound with integrity."

"Am I really?" Hale said. "That's the nicest thing anyone's said all week. I'm going to write that down."

"D'you know a game called 'Journey to a House'?" she asked.

"How does it go?"

"Oh, it's just one of those idiotic games people end up play-ing at parties at two in the morning. You have to describe a journey through a wood, across a river, over a wall, and up to a house. In detail."

"Hmm." Hale closed his eyes. "This wood . . . it's really a forest. Tremendous great oaks and beeches, with the occasional giant redwood. The undergrowth is dense, very dense, but I hack out a path and I reach this stream."

"Just a stream?"

"Well, it starts as a shallow stream with stagnant pools but it soon becomes a raging torrent with thundering waterfalls leading to a mighty river which dwindles to a trickle in the dry season. O.K.?" He looked up.

"Yes, if that's the way you see it." Carol's eyes were large with enjoyment.

"Anyway, I swim across. That takes about three hours. On the other side is a high wall—"

"Wait a minute. Is there a door in it?"

"I'll have a look. . . . Yes."

"Locked?"

"Padlocked, and it's a combination lock. You can only open it if you know the secret word, which has seven letters. Did I mention that the wall is made of glass bricks? So everyone can see the house on the other side, a vast and sinister mansion, like a cross between Wuthering Heights and Euston Station." He sat back and nodded.

"Very interesting."

"Wait, I nearly missed something: *the east wing is on fire.*"

"Oh, perfect. Now d'you want to know what it all means?"

"Please."

"Well, the house indicates how you see yourself."

"Oh my God."

"Yes, it looks pretty forbidding, doesn't it? All gloom and doom, with a touch of disaster. Poor you."

"Never mind. . . . What about the wall?"

"That shows how you think you get on with the rest of the

world. Some people don't have any wall at all; I suppose they're complete extroverts."

"My wall is very high."

"But transparent."

"Yes, absolutely. What d'you make of that?"

"It sounds to me rather like a love-hate relationship."

"Ah. . . . Is that why I set fire to the house, d'you think?"

"Maybe. No, probably not. Setting fire to the house is obviously a cry for help."

"Yes. . . . You know, if only that damn wall weren't so high, we could carry water from the stream."

"I wouldn't, if I were you. That stream represents your sex life."

"Really? I'll let the old dump burn to the ground. Can you dredge anything interesting out of my stream-torrent river?"

"Oh, plenty. You're either impotent or normal or insatiable or . . . or phenomenal. Or confused. Or bragging."

"Oh my God again."

"It all sounds very uncomfortable. I really think you ought to make up your mind, don't you?"

"It's out of my hands," Hale said. "If you'll pardon the expression."

She laughed. "At least you're not queer."

"Don't speak too soon, I've just remembered the whirlpools."

"*Whirlpools?* Rubbish!"

"Funny you should say that. 'Rubbish' is the secret word that opens the padlock."

"What? Oh . . . I'd forgotten."

"Ah, but I hadn't. Rubbish is the key to it all. I *know,* you see. I've played this game before."

"What a swindle."

"Aren't you going to finish me off? You haven't done the forest yet."

"No, and I'm not going to."

"Pity," Hale said wistfully. "I felt rather proud of my giant redwoods. What is it they represent? Virility?"

"I'm not going to tell you."

"Perhaps you're right. It can be dangerous to probe the Unknown. Besides, we've only just met, so it's a shade premature to go shooting the rapids."

"Premature?" Carol thought about the word. "Premature. I was premature. I shouldn't be here at all, so they said. It's a funny feeling, knowing that. It makes you want to get on and do everything, quickly. I suppose it makes you greedy."

"I find it hard to believe that you're greedy," Hale said.

"Do you swim?" she asked.

"Yes, quite a lot. Do you?"

"No, I hate swimming. But I'd like to watch you swim. Do year wear tight trunks, or shorts like footballers?"

"Trunks."

"Oh."

Hale waited for her to go on, but apparently that was all she had to say about swimming. Still the evening was a success. As they drove into London he felt pleased and capable. "About tomorrow," he said. "How do you feel about a film?"

"I have a date tomorrow," she said.

"Oh." They drove for a couple of miles in silence, while he digested the news. He stopped at a red light, cleared his throat, and said, "Sunday?"

For a moment she looked at him without speaking; then said, "David, have I got good legs?"

"Very good legs." The lights changed. "Wonderful, marvelous, *superb* legs."

"All right. It's just that . . . every so often I feel the need to open your safety valve. You're so wound up. We should spend an hour just talking about my legs, so that you can relax a bit."

Hale squinted at an oncoming headlight, and grunted.

"I'm sorry," Carol said. "Greedy again, you see. But yes to Sunday. Why don't you come round in the evening?"

"O.K. I'll get us tickets for something."

When they reached her flat she asked him up to meet the

other girls, three stewardesses. But when she opened the door the atmosphere was hostile and the faces were stiff. "Oh dear," Carol said. "Trouble." Hale left.

St. Nicholas-nither-Fleet was a handsome old church, lost in the tangle of alleys and narrow streets between the bottom end of Fleet Street and the Thames. Evensong was at six-thirty. Hale got there at six in order to have a good look round. He stood in the middle of the aisle and took in the tattered battle standards, the marble memorials, the brass plaques. He wondered who had chosen St. Nicholas's as a rendezvous, and why. The air was still and ancient, and the place smelled like the Archbishop of Canterbury's old toy-room.

By six-twenty-five the church was nearly half full. Hale climbed the stairs to the gallery at the far end from the altar. The stairs were steep, and he found only a few people up there; Kamarenski was not one of them. Hale sat in the middle, on his own.

Midway through the opening hymn, Kamarenski arrived.

He went very slowly to a pew two rows in front of Hale and made no attempt to join in the singing, but stood staring at the people below. Hale edged towards the gangway, and in the business of settling down when the hymn ended, moved forward and sat in front of Kamarenski. Nobody paid any attention. The usual prayers followed, the minister and the congregation serving phrases to each other with the competence of tennis players warming up. Then a psalm was announced. Hale fumbled with his prayer book, and finally turned to Kamarenski for help. The man leaned forward, Hale showed him the passport-type print taken from Kamarenski's own photograph which he was holding between the pages; he checked the page in Kamarenski's book just for the sake of form; smiled; and turned back to the chant. Kamarenski's prayer book was trembling like the last leaf of autumn, and the rosettes of muscle at the corners of his jaw were bunched up tight. He had looked at

Hale with great fear, as if Hale might reach out and scar him. The psalm ground on, stopping and starting like rush-hour traffic. Hale wondered what Kamarenski made of all this. He wasn't singing. Perhaps his stammer prevented it.

The psalm ended. More prayers. Hale did not kneel, but sat more or less upright with his head well bowed. Kamarenski knelt and put his elbows on the back of Hale's pew and held his head in his hands. The smell of his sweat made Hale's nostrils twitch.

Under cover of a heavy response by the congregation, Hale muttered sideways, "What have you found?" There was a brief solo from the minister, then the congregation was off again. Hale heard Kamarenski's teeth chatter gently as he strained to speak; then there was a fast shuddering gasp of breath. Hale could hear the air whistling in and out of Kamarenski's long nostrils: he glanced back and saw the man's fingers pressed hard against the damp skin. Kamarenski's face was a shiny grey, like fresh cement. Hale hoped he wasn't going to faint.

The prayers changed key: a long set-piece by the congregation began, uncertainly at first, then settling into a gloomy rhythm. Hale tried again. "What's going on?" he muttered. Kamarenski opened his mouth, but nothing came out except a fine spray of saliva, which flecked Hale's back. Hale listened to the noisy breathing, broken occasionally by a swallow, and wondered what to do next. Take him somewhere private, probably. Perhaps drive him around London while he talked. If he talked. If he came.

Kamarenski's forehead struck the rounded top of the pew with a smack like a steak on a butcher's block. Hale turned and half-rose. A few faces looked across curiously, their mouths still praying. He took hold of Kamarenski's shoulders, his hands gripping the bony flesh under the old brown suit, and shoved him back. The eyes were closed but the mouth was open; Hale glimpsed gold, and a thin dribble stretching between the bloodless lips. Holding him steady with one hand, he climbed into the other pew and hoisted him onto the seat, shoving the skinny buttocks back, and with his leg, forced the feet apart so that he could stuff Kamarenski's head between his knees. He sat beside him, holding him by the neck, and with his free hand searched for the pulse in his wrist. But before his right hand could find the pulse, his left hand had found the hole in the back of Kamarenski's neck, and the hotness that came seeping out of the hole. He looked behind him but there was nobody there. He let everything go and ran along the pew and up the stairs to the little landing outside, while Kamarenski slipped sideways and slid quietly to the floor. Some people had stood up, uncertain whether to risk the embarrassment of interfering. Hale plunged down the outer stairs, grabbing pillars as they came, and pounded across the empty vestibule and into the empty street. Perhaps he heard a car; perhaps it was just the organ. He ran back upstairs. He reached Kamarenski just as the first person was about to touch him, and grabbed the man's arm. "Go down and call an ambulance," he said. "I'm a doctor. Go now."

The inside of the ambulance stank of that purple antiseptic raw-alcohol smell you get in the bloodier parts of hospitals. It was worse in the ambulance because it was enclosed and there seemed to be no ventilation, but maybe that was all in Hale's mind, which was also enclosed and lacking ventilation. All he could think of was failure. Divine had sent him on a simple job and he had allowed someone to shoot the job dead in the back of the head. Total failure.

He found a handkerchief and wiped his face. His head was sweating but his body was cold. It had taken a little while for the sickness of death to catch up with Hale. He had never seen a shattered skull before; he had never before touched with his fingers the actual seeping cavity through which death had just entered at approximately two thousand miles an hour. It had not been easy to grasp the fact that he had been sitting only three feet away while a tiny act of demolition was performed on the back of Kamarenski's skull; a calculated, craftsmanlike act, involving a small calibre and an economical charge, since the bullet had remained inside Kamarenski's brain instead of punching a good deal of it out. All this had not been easy to grasp, and once grasped it turned out to be impossible to discard.

Hale tried not to look at the lumpy red blanket spread over the stretcher; that colour, and the way the lumps slid from side to side as the ambulance turned corners, seemed to strengthen the purple hospital smell, as if it were an aura being released by the body.

"You all right, are you?" the ambulanceman asked. Hale nodded. He wiped his face again. It felt as if he had walked through strings of fine cobwebs. "You don't look too good," the ambulanceman said. "In fact, you look bloody awful." He watched Hale for a moment, and then reached under his seat for a plastic bowl. "Just say the word if you need this," he said. "Don't be shy." Hale looked at it and nodded. His stomach felt too numb to move. His whole body felt stunned. Coming like this—silently, invisibly, casually, brutally—death was an obscenity which made life seem a presumption.

The ambulanceman watched him obliquely. It's all very well for him, he thought. He doesn't have to clean it up afterwards.

The police car followed the ambulance into the hospital, and the policemen followed Hale and the stretcher into a white-tiled room. The ambulancemen put Kamarenski on a table and removed their blanket and went out.

One of the policemen ran a finger along Kamarenski's toes. "What happened to his shoes?" he asked.

"They must have fallen off," Hale said. The shoes were in his raincoat pockets.

"Lucky you happened to be sitting next to him, Doctor," the other policeman said. "Not that there's anything anyone could have done."

"I'm not a doctor," Hale said, "and I've got to go now." They looked at him sharply, resenting the loss of initiative. Hale took out his wallet. "You'd better see this," he said.

They took his K2 credentials and read them. They did not like them. "I'll have to see about this," one of them said. He went out to the car.

"You've got the evidence of the people in the church," Hale said. "You know I didn't kill him." The other policeman said nothing. He looked at Hale and played a tune on his teeth with his ballpen and said nothing.

His colleague came in. "I might have bloody known it," he said. He gave Hale back his papers. "All right, Superman, fly away." He sounded disgusted. "Why do you always have to do it on somebody else's doorstep? You should have sent for the dustcart, not the police."

Hale picked up his raincoat. The shoes in the pockets bumped against his side.

"Where does your skinny friend belong, anyway?" the other policeman asked.

"He's a Russian," Hale said. "Try the Embassy."

"That sounds familiar," the policeman said. "I must have seen the film. Who was in it, again?"

The other policeman straightened Kamarenski's tie. "It wasn't Shirley Temple, anyway," he said.

Divine had already reached his office when Hale got there. The lights were on, and he was talking into the telephone. Hale saw that he was wearing bottle-green golfing trousers and an Aran Island sweater. A pair of string-backed driving gloves lay on the desk.

"Knowing your well-deserved talents for putting the diplomatic boot in," Divine was saying, "I'm sure we can depend on you to wear size twelves at the very least. . . . Good. Yes. I will." He hung up and looked at Hale. "Well, David. A touch of the thud-and-blunders. Are you all right?"

"Yes, fine. Sorry to bust into your week-end like this, Major."

"You don't *look* all right. You look quite frightful. You'd better have a drink, before one of us bursts into tears." He took a bottle of whisky out of a filing cabinet and made two drinks. Hale had a good swig and felt it flickering hotly as it went down.

"Tell me what happened," Divine said.

"Well, he's dead," Hale began. It sounded more like the end than the beginning. "Somebody shot him. In the church. We were all supposed to be praying at the time, so not many people noticed it."

"Where were you?"

"Right in front of him. He was shot from behind. Hit in the back of the head. In the neck, really."

"Why didn't you sit behind him?"

Hale immediately thought, Because then I'd have got it in the neck too, but that made no sense, and he said, "I had to hear him, and he had to see me. The best place for me was in front, so that he could whisper."

"And *did* he whisper?"

"He tried. He couldn't get it out. He was too scared, Major. He couldn't speak, he could hardly breathe. He was terrified. Scared silly."

"And with reason, it appears. I suppose nobody saw who shot him?"

"Yes, one of the sidesmen or vergers or whatever they are saw something. He saw a man standing at the back of the gallery with a cine camera. They sometimes have trouble with tourists using cameras during services, and he was going to go up and stop him. Next time he looked, he'd gone."

Divine wrinkled his nose. "It's become a rather dreary cliché, hasn't it? Almost as bad as violin cases."

"It worked. I didn't hear a damn thing until Kamarenski collapsed."

"And what then?"

"Oh . . . we went through the motions. Nine-nine-nine, ambulance, police, hospital. The police were fairly annoyed when I took off my false beard and left them lumbered with the remains." Hale was starting to loosen up now; Divine had taken Kamarenski's death surprisingly calmly. "They know he's a Russian with some kind of official status over here."

Divine gave him more whisky. "Your first body, David?" Hale nodded. "Well, I'm glad to see that you're treating it seriously. Death is not a joke. At least, I've never heard a funny joke about death." Divine was strolling around the room, unstraightening pictures so that he could straighten them again. "We see our fair share of corpses at K2, but personally I've always regarded killing people as a confession of failure, although there are those," he said, looking at the ceiling, "who use it as an index of efficiency. The head of the department, you know, is quite keen on marksmanship. In his case I think it's more from a character-building point of view. Did you get his shoes?"

"Yes." Hale went over to his raincoat. "I went through his pockets, too, before the police arrived, but there was only this." He gave Divine a silver cigarette case.

"My God," Divine said, "he shouldn't have bought that. Far too conspicuous." He sniffed the cigarettes. "Best desiccated yak's dung, as usual. Just the left shoe, please."

Divine unlaced it and peeled back the inner sole, then held it up to the light and looked closely inside. "Pooh," he said. "Remind me to send Starin a case of talcum powder." He put his thumb inside, pressed, and swivelled it. Hale heard a faint click. Divine took a good grip of the shoe with his left hand, wrapped his fingers around the heel, and gave it a wrench, counter-clockwise. The heel turned stiffly, grudgingly, through one revolution, and then spun off fast.

Hale leaned over to look. There was a small aluminium canister, packed around with wedges of paper.

"Talking of clichés," Hale said, "I thought the hollow heel went out with Bulldog Drummond."

Divine corked the whisky. "Can you think of anywhere better?" he asked. He put the canister on his desk and began smoothing out the paper packing.

"No, but . . . Surely that's the first place anybody would look, if they thought Kamarenski—"

"My poor oaf, if they really thought Kamarenski was hiding something, they'd find it in ten minutes even if he'd gone to the trouble of having it engraved on his heart in Esperanto. This bit of nonsense wasn't meant to baffle Starin, it was meant to reassure Kamarenski, that's all. Help him sleep at night."

"Oh. What's inside?"

"Film, I hope. Candid scenes of vice and viciousness revealed within the sinister precincts of the Russian Trade Mission. Another great first for Kamarenski and his trembling hand-held screwdriver. Maybe. Or maybe it's ten feet of nothing. What d'you make of *that*?" He gave Hale a piece of the paper.

"It looks like a sheet of toilet paper."

"Yes, but the *quality*."

Hale fingered it. It crackled. "Not too lush," he said.

"Lush? It's like sandpaper. No wonder they're so suicidal. I've heard of having a death-wish, but mortifying the flesh with this stuff is a needlessly longwinded way to go. Incidentally, I wonder why they didn't shoot you too."

Hale's shoulders twitched. "Why should they?" he asked defensively. "I hadn't done anything."

"They didn't know that. You'd just met Kamarenski, and they shot him. Why not you?"

"Too big a risk. They didn't know who else might be there, besides me. They didn't even know I was there to meet him."

"You spoke to him."

"Six words, that's all."

"In the circumstances, more than enough. It looks as if Starin had Kamarenski followed. Maybe he suspected him, maybe it was just routine. Whoever was following him didn't like the idea of Kamarenski going to church, especially when you and he began putting your heads together, so he cut it short there and then."

Hale squeezed his thighs and stared into space. "He *should* have shot me, shouldn't he?" he said.

Divine put the bottle back in the filing cabinet. "I can only assume that Kamarenski was in the way," he said. "He was right behind you, so perhaps he shielded you."

"It was during prayers, too. He was kneeling, but I was just sitting and leaning forward."

"It looks as if you were saved by faith, then. And Kamarenski was perhaps unsaved by unfaith. And maybe we were all saved by Starin's faith, since Starin was trusting that Kamarenski hadn't given anything away, and Starin didn't know about the film." Divine picked up the canister and tossed it to Hale, who was thinking about Kamarenski's stockinged feet at the time and fumbled the catch badly. "I want that developed. Not here, they're far too slow on week-ends, we wouldn't see prints before midnight. There's a man in Shepherd's Bush I sometimes use. I'll call him while you're driving there." He gave the address.

Half-way to Shepherd's Bush, Hale pushed his foot to the floor to beat some traffic lights, glanced nervously at a cab nosing into the traffic, and looked up to find flaring brake lights dead ahead. His tires laid a track of burnt rubber to within inches of the car. As the suspension recovered itself and heaved him back, he slumped and rested his head on the wheel. "You bloody idiot," he said aloud.

"You're the bloody idiot, mate," the cab-driver said. Hale didn't look at him.

The man at Shepherd's Bush took an hour and a half to develop and print. He said nothing at all until he gave Hale the results, tightly sealed in a flat cardboard box. He was bald and ruddy, with splayed teeth like an adult thumbsucker. "How's George Divine these days?" he asked. "Is he running the show yet?"

"I don't think so," Hale said. "I'm not really sure."

"Ambitious bugger, old George. Always working his way up

the ladder. I expect he's about four rungs from the top by now, and stamping on as many hands as he can reach. Don't forget your coat."

Divine was on the phone when Hale got back. "No, no, no, it's not that," he was saying. "Naturally I'm flattered to be asked. But look at my workload at the present: fourteen separate projects." He glanced across at Hale. "Wait a minute, I forgot one: fifteen. It's just not possible. Hang on a moment." He covered the mouthpiece. "Is that it?" Hale gave him the box. "Well done. See me in the morning." He swung his swivel chair away. "You see my problem, old boy? Now what I suggest . . ."

Hale drove home, suddenly weary with the fatigue of anti-climax. He let himself into his flat and realized, with the shock of a man treading on a non-existent stair, that he should have been somewhere else all evening with a girl whose face that moment he didn't even have the courage to picture.

———

Monday morning turned out to be that peculiarly London weather which has neither the guts to be lousy nor the gall to be bright. The sky was grey and remote like a coat of distemper on a distant ceiling. Hale arrived early at K2, feeling both weary and refreshed, as if he had spent the week-end climbing hills. He was eager to see Kamarenski's film.

There was someone else waiting to see Divine; and the Major himself was in a meeting, so Hubbard said. Hale sat on a chair and watched Hubbard organizing the coffee. This was not what he had expected. Divine had dismissed him the night before, but there could have been a reason for that, for instance if the film had showed up something really big. . . . Of course, Divine couldn't have known that until after Hale had gone. . . . So it looked now as if Kamarenski hadn't found anything important. . . . Unless, of course, he'd found something absolutely tremendous and that was what this meeting was all about. . . . Then Hale remembered Divine's workload, the fourteen *other* separate projects he said he was handling. Maybe Kamarenski wasn't top priority after all.

Hubbard was ready to wheel in the coffee. "Could you let the Major know I'm here?" Hale asked. Hubbard pursed his lips and narrowed his eyes and indicated that he would do his best. He opened the door and came back for the trolley, and Hale saw a stranger sitting at Divine's desk, a younger man, perhaps only forty-five, expressionless but with wide-awake, thoughtful eyes. Then Divine appeared, helping to guide the trolley. The door closed.

So it wasn't even Divine's meeting.

Soon Hubbard came out. He glanced swiftly at Hale and the other man, just counting them to make sure. The other man was reading a newspaper. He didn't look up.

Hubbard opened his desk, sorted through his paper-clips, uncoupled a pair which were behaving suspiciously, closed his desk, and said, "I hear Mr. Kamarenski has severed his connection with us."

Hale said, "That's right."

"He didn't last very long, did he?"

"No, unfortunately."

"I can't say I agree with you, Mr. Hale. I never liked him, you know. *Dirty*." He was like an old maid describing the children next door. Hale was startled at his callousness.

"Do you know what happened to Kamarenski?"

"No, but the Major left me a note saying that we should stop crediting his account, so I assume his usefulness has come to an end."

Forty-five minutes later the meeting ended. Six silent men came out and went away. "Hoo-ruddy-ray," said the other man who was waiting. He dumped his newspaper in a wastebin and trod it down. "At last, the Divine resurrection," he said. Hale saw him full-face; he had a slight hare-lip.

Hubbard took the other man in to see Divine and came out carrying a flat cardboard box. "Major Divine would like you to see these," he said. They could have been wallpaper patterns, the way he said it. Hale took the box and looked at the torn seals.

"You can come back after lunch," Hubbard said. Christ Almighty, Hale thought, get me out of here! Hubbard held the door for him. He used both hands.

Hale tried to find an empty office, and failed. He took the lift down to the ground-floor coffee shop, but there were no empty tables and he didn't want to share Starin's secrets with some needle-nosed shorthand-typist. He thought of going out and sitting in his car, decided against it without knowing why, and went back upstairs to K2's offices and locked himself in a cubicle in the lavatories. There was no lid to fold down, so he sat on the edge of the seat. Someone had written on the wall, *Don't shit! K2 gives nothing away.* Someone else had added, *So quote me a price for it, then,* Hale rested the box on his knees and looked at the words. The whole scene was less than reassuring. He took the lid off the box.

The prints were big, about eight-by-ten, matte, black-and-white. The top one looked like a picture of a blizzard. The second one looked like a blizzard at midnight. Pictures three to seven looked like dense fog with gales, and picture eight showed a page of scientific calculations. Handwritten. In ink.

Hale stared, trying to work out what was odd. For a moment he thought it was in Russian; then he realized that it was upside down. Reversed, it looked better; obviously English, because he recognized some of the symbols; and the alterations and corrections were plain. It all flowed like an orchestral score, except that Hale couldn't read the music.

He looked at the next print. More of the same. He went on looking. The scientific symphony played for ten pages in all. The next and final print was of the cover. The work was called Project 107. No name, no address; just *Project 107* scribbled across the centre of the page. And a rubber stamp slammed diagonally on the top right corner. It said MOST SECRET, inside a strong rectangular frame. Hale felt the blood beating up into his head. The enemy was in action.

"I may have to kick you out," Divine said. "I'm expecting a call from upstairs at any time. What did you make of it? Not particularly gripping, is it?" He was cleaning up his desk, sorting papers, throwing stuff away.

"It's hard to say," Hale said. "But it looks as if Kamarenski earned his fifty quid a week, at least."

Divine grunted. "When he managed to remember to take his thumb off the lens," he said. "Anyway, what's all that scientific gibberish about?"

Hale was taken aback. "That's what I was going to ask *you*, sir."

"Me? I haven't even had lunch yet, so I certainly haven't had time to—" The black telephone rang. "Divine," he grunted, listened for six seconds, and then interrupted the caller. "Not a hope." He hung up. "What is it, anyway? Physics? Chemistry? Molecular biology?" He initialled something and slapped it in a tray.

"Nobody knows; nobody in the department, that is. They all seem to think it must be something pretty unusual, sir. Probably something very high-powered, too."

Divine ripped a yellow file in half and tossed it into a bin stencilled DESTRUCT. "There's only one decent scientist in K2, and he's a chronic liar, so don't put any faith in what you're told around here," he said.

"What about Starin?" Hale asked. "Does his opinion carry any weight?"

"Starin's opinion?" Divine abandoned his desk-cleaning with a shrug of disgust. "Bloody bumf, I swear it breeds in the night. What about Starin?"

"Well, sir, presumably Starin considers this stuff fairly important."

"What makes you think Starin even knows it exists?"

"It must be someone fairly senior to be handling a document stamped MOST SECRET. And you told Kamarenski to watch Starin."

Divine put his hands in his pockets and looked at Hale as if Hale were modelling men's wear with no great skill. The black telephone rang; he killed it by lifting and replacing the receiver. "Granted, for the sake of argument, that this was on Starin's desk," he said, "so what?"

"Well . . ." Hale looked at the photograph for reassurance. "Surely it means that Starin has decided that this scientific statement or document or whatever it is must be . . . be, you know . . . valuable, or something."

"Or something. I see. Are you sure you don't mean 'by and large, generally speaking, and so on and so forth'?" Hale turned red, and said nothing. "I can't stand a sloppy prose style," Divine said. "We may not have much taste in K2 but at least we don't abuse the language." He put his foot on a chair and began tightening his laces. "In any case, I don't see what it's got to do with us."

"But . . . it's in English, sir, isn't it? If Starin got it here—and he probably did—then he won't have far to look for the man who wrote it."

"Another unknown factor."

"Well . . . not entirely." Hale searched through the prints until he found one where the calculations took up only two-thirds of the space. "This seems to be the last page," he said, "and it's been initialled at the bottom, and the initials look like 'M.J.' My guess is that Starin is after this M.J."

"I shouldn't be in the least surprised," Divine said. "He probably wants him to address the Soviety Academy of Angst, in Tomsk." The red telephone rang, and he turned away from Hale to answer it.

"Right," he said quietly. "Yes, of course. Shall I come up? Right." He straightened his tie and picked up a clipboard.

Hale got to his feet. "This could be very serious, though, Major," he began.

"No doubt. At the moment I'm responsible for at least ten things which *are* serious, and four which are positively bloody, so forgive me if I don't get agitated about a dozen snapshots." Hubbard was opening the door from the other side.

"Yes, but Major . . . Aren't you forgetting? I mean, Kamarenski . . .'. Doesn't that prove Starin has something to hide?"

Divine was through Hubbard's office and walking into the lift. Hale saw the lift doors close and heard the dental whine as Divine went up and away. He looked at the big photograph in his hands, at the lines of unfamiliar script, slightly fuzzy on the grey and grainy background, like a weathered legend on an old tombstone. Whatever their meaning, they were Kamarenski's epitaph, and there was something fundamentally askew about Divine's indifference to them. The balance was wrong. It wasn't a question of revenge or retaliation or correcting injustice. It was a question of straightening the balance.

Hubbard was dusting his typewriter with a long camel-hair brush. Hale stood in front of him and showed him the M.J. photograph. "I want to find out what this means," he said. "I want to find out *now*, today. All I know about it is it's complex, and unusual, and probably classified. Where do I go?"

For a few moments they had a little staring-out match. Hubbard's eyes flickered first. He unlocked a drawer and took out a small, thick directory. Hale watched him select names and numbers. Hubbard was trying to grow a thin, shoe-salesman's moustache. It made a tiny hedge along his upper lip, separating the mouth from the nose in a way which eliminated all possible confusion.

When Starin was shown in to the Embassy library he did not at first see the Ambassador, who was on top of a stepladder, against the shelves, half-hidden by the door.

"Oh, you're here," the Ambassador said. The servant carefully closed the door from the outside. The Ambassador finished reading a paragraph, and put the book aside. "I've got to make another speech," he said. "I don't suppose you know any decent jokes. . . . No, I thought not." He made himself comfortable on the padded top of the ladder. "I had a rather sudden summons this morning, on account of your Mr. Kamarenski. The British take what they call 'rather a dim view' of what happened with Kamarenski. I must say I agree with them."

"Is that why you called me over? Because of Kamarenski?" Starin did not hide his indifference.

"Yes, that *is* why. I don't know how much Kamarenski mattered to you—"

"Mattered? He didn't matter a damn. He was a lousy incompetent snooping handyman, that's all."

"Well, I can assure you that he, or you, or both of you, succeeded in giving me an extremely uncomfortable twenty minutes this morning. They told me that they aren't treating it as murder, and they as good as told me why: because we are responsible for cleaning up our own mess. Furthermore, they made it quite clear to me that, as messes go, this mess was made at the wrong time in the wrong place and in the wrong fashion, and if we could conduct our internal affairs with less of a public shambles in future then Her Majesty's Government would be greatly obliged, thank you and good-bye."

Starin scoffed. "Balls to them. They tried to buy their way into my Mission and they wasted their money on a thimble-wit. So they failed! Are they surprised at that?"

The Ambassador looked down at him. He changed his reading glasses for his regular glasses and put his head forward and looked hard at Starin again. "You talk as if you're in the C.I.A.," he said. "You seem to think this is Guatemala City, or Brazil, or the Philippines. You go about solving your problems like a cowboy. I have news for you, my friend. This is London, and I have to get along with these people, try and persuade them to do things, trade, negotiate, plan. It is not so damned easy. The British can be very difficult, especially when item one on the agenda is a discussion of how one of our staff comes to be shot dead in one of their churches during evening service."

"They know damn well why. Besides, it's only one man, one body. Not an international incident."

The Ambassador threw a book down to Starin, who caught it. "That is only one book," the Ambassador said. He threw a second book, a third, a fourth. Starin dropped the fifth. "Think about it," the Ambassador said. He sounded angry.

Starin looked at the books in his hands. "Take my advice, Mr. Ambassador, and stick to jokes," he said. "Leave all the funny business to me." He dumped the books in a wastebasket and went out.

It was six o'clock when Hale got back to K2, and three people were waiting to see Divine: two middle-aged women and the man with the hare-lip. Hale halted inside the door and looked at them in dismay. The man with the hare-lip grinned crookedly. "Don't worry about me," he said. "I'm only selling encyclopedias." The two women looked across. "And they play duets at two pianos," he said. They looked away. "What do you do?" he asked Hale.

"I don't know," Hale said wearily. "Sometimes I'm not even sure I exist." He found a chair. Hubbard typed and paid no attention to anyone.

After fifteen minutes the man with the hare-lip got up and fished his newspaper out of the wastebasket. He smoothed it flat, held it by the fold, and began tearing. As he tore, carefully working to some invisible pattern, he whistled an elaborate version of "Sally," all trills and grace notes. Hale and the women watched stolidly; even Hubbard glanced across. The newspaper was thoroughly shredded when Divine walked in.

"Ta-dah!" cried the man. He opened the paper with a confident flourish. It disintegrated into hundreds of tattered scraps which fluttered around his feet. "Back to the drawing-board," he said resolutely. Divine put a hand on his shoulder and steered him into his room. Hubbard and the two women looked at the mess of paper.

Five minutes later the man with the hare-lip came out. "And now, by special request," he said, wading briskly through the torn-up paper as he left. The women got up and went in. Hale began to feel hungry. After a while the women reappeared, looking shaken yet satisfied, as if they had been acquitted of allowing their dogs to foul the footpath. At last it was Hale's turn.

Divine was standing by the open filing cabinet, in his shirt sleeves and with his shoes off, mixing a gin and tonic. "One for you, David?" he asked. He seemed remarkably cheerful. Hale took the drink. "Love conquers all," Divine said, making it a toast.

"Love of what, though?"

"In this case, love of one's fellow man." Divine stopped trying to contain his pleasure, and laughed aloud. "It's quite made my day, really. Two Hungarians, just the ordinary sort of tenth secretaries or semi-demi-attachés, but they've been unusually furtive recently, so I had people watching them. Today we found out what it's all about. They've just eloped."

"With each other?"

"Certainly not. One's gone off with a lorry-driver and the other with a professional footballer."

"Is that good?"

"Good? I think it's priceless." He snapped his braces. "All those messages we've been intercepting, full of measurements and colours and angles—we thought it was some kind of code, I never suspected that they meant every word. Quite astonishing."

Hale allowed Divine's delight to weather a little, and said, "A little bit of astonishment came my way this afternoon, too."

"Yes?" Divine was looking for his shoes.

"Yes. I showed those photographs to a man at London University who was so very busy and so terribly important that he could spare me perhaps two minutes at the very most, and an hour and a half later he still had his nose in them when he remembered that he should have been lecturing somewhere, and he called up and cancelled the lecture."

"Indeed?" Divine found one shoe, and put it on. "What did he make of it all, finally?"

"He was still working on it when I came away."

"You left the prints there?"

"Yes. He's got security clearance. He knows how to look after them."

"All the same, I'd rather you stayed with him. And with them. I don't trust academics. They keep coming up with ideas of their own. You'd better go back."

"Major, it occurred to me while I was waiting over there that what really matters at this stage is not what the cream of London University thinks of Project 107, but What Starin thinks of it."

"Why should that make any difference? Starin's a scientific illiterate. He wouldn't recognize the square root of minus one if you served it up with an apple in its mouth."

"Perhaps not, sir. But that won't stop him going after the man behind Project 107, if he's got faith in it."

Divine limped around the room looking for his other shoe. "What are you driving at?" he asked.

"Suppose we were to start by offering to sell those photographs to him. Presumably he doesn't know that we know that he has details of Project 107, and if he wants to keep it to himself, and someone starts flashing pictures of it about—"

"Someone? Who?"

"Well . . . ostensibly a free agent, some kind of independent free-lance trader who does business in this kind of thing." Hale looked away; it sounded vague and wishful; limp. Then an idea came rushing to his aid. "The sort of chap who probably got hold of Project 107 for him in the first place," he said quickly.

"It boils down to this, then: you're proposing to try and sell those photographs to Starin. Anonymously."

"Yes. His response should define his general attitude."

Divine stood like a stork, left sole on right calf, hands on hips, and thought about it. "Well, I suppose dottier things have happened," he said. "Like Hungarian faggots running barefoot through the dawn with British lorry-drivers."

"Given a good man handling it, I think it should stand a fifty-fifty chance, Major. Maybe better."

"That's what's worrying me." Divine found his other shoe at last: it was under Hale's chair. "We haven't any good men. They're all out working. So you'll just have to do it yourself."

Hale sat very still and held his empty glass by the extreme tips of his fingers. He could just taste the tail-end of his lunch coming up. He swallowed heavily to drown it.

"How can I contact him?" he asked.

Divine flapped a hand without even looking. "Use your brains. How would you set about propositioning the Prime Minister? The Archbishop of Canterbury? Elvis Presley?"

"God knows."

"Then go and ask Him. Just stay out of churches, that's all. Good-bye."

Hale went home and tried to use his brains. He took a shower and wondered why Divine had picked on Elvis Presley. He drank a can of beer while he heated something out of a tin, and let the whole problem go round in his brain at the speed of the wooden spoon in the saucepan. He realized that nothing much was happening between the ears. The brain was at its post but it was not on its toes.

He ate the food and drank a second beer while he worried the problem. Each time he tried to focus on the idea of approaching Starin he ended up with an image of himself ringing the doorbell at the Russian Trade Mission in Islington, being seized by snarling Tatars in double-breasted blue suits, dragged down to the basement, and castrated with blunt secateurs behind the central-heating boiler.

After an hour of this he called Carol Blazey.

"She's washing her bloody hair again," a girl told him.

"Oh. Well, I'd better . . . I suppose . . . I'll call again later."

"Do that thing."

He tried to forget all women and get on with the problem. How could an unknown salesman with unknown goods make a pitch to a hostile foreigner? The more he thoeught about it, the more advantages he saw in Mata Hari. He pictured Mata Hari ringing the doorbell at the Russian Trade Mission. Several things happened, but none involved secateurs.

The phone rang; it was Brandon, from Flekker Handyside.

"At last," Brandon said. "Where've you been? Your secretary told me Handyside's given you a special assignment, or something."

"That's right."

"What's it about?"

"It's confidential."

"Well, *everything*'s confidential in this business, but you can tell me."

"No, I can't. If you really need to know, you'll have to ask Handyside himself, I'm afraid." Hale was speaking the lines which K2 had told him to speak in this situation.

"Oh." Brandon was not about to go and ask Handyside, and they both knew it. "I see. Well, I may have to take over your Lavagarde deal."

"Why? I can still handle it."

"It really needs someone here. You know, someone who can keep an eye on the general situation, so to speak." Brandon cleared his throat.

That smells, Hale thought. Flekker Handyside was a good merchant bank, but Brandon was ambitious, and sometimes his ambition led him along short-cuts which turned out to be back alleys. "Are you thinking of changing the deal?" he asked.

"No, no, of course not. It's just that Lavagarde and Petrolex are both clients of ours, both operating in the same area, and if we can arrange anything to their mutual benefit, then obviously we should."

"Petrolex? Petrolex is a gamble. I mean, looking for off-shore oil is the *biggest* gamble, we all know that. Lavagarde's project is something completely different, he's building a new agricultural industry. Everything's costed, down to the last sack of seed."

"Absolutely. But don't forget that the same little old African country stands to benefit from both plans."

"Sure! and Banzania's staking half its income for the next five years on Lavagarde, not Petrolex, because you can't eat oil. It's as simple as that."

"Granted. On the other hand, if we can drum up some more support for Petrolex, maybe your Banzanian friends can have some oil to cook their food on, or in, or however they do it."

"You mean Petrolex is getting cold feet, and now you want Banzania to help finance them."

"I didn't say that. But you must agree, it's perfectly obvious that Petrolex will try a damn sight harder once they know Banzania's behind them."

"Try harder? Yes, I suppose they will. Trying harder won't create oil if there's none there, though, will it? Frankly, I don't give a damn about Petrolex, but Banzania's got a per-capita annual income of about fourpence. They're *poor*. They can't *afford* to gamble."

"It doesn't have to be their money. We could raise a loan for them."

"That simply assumes success. If Petrolex flops, how the hell is Banzania going to repay?"

"Well . . . Lavagarde's project should be reaching fruition by then, shouldn't it?"

Hale let the phone slide out of his hand and hooked his fingers around the cord so that it swung free while he sat and stared at nothing in particular. You bastard, he thought. You desiccated bastard. He got the phone back.

"You still there?" Brandon said.

"If I thought that Flekker Handyside was trying to con Banzania into mortgaging half its food for a generation to come, simply in order to make Petrolex happy," Hale said, "I would immediately come over there and strangle someone."

"Just a thought, old boy," Brandon said. He hung up.

Hale brooded for five minutes, and then called Carol again.

At first he didn't recognize her voice; she sounded very flat. "I just called to apologize," he said.

"Who is this?"

"David Hale. Sorry."

"Oh. Yes."

"I had to work, and it went on much longer than I thought. We had a bit of a panic, and I just couldn't get away."

"I wondered."

"If it hadn't been so serious I'd have been able to call you, but there was no way out. It was absolutely unavoidable."

"I've forgotten what you do."

He closed his eyes. "Merchant bankers." She said nothing. "I tried to call you at your office. I feel very badly about the whole thing." In the background, he heard a girl say, "How much longer are you going to be on that phone?"

"It doesn't matter," Carol said to him.

"It does to me." There was a pause, tense with uncertainty. "How are you, anyhow?"

"Headache."

"Oh. Have you taken something for it?"

He heard her suck in a deep breath. "If you don't mind, I think I'm going to bed, or something."

"How about . . . uh . . . I mean, d'you think—"

"Bed." She hung up.

Hale spent twenty minutes staring at the furniture, and suddenly, almost effortlessly, he realized what Divine must have meant. There was, of course, only one sure way to contact Starin, just as there was only one sure way to contact the Prime Minister. He got to work.

Mikhail Starin laughed loudly. When something amused him he opened his mouth and let the laughter come tumbling out like bricks out of a dump-truck, and when he had delivered

enough laughter he stopped. Now he was laughing so loudly
that the man had to knock twice.

Starin put the book on the desk, face-down to keep his place.
"This Kingsley Amis is very funny," he said.

"A telegram for you, Colonel."

Starin took it and did not look at it. His eyes were on the
man's face. "Why didn't I get this with the rest of the mail? Who
has seen it?"

"Nobody, sir," the man said. His voice was flat but firm.
Starin stared, searching for signs of nervousness, but the man
simply looked at him.

Too young, Starin thought, well under thirty. They don't
worry like they used to; more fools they. He looked at the
telegram.

It was an ordinary, buff, British Post Office telegram envelope. He slit it open, using the nail of the little finger on his
left hand, a nail which he had allowed to grow until it was an
inch beyond the finger-tip.

The telegram had been handed in at Piccadilly less than an
hour before. It read:

PROJECT 107 VALUABLE FIRST EDITION AVAILABLE. PROOF
WILL BE DELIVERED TOMORROW TUESDAY MORNING PLUS
TELEPHONE NUMBER. CALL AT NOON. BETTY.

Starin read it twice and spread it on his desk and read it
again. It could be good news or it could be bad news. Or it might
add up to nothing at all. But even nothing would be wrong,
because there must be somebody behind the nothing, an interfering somebody who knew more than he should. . . .

"When did this arrive?" he demanded.

"I brought it straight in, Colonel." He brushed a loose hair
from his face, glanced at his hand, and looked politely back at
Starin.

"And now, I suppose you want to get back to your television
set."

The man almost shrugged; he damn near shrugged; his

shoulders certainly shifted. Starin's eyes widened with anger. The man said, "Unless you require—"

"Come here. Show me your hands."

The man walked forward and presented his hands. Starin tapped aside the left hand and examined the right. He squeezed the pad of flesh in the palm below the thumb, making it bulge. "A man without fear is a man without imagination," he said. He laid the sharpened overhang of his fingernail against the pad of flesh and made a quick, deep incision. The man gasped and jerked, but Starin held his wrist until they had both seen the thick red blood surge out and start to leak along the creases of the palm. Then Starin let him go.

"Well now," he said, wiping his finger on the blotter, "were you expecting that?"

The man shook his head. His stomach made a shifting, gurgling noise.

"Then you have learned something. Show a little more respect for the unexpected in future. Understand?"

The man nodded. He was holding his right hand in his left, and both hands were red.

"Good." Starin looked at the telegram again. "Because next time I shall cut off your head. Now leave me before you soil my carpet."

At eleven o'clock, Hale parked his car near the most isolated telephone box on Hampstead Heath. Nobody was about. He taped up three large OUT OF ORDER signs, one on each glass side. It was two minutes past eleven. Fifty-eight minutes to wait.

Time passed very slowly. The morning was grey, and the view from inside the box was limited and unexciting. Occasionally someone walked by, and Hale imitated a telephone repairman; for most of the time he had nothing to do but read the dialling-instruction cards and kick the cigarette ends into a corner.

By eleven-twenty he'd had enough of the kiosk and its stale air. He came out and walked around. The OUT OF ORDER signs looked adequately official and discouraging; there was really no need for him to occupy the booth. He sat on the grass.

Fifteen minutes later a woman walked across the Heath and stopped on the other side of the road. She was about forty-five, solidly built, respectfully dressed in a sensible coat. She had a hat and an umbrella and a pleasant expression, and she was carrying a large parcel wrapped in brown paper. She saw Hale and included him in her pleasant expression, and then politely looked elsewhere.

Hale watched her. She seemed to have arrived; this was where she wanted to be. Nobody else was in sight. She was standing exactly opposite the phone box. In all the acres of Hampstead Heath, this was the spot she had chosen. And it was nearly a quarter to twelve.

Hale got up and walked into the middle of the road. "Can I help you?" he asked. She looked at him so sharply that for a moment he wondered if she might be a police decoy, on patrol. Then her mouth opened and the scrubbed-porcelain gleam of dentures reassured him. "No, thank you," she said. He went back.

For a few more minutes she stood on one side of the road while he sat on the other. Then rain pattered over the asphalt, and they both looked at the black spots on the matte grey. The rain came again, this time with a lick of wind to help it, and Hale remembered that his car windows were open.

He began to walk, but he could see the Heath bending before the wind so he ran to the car and got inside just before the really serious rain swept down. By the time he had wound up the windows, the windscreen was streaming. He switched on the wipers. The parcel lady had gone.

"Good," he said aloud, and then wondered where; and at once he saw her shape inside the phone box. "Bollocks!" he muttered. It was eleven-fifty. If the Express Messenger Service had done its stuff, Starin would have got the evidence ten minutes ago, and he should be calling this number ten minutes from now. She had to go, very rapidly. He ran through the rain and yanked open the door. "I'm terribly sorry," he said. "I'm afriad you'll have to leave."

"Don't be ridiculous."

"I'm sorry. It's urgent, it's an emergency."

"What? It can't be." She pointed at a sign. "This phone's broken."

"Yes, but I'm an engineer, I'm working on it."

"*Working?* You've been sitting out there on the grass. I saw you. Don't be ridiculous."

"*Please,* lady, I'm getting soaked and—"

"Too bad, serve you right, you should have thought about that earlier. Now you want *me* to get soaked. Go away. I'm waiting for my friend."

"Look," Hale said, "you can go and wait in my car. It's not locked."

Her eyes flashed. "You must think I'm simple! Get into a total stranger's car, out here in the middle of Hampstead Heath? I'm not daft!"

"Honestly, this is really urgent," he pleaded.

"Rubbish! How can it be? And you just stay away from me."

The phone rang.

Hale stared, unbelieving. It was far too early. As he checked his watch she lifted the receiver. "Hallo," she said pleasantly.

"That's for me!" he shouted, but she turned her back on him. "Betty?" she said. "Nobody of that name here, you must have the wrong number. This phone's out of order, anyway."

Hale reached over her shoulder and grabbed the phone. She squealed and ducked away. "Hallo, hallo!" he cried. The dialling tone purred hoarsely back at him. "Blast!" he snapped. He banged the phone onto its cradle and glared at her. "See what you've done now? You've cocked it up!"

"Keep away from me!" she shouted. "Go back where you belong!"

Hale looked at her furious eyes, and made a quick decision.

He seized her by the shoulders and swung her through the doorway and out into the bucketing rain. "Beat it!" he ordered. He slammed the door and took a good grip on the handle.

For a moment they stood and hated each other. Come on, Hale told the telephone, ring, you bastard, ring. She hauled on the door and got nowhere. "Get out!" she shouted. He braced himself and concentrated on the silent phone. She beat on the door with her umbrella.

Hale glanced at his watch. Come *on*, Starin. . . . He pressed down on the receiver, making sure it was cradled properly. She appeared suddenly on the opposite side and pounded on the streaming glass. "How dare you!" she cried. Hale turned his back, which enraged her. She kicked the kiosk and hurt herself. "Bastard!" she bawled through her tears.

Hale wondered what Starin was thinking. A wrong number? An error? A hoax? His fingers were getting stiff. Why had Starin telephoned early? A sudden *crack!* made him jump: she was back at the door, hammering with her umbrella. Hale clenched his teeth. The thought scuttled into his head: Maybe the phone really is broken. Maybe—

The bell shrilled.

Hale was so startled that it rang again before he grabbed the receiver. "Hallo!" he said.

"Hallo indeed."

"This is Betty." He realized that he was shouting; the racket from the door was deafening.

"Yes? At last."

"Sorry about that. Did you get my letter?"

"Of course. How else would I have known where to telephone?"

"Good," Hale said. The umbrella-pounding vibrated through his fingers. "You've seen the picture, then."

"I saw a part. Is that what you sent, a part?"

"Yes, a part." The top of the print of the cover, cut diagonally so as to show a bit of the rubber stamp and half the title. "Does it interest you?"

Glass shattered as Starin replied. Hale jammed the receiver against his ear. "Sorry . . . what did you say?"

"I said: should it?"

"I think so." Hale turned and splinters crunched underfoot. *"Bleedin' great bully!"* she shouted at him through the hole in the door. He said rapidly, "I should have thought it quite likely to be of interest to you."

"Indeed."

There was a pause, and she thrust the umbrella through the hole and jabbed Hale in the ribs. "For God's sake!" he shouted. He jammed the sole of his shoe against the hole, but she dragged the umbrella out.

"Betty," Starin said, "what the hell is going on with you?"

"Nothing, just . . . just somebody trying to—" His voice was drowned by furious hammering as she attacked another part of the door. "Listen," he shouted, "d'you want the rest of these prints or don't you?"

"You give me a reason why I should want them, Betty, and perhaps I will."

"Certainly I'll give you a reason. If *you* don't take them, I'll put the whole damn lot up for auction. I know at least three governments who'd be more than interested, starting with the Americans."

"The Americans? Why should they care?"

"For the same reason that you care, because it's important, because—" The umbrella handle pounded away. Hale switched the phone to his other ear.

"Yes? Because?" Starin asked.

She wrenched the door open and screamed, "Bloody swine!" The umbrella slashed across his shoulders, and hurt. He grabbed it and tried to shove her out but she twisted and kicked him. Her hair was in her eyes and a shoe was missing. She was frantic with rage and too much for one hand to fend off.

Starin said, "You seem to have visitors again—" before Hale had to drop the phone.

He wrestled the umbrella from her and used it to drive her

out, while she spat and tried to scratch his face. He slammed the door and held it closed while he found the telephone, which was still swinging and banging itself against the wall. "Are you there?" he asked, breathing hard.

"Betty, I am genuinely *worried* about you," Starin said earnestly. "Those people sound most *dangerous*. Should I contact the police?"

"Just give me an answer, for Christ's sake. Don't worry about me. . . . *Fuck off!*" he bawled in exasperation, as she put her face to the hole in the door. "Not you," he said wearily to Starin. She was cursing, but hoarsely and incoherently.

"I think we should meet," Starin said.

"So you want them. Five thousand quid, in notes."

"Don't be absurd."

"That's the price. I've got other people to pay."

"How sad for you all. Two and a half thousand for the prints *and* negatives this afternoon. Otherwise nothing."

Hale took a huge breath. Starin had bitten. Everything seemed to slow down and relax. He realized that the screaming and swearing had stopped. She had gone.

"O.K.," he said. "Two and a half thousand, in five-pound notes. Where?"

"It doesn't matter."

"Kensington Gardens. The Albert Memorial. When?"

"Three o'clock." The line went dead. It was done.

Hale slumped into a corner of the booth. He felt as if he had won first prize in a raffle and discovered that it was a boa constrictor—a valuable beast, no doubt, but still a hell of a thing to have to go and collect. Then he heard a horn blaring in the rain.

She was sitting inside his car. He went over and looked at her. The rain washed down his sweated face and cooled it. "I'm sorry," he shouted. "It was an emergency." He tried a door; she had locked it. She put out her tongue at him. "Please," he shouted. He tried to use his key but she had her elbow on the locking button. The rain on the window blurred her stiff face.

He was too weary to be angry, but he was getting very wet. He went back to the booth and saw her parcel.

He took it out and showed it to her. She hit the horn again. He turned and walked away. She scrambled out and ran after him. He threw the parcel and she almost fell as she caught it. By then he was running back to the car. As he drove away she slashed at it with her broken umbrella, and scored. The old girl's got spirit, he thought.

Starin kept a heavy jackknife to use for sharpening pencils and cutting string and chopping bits off the telephone. He sat now, hunched at his desk, and let the weight of the blade fall and scar the black plastic. When the door opened and a man came in, Starin did not look up. His arm rose, paused, fell; the telephone rattled under the blow.

"Shall I attend to him?" the man asked. "I mean, Kensington Gardens. . . ." He made it into a joke.

"No." *Chunk* fell the knife. "Use your brains, Grobic. What if he is from some department? What then?"

Grobic thought about it. "I don't believe he's from a department," he said. "All that chaos and confusion. All that hamfistedness. I mean, some things just cannot be faked. And in any case, why try?"

"If he's not from some department then he must be on his own." *Chunk,* and the blade sent a black fragment flying. "Either way, we can't just ignore him. I paid a hell of a lot of money for that report, and I was *told* it was unique. That was half its value. Now here's someone threatening to sell copies of it in the street."

"Perhaps they're not real copies, Colonel."

"I still have to find that out. He sounds confident enough, but . . . Maybe he can be bought off."

"Sometimes that only encourages them."

Starin poked the point of the blade into the dial and turned it at random. "It's a gamble. It's all a gamble. I can't ignore him and I can't risk a fuss, not at this stage. It's all too . . . delicate."

Grobic half-hid a yawn. "I'm afraid delicacy was never my long suit, Colonel," he said.

Starin threw the jackknife into a drawer. "Your deficiencies are plain enough already, Grobic," he said. "Do us both a favour and don't remind me of them."

The rain rapidly worked itself out of a job. Within thirty minutes the sun was shining and the streets were steaming, and Hale drove into a London which looked unnaturally fresh, like a tourist poster, except that it was full of tourists. He left his car with a garage and sidestepped smartly through the lunchtime mobs. It was ten to one when he reached K2. The duty man in the security lock was painfully slow checking him through. Hale ignored the lift and took the stairs three at a time, and strode briskly down the corridor to Divine's office. Good news travels fast.

A blind man was sitting in Hubbard's room. That stopped Hale. Black glasses, white stick, slightly elsewhere expression. Good God, was Divine using blind men now?

"Hubbard is out to lunch," the blind man said. "Of course, in the greater sense, you might say we are all out to lunch."

"Really?" Hale's wits were still coming up the stairs. "I mean . . . Well, yes. No doubt." Perhaps he wasn't really blind at all.

"You want Divine, I suppose. Better go in. They're only showing their holiday slides."

Hale tapped on the door and opened it, sending a wedge of daylight into the gloom. The venetian blinds were closed; tobacco smoke shifted sluggishly in the draught. Divine got up from a chair and waved him in.

Three other men were there, one operating a slide-projector, the others just sitting. All had their backs to Hale. He blinked at the grey sting of smoke, and tried to adjust his eyes to the picture on the screen. It was poorly focused, or perhaps the fault had been in the photography; at any rate it looked like

a close-up of several fuzzy balloons, some only half-inflated.
. . . Unless it was a medical shot, because wasn't that an elbow
. . . and those looked like buttocks. . . . Were they wrestling, or
swimming, or . . .

Hale swayed backwards as he realized exactly what they
were doing. The projector gave a double click; the next slide
was in focus; and Hale felt a lurch in the groin. He stared,
fascinated.

"Arthur's in good condition for his age, isn't he?" one of the
men said.

"He's made for golf," Divine said. "Nine holes a day."

"There must be a joke about that," the other man said.
Nobody laughed.

Divine took Hale by the elbow and led him away. "What
news?" he asked.

"Nudes, Major?"

"News, my dear chap, news."

"Oh, *news.* Yes. Well, I propositioned Starin and he says he's
ready to do a deal, Major. Two and a half thousand for the negs
and prints provided he gets them today."

"How did he sound?"

Hale hesitated. "Hard to say. It was a very bad line."

"And what about the clotted cream of London University?"

"Oh, he's bashing on. I called him at eleven, and he said he
was still double-checking. He should have a result this afternoon."

"And how did *he* sound?"

"Very impressed. In fact, slightly stunned, but that could be
because he didn't get much sleep last night. Project 107 has
really got a grip of him."

Click, click went the projector. "Not *that* again," said one
of the men. "I thought the diplomatic corps was supposed to
have imagination and initiative?"

"Arthur had to do just about all the work," the man at the
projector remarked. "Very one-sided, he said it was."

"Thank God for Arthur, that's all I can say."

Divine looked back from the screen. "He must have *some* idea what it's all about, though," he said. "Extra-super antibiotics or double lasers or something."

"He wouldn't tell me. I asked him, but he said that with something as extraordinary as this he wanted to be absolutely sure."

"He said it's 'extraordinary'?"

"That's the word he used, sir."

Divine grunted. "Extraordinary. . . . What are your arrangements with Starin?"

"Kensington Gardens at three o'clock. The Albert Memorial."

"Kensington Gardens." Divine squeezed his chin. "Why Kensington Gardens?"

Hale sought a good lie and fell back on the truth. "It was the first place I thought of, sir. I suppose it's handy and easy to find."

Divine propped a buttock on the edge of his desk. "Awfully exposed, though. I'd have gone for somewhere indoors. Safety in numbers yet lost in the crowd. We've found that very useful." He took a coin from his pocket and tried to spin it on his desk.

"I didn't have much time to decide, that's all."

"Ask Hubbard next time, he'll help you." The coin wouldn't spin on the blotter so he tried it on the polished wood. "The last time one of my chaps was playing post office with one of their chaps, Hubbard booked two seats at the Festival Hall." The slides were all finished; somebody opened the venetian blinds. Hale looked across and recognized the man with the hare-lip. "It's good and safe," Divine said. "Nobody's going to make a fuss in the middle of two quids' worth of Tchaikovsky." He snatched the coin as it ran off the edge.

"I suppose so." Hale watched Divine's hands. He had strong, soldier's fingers; the kind that would test a cobweb and make a great gash in it. "To tell the truth, sir, I can't see Starin going to the Festival Hall for anybody. Certainly not for me."

"Doesn't have to be there, you know. Old Vic, Covent Garden, Leicester Square Odeon. . . . Oh!" Divine had done it; he watched the coin shimmering slowly across the desk, his face blank, his eyes wide and unblinking. Over by the window, the three men were talking about Arthur and what a great job he had done.

"I honestly don't think it matters much where we meet," Hale said. "If Starin really wants those pictures he won't try to touch me until he's got them." At last the coin slowed and fell and subsided with a tiny metallic drum-roll.

"And after that?"

"I'll just have to be ready to jump, Major."

"Yes." For the first time, Divine really looked at him. "I hope you're not thinking of wearing that suit. You look as if you fell in the river." He walked over to the three men. "Keep in touch," he said.

At five to three Hale walked across the vivid, rain-fed grass towards the Albert Memorial. Under his ribs he felt the same tension, the same pressure on his breathing, which he had felt when he watched Carol Blazey at the party.

The Memorial rose like an Italian-American wedding-cake, elaborate and glittering and hectic. More than Italian-American; it was Neapolitan-Texan. He climbed the steps and stood under the huge canopy. The extravagant setting did nothing to soothe him. He tucked the big white envelope more tightly under his armpit, and twitched his knee-caps to an invisible rhythm. The sun was too bright, he should have worn shades. Damn it.

Starin came round a corner and walked up the bright gravel path. He was smaller and looked younger than Hale expected from his photograph: not the chunky, bearish figure which would have matched his reputation, but trim, like a gymnast, swinging his heavy leather satchel, trotting easily up the steps. Then he stood and looked at Hale, and Hale saw how old the eyes were. Starin could keep his body up to scratch, but those eyes could see nothing new; only repetitions of things past, differently dressed.

"I'm Betty," Hale said.

"Show me proof."

"Balls." Hale walked over to a pillar and sat down with his back to it. He was disturbed by the violence of his own reaction, but it was too late now. "Sure you want proof. You'd like my driving licence and my gun permit and my latest chest X-rays. I recognized you, didn't I? That's all the proof you need."

Starin looked away and chuckled. He shook his head, found some unused chuckles, and looked back. "What it is to be twenty- . . . seven? I remember when I was your age. . . . No, that's not true. When I was your age I was sixteen and not quite so foolish. Who do you work for, Mr. Betty?"

"I work for myself."

"Oh no. You work for a department."

Hale's fingers uncurled. "Which department is that?"

"It doesn't matter. Was that your secretary I heard cursing when I telephoned?"

"No, that was my mother. She was drunk again. She wanted to offer you a round of golf. Mother gets confused when she's in her cups. She mixed you up with Mahatma Gandhi. You see, she believes that Gandhi won the British Open in 1938. Mother was drunk then, too." Hale stopped because Starin wasn't listening; he was watching Hale's face, studying it as if it were a picture, interesting despite its flaws. There was a pause.

"Your mother drinks a lot," Starin observed.

"That's nothing," Hale said. "You should see how much she spills." He pressed his knees together. This was all too bad to last.

Starin looked up at the Memorial. "It's interesting that you should choose such an ugly place to meet, isn't it?"

"Fascinating. It is not generally known that the masonry is stuck together with a mixture of sweat, blood, and tears, generously donated by child labour. Also that Albert, up there, isn't really Albert at all, but a well-built revolutionary who was hanged for tugging his forelock with the wrong hand. They poured bronze over him and propped him in a corner to dry." Hale made himself shut up.

"Will you get a big bonus for this job?" Starin asked.

Hale got up and looked at his watch. "Time I was moving on. Can't afford to keep the Chinese waiting, you know."

Again Starin surprised him. He came over and put his arm around Hale's shoulder, gave a little hug, and steered him down the steps which led into the Park. "It is good to meet you again, Mr. Betty, and in London of all places."

"Again? I don't think so."

"Oh yes, I have met you before in every generation and in many countries. Unhappy young men, walking about with bombs in their pockets and looking for something to blow up. Really you want to blow up everything."

"Really. I must remember to tell Mother." They reached the grass, and Hale tightened his grip on the white envelope.

"You are a funny young man, Mr. Betty. Very stern. Very old-fashioned. Very suspicious. You suspect me, isn't that true?"

"Well, Mother warned me." Starin's arm was still round his shoulders. Hale felt acutely uncomfortable.

"Of course. And yet *I* am the real conservative—I fight to preserve the revolution, because the revolution is successful. Whereas *you* are truly the romantic and the revolutionary, but you don't know it."

"But I don't know it," Hale said. "Poor me."

"Exactly. And you must blow up something, even if it turns out to be yourself."

"Surely not. This is England. We don't go in for bombs. We have soccer and bingo."

"Ah, the famous British sense of humour. That is a bomb, too, a toy bomb to play with, like your Albert Memorial. Look at it. There is *your* England, Mr. Betty. That's why you brought me here: to hit me over the head with your Albert Memorial. Perhaps if you hit me hard enough you will break it to pieces."

"I don't know what the hell you're talking about," Hale said.

"It is just that you are on the wrong side. Probably that is why you are doing it so badly."

"I'm not on anybody's side, I'm in the middle. So can we please, for Christ's sake, get on with it. Here are your negs and prints. Is that the money? And stop bloody fondling me. I'm not for sale."

Starin laughed, full and free, and while the laughter was tumbling out Hale felt a searing pain on his neck, behind the left ear. He jerked and spun away. I'm stung, he thought; but his hand showed blood across three fingers. He felt again, and flinched. "Christ Almighty!" he said. He found a handkerchief and mopped his neck. Then he noticed Starin.

Starin also had a handkerchief, but he wasn't using it. He was examining the little finger of his left hand. Hale saw a smear of blood on the inch-long overhang of nail.

"You little bugger!" Hale said furiously.

Starin said nothing. He stood with his satchel between his feet and looked at Hale sideways, emptily.

"You *bastard*," said Hale. "You sadistic little *bastard.*" He went for Starin and kicked him in his backside. Starin tried to dodge but his bag was in the way, so he turned with the impact and kicked Hale on the shins. Then he scooped up the bag and moved away.

Hale was more astonished than hurt. He caught up with Starin as they reached three women, chattering over their prams. Hale and Starin walked past, a yard apart. Starin's face was blank, but Hale could not hide his fury. The women didn't even look at them.

As soon as they passed a screen of bushes, Hale rushed at Starin and punched him in the head. Starin slammed the end of his satchel into Hale's stomach. Hale covered up, kneed him hard in the left buttock, and felt the impact jar his whole body. Starin slashed at Hale's face with his left hand stiff; Hale stopped the blow with his forearm and took a nick in the wrist.

And so they strolled across the park, closing and scuffling and moving apart and closing again. When they got near anybody, the scuffling stopped and they walked by, breathing hard and flushed in the face. Then they resumed. Hale dodged an elbow aimed at his windpipe, and slammed his own elbow against Starin's heart; in return he suffered Starin's shoe, once on the ankle and once on the knee.

From a distance, it must have looked like a game; two foolish young men who kept drifting apart, swaying outwards and back like lovers who separate for the pleasure of meeting. Up close, it was all gasping breath and rumpled clothes and hair over the eyes. And closer yet, Hale's face was vengeful, while Starin's was intent, almost businesslike.

The end came unexpectedly, even farcically. They lurched out of a hollow as a detachment of mounted police jingled by: a dozen policemen on heavy-rumped mounts, beside the two sweating civilians. When they had passed, Hale looked at Starin and smoothed the squashed and bloody-fingerprinted envelope.

"I always wondered how you people got your jollies," he said. "Now I know."

Starin shook his head. "No, no. We know each other much better now. Isn't that so?"

Hale held out the envelope. Starin held out his satchel. For a moment they stood, each grasping both packages, until Hale said, "One-two-three *go!*" and let go of the envelope as Starin released the satchel. He backed off and undid a strap and glanced at the bundles of money, while Starin used his nail to slit open the envelope.

"We have done a deal, correct?" Starin said. He waggled the envelope. "I have the prints and the negative, you have the money. And perhaps a duplicate negative too? Don't use it, Mr. Betty. You will suffer very severely if you do." Hale mopped his neck and looked at the spreading stain on the handkerchief. He felt impatient, hungry for more fighting. "Just get stuffed," he said.

"I may need you again soon. Keep looking in the *Times'*

personal column for a message to Betty. It will be worth your while."

"Get stuffed and get knotted," Hale said.

Starin looked surprised and amused. "Don't you like dealing with me, Mr. Betty?"

"One day I'm going to kick the Russian shit out of you," Hale said, "and then there won't be anything left to separate your boots from your bonnet."

Starin laughed with genuine pleasure, and strode off.

———————

Hale limped into Hubbard's office and sat on the nearest chair. "Add me to the queue, would you?" he said. Four people were waiting: two civil-servant types carrying bowler hats; a woman like a young headmistress; and the man with the hare-lip, who was sketching the other three.

Hubbard looked up from the electric kettle; he was making tea. "What splendid timing," he said. "The Major was just asking for you."

"Yes? What's happened?" Hale's lip had puffed up, and it gave him a small, tough lisp.

"A visitor. From London University." Hale came over, and Hubbard cocked his head to see the thick plaster on his neck, the stains on his clothes. "Oh dear," he murmured. The kettle boiled.

"Usher the lad in, Hubby, usher away," urged the man with the hare-lip. "I shall make the tea and guard it until you return in case masked raiders burst in and steal it, the rotten bastards, sorry madam, lousy bleeders, I can't help it, the environment's to blame, hurry along, Hub." He crossed the room, rapidly playing the zip of his fly up and down like a one-stringed instrument. The young headmistress closed her eyes.

Hubbard knocked and carefully opened Divine's door, using both hands, as if the hinges were kept together with button-thread. "Ah, tea," Divine said. Hale went in. "Oh well, you're better than nothing, I suppose. . . . You've met Hale, of course."

Hubbard closed the door, still using both hands.

The cream of London University was called Lipman. He was tall, fat, and moist about the chops, either because or in spite of the way he kept licking them. He was about sixty, and he blinked fiercely at strangers as if he suspected them of wasting his time. He had given Hale the fierce blinks when they first met; now he batted out another barrage. Hale nodded neutrally.

"You haven't missed anything; we've only just started," Divine said. "Dr. Lipman tells me he's gone as far as he can with what we gave him on Project 107." He flicked back his jacket to put his hands in his pockets; there was a flash of scarlet lining. "He tells me he's awfully impressed."

"There are gaps, mind you." Lipman's forefinger swung like a metronome. "Not exactly gaps but . . . threadbare patches, areas still to be fully explored. Perhaps serious obstacles . . . ?" He used his sleeve to wipe the spray from "serious obstacles" off the prints. "Here, you see, he never quite . . . ?" He found another print and hit it with his finger. "And look at that, now, just look at that *long-jump*. I'd like to know how . . . ?" Another print, another stab. "That's awfully thin ice there. . . . And *this* bit doesn't altogether . . ." He sucked in his breath. "If you want to know what I think," he said.

"Please," Divine murmured.

"*Brilliant leap-frog*, that's what it is."

"Ah." Divine watched Hubbard bring in the tea. "And assuming that the leap-frogging comes off, doctor, where does it take us? What scientific field are we in?"

"Nuclear physics, of course." Lipman held up the photographs as evidence. "What else?"

"Yes, of course. And what aspect of nuclear physics is involved in Project 107?"

Hubbard gave Lipman a cup of tea. "Ordinary water," Lipman announced. "It's an exploration of the feasibility of using ordinary water as a source of atomic energy."

"Good God."

"Exactly. Good God! Providence has seen fit to provide nuclear energy throughout this universe. We can release it from uranium and plutonium. Why not from water?"

Hale said, "And if this really works, what are the implications?"

Lipman had forgotten Hale. He found him again, and gave him two seconds' thought. "If it works . . ." He shrugged, spilling some tea on the carpet. "The consequences can only be immeasurable. Sorry," he said to Hubbard. "I never drink the stuff." Hubbard took the cup back.

"Ordinary water," Hale said. "Atomic fuel. What a staggering idea. . . . Tremendously cheap, I suppose?"

"I expect so. Cheap to get, obviously; and fairly cheap to use. Also clean, quite fast, fairly simple, safe—that is, as safe as any nuclear plant can be—and relatively silent. I mean, what else do you want?"

"You say it's simple, doctor," Divine said. "Yet Project 107 seems rather complicated."

"Certainly, it is; fiendishly complicated. Put it this way: the route is challenging, but the destination is clear. To a scientist there's nothing new in that. Now then, who did all this?"

Hale said, "I was hoping that you might know, sir. You saw the initials? 'M.J.' "

"I saw the initials. They mean nothing to me, but then I don't know everybody in this field. Where did the stuff come from?"

Hale looked at Divine. Divine looked out of the window.

Lipman twitched his nose. "Sometimes I think you people make a meal out of a mystery," he said. "I can only say it is an attitude in which I can find nothing wholesome."

When Lipman had gone, Divine said, "What happened to you?"

Hale fingered the plaster on his neck and tried to find suitable words. "Well . . . Starin . . . It's hard to explain. Anyway, we ended up having a sort of a rolling brawl across Kensington Gardens. He started it, I may say."

"Why?"

"No reason."

"There must have been a reason. One doesn't . . ." The phone rang. Divine listened. "I know all that," he interrupted. More talk. "Five minutes," Divine interrupted again. *"Five."* He threw the phone down, and Hale watched the pressure slowly fading from his lips as Divine reminded himself of Hale's problem. "What did you call it? A rolling brawl? In Kensington Gardens? Starin must be mad. Was he drunk, or what?"

"No, he seemed sober. And you see, sir, he *did* buy the photographs." Hale gave Divine the satchel. "There was never any dispute about the deal. The fight was just . . . an extra."

Divine dumped the banknotes on the carpet. "Not bad leather, I might keep that. Two thousand?"

"Two and a half. I haven't counted it."

Divine stirred it with his foot. "Peanuts to a wheeler-dealer like you from Flekker Handyside, I suppose. . . . It must have hurt Starin, though. You've no idea how many forms they have to fill in to get foreign currency, it's quite frightening. What do you make of it all?"

"I don't quite know, sir. It's complicated, in a straightforward sort of way, isn't it? Obviously Starin has something to hide, and obviously he values Project 107 pretty highly. On the other hand he didn't seem to know what to make of *me.* I had a feeling he wanted a lot of answers but he couldn't think of the right questions, so he finally hit me—no hard feelings, it was just a way of getting to know each other."

"Did he say anything about 107?"

"No, nothing." Hale stared at the tea stain on the carpet. "But presumably he knows as much as we do. Maybe more."

The telephone rang. Divine opened a desk drawer, put the telephone inside, and closed it on the cord. He glanced at his watch. "You've got sixty seconds left in which to point out the obvious."

Hale was startled. He wasted twenty seconds working through everything that had happened since he'd left Flekker Handyside. Divine tidied up his desk. Hale reached now, the present, the future, the obvious. "I suppose we ought to find M.J., sir," he suggested.

Divine didn't even look up. "See Hubbard," he said. "Send the next customer in."

———————————

"This may sting a little," the Embassy doctor said. He washed the dried blood off Starin's ankle. Starin stood in his shirt and underpants and watched Grobic trying to make sense of the photographs. It was just like Grobic, he thought, shuffling and studying them as if those ranks of chemical and mathematical formulae might contain a hidden clue, like a children's competition in a newspaper where the man's face is part of a tree. The doctor's fingers probed and Starin flinched.

"That hurt," he said.

"Well, I told you it would," the doctor said.

"He seems to be able to look after himself," Grobic remarked.

"He'll need to, because he obviously can't take care of anyone else. I could have snapped his wrist in the first minute and blinded him in the second. He has no technique, only anger."

"So why didn't you, Colonel?"

"In Kensington Gardens? His screams would have interfered with business. I wanted those photographs. And besides, I may need him again."

Grobic was puzzled. "I can't see the point in attacking him, then. Surely if—"

"I hit him because I could see that he wanted me to hit him. He wouldn't answer my questions, and he couldn't find any questions of his own to ask me, so we took up the dialogue of violence."

"Keep still while I do something to this bit of punctuation on your thigh," the doctor said.

Grobic still could not understand. "But then, if he hasn't been trained to fight, why did he go on with it?"

"Exactly. What would you have done in his place, Grobic?"

"Me? I suppose . . . I'd have kept my distance and let you cool down, Colonel, and then tried to get on with the deal."

"Quite right. His response was all wrong. Thoughtless, impetuous, inefficient, not at all the way a trained agent should behave."

"Well, we knew that already," Grobic said. "This fellow blunders about like a fly in a thunderstorm."

"I wish I had some real evidence," Starin said.

"I've found something here, half-way down your leg," the doctor said. "It looks rather like a knee-cap."

The door opened and the Ambassador looked in. "My goodness," he said. "Did you trip over your cloak and fall on your dagger?" Starin looked at him wearily and then looked away. The Ambassador came in. "My information department has some news for you. Apparently you wanted them to look for an eminent British atomic scientist with the initials 'M.J.' "

"That was a week ago. And I didn't say 'British.' 'In Britain' was what I told them."

"I do beg your pardon. They will have got it right, I'm sure; my information department is frighteningly thorough. Anyway, the message I have for you from them," the Ambassador declared proudly, "is that there is no eminent atomic scientist in Britain with the initials 'M.J.' "

"Balls," said Starin.

"Cough, please," the doctor said.

"I have a report signed by this man," Starin told the Ambassador angrily. "A recent report. Tell them to look again."

"They've already looked again. They've made three separate checks."

Grobic said helpfully, "There can't be all that many atomic scientists."

"Can't there?" the Ambassador said. He took out a piece of paper. "In this country nuclear research is at present being carried out in forty-two different places. Of these, twenty-three are colleges or universities, nine are government laboratories, and the rest are run by private industry. In addition, four medical centres employ senior men with qualifications in nuclear physics."

"So he must be in there somewhere," Grobic said.

"Those are the *obvious* places to look," the Ambassador said. He turned the paper over. "Furthermore, each of the armed forces carries out its own secret programme of specialized nuclear research, and the Ministry of Defence has a team up in Cumberland doing something with plutonium which we're not supposed to know about." He put the paper to his lips, edgewise, and whistled. "There are *that* many atomic scientists."

"But not all with those initials," Grobic said.

The Ambassador turned the paper upside down. "Enough," he said. "Did you know that there are three thousand nine hundred and seven people called Jones in the London telephone directory alone? And six hundred and ninety-nine Jenkinses? Two thousand and ninety-four Johnsons? That gives you some idea. My department found *one hundred and seven* men and women with the initials 'M.J.' who are connected with nuclear physics."

"Holy cow," whispered Grobic.

"Naturally, most of them are laboratory assistants, technicians, secretaries, and the like. However, my department identified *seven* who are qualified enough to merit further investigation."

"Seven," Starin said.

"Yes, seven. Four are in teaching jobs; they haven't done any research for some years. One is on a course in America. Another has resigned to stand for Parliament in a by-election."

"That still leaves one," Grobic said.

"Yes. He went to jail a month ago. Dangerous driving, I believe. Of course," the Ambassador said to Starin, "if you insist, I suppose I could ask my people to make a fourth check on the lab assistants and secretaries and so on."

"Listen, this man's *brilliant*," Starin said. He tried to hold the Ambassador with a stare but the Ambassador was sitting down and lighting a small cigar. "I sent his report home by courier—not just in the bag, but *by courier*— and that courier didn't get any sleep until he reached Ulan Bator."

"Nuclear City," Grobic said automatically. Nobody paid any attention.

"And nobody in Ulan Bator got much sleep *after* that, either," Starin told the Ambassador forcefully; but the Ambassador was examining a green blemish on his cigar. "Nobel stand-ard!" Starin shouted at him. "Our own people rate this man's work at Nobel standard, and that pack of blind deaf-mutes you call an information department can't even find him!"

The Ambassador had found a loose thread on a button, and he began burning it off with the end of his cigar. He said, "Ulan Bator also reported that his brilliant work is full of brilliant holes, through any one of which several Nobel prize winners could walk without removing their top hats."

For a moment Starin stopped breathing. The doctor reached up and took his pulse. "Who told you that?" Starin demanded. The Ambassador tugged his jowls. "You're hiding him," Starin accused. His legs were stiff, and his left thigh muscle kept twitching as if touched by flies. "You've found him and you're hiding the bastard. By God, I'll—"

"No, by God, you won't," the Ambassador growled. Grobic stood very still. "This is *my* embassy and, by God, you'll get out of it right now." Everyone was very still: Grobic holding the prints, the doctor holding Starin's wrist, Starin squeezing air in his fists. The Ambassador heaved himself out of his chair. "If my people tell me that there is no big atomic scientist with the initials 'M.J.' working in Britain, you had better believe it, my friend, because it is true." He lumbered towards the door, and his hip brushed Starin's trousers off the back of a chair. He stopped and turned back. "And there is one other thing you had better do. Give my accounts department a damn good reason for letting you go off with several thousand pounds on a glorified petty-cash slip." He turned again and walked over Starin's trousers, breaking something in a pocket. He went out.

The doctor let go of Starin's wrist. The pulse was fast, but in the circumstances that was normal. He gathered together his bits and pieces and followed the Ambassador.

Grobic released a great gush of breath. "Well, well, well," he said. He put the photographs back in the envelope. "It looks as if you stepped on Kamarenski just in the nick of time, Colonel."

Starin put on his trousers. "Grobic, you're what the Americans call a brown-nose," he said.

"Yes? What's that, Colonel?"

"Two pounds of shit in a one-pound bag. Kamarenski didn't take those pictures." He took the envelope and shook them out. "D'you think I would leave a handyman alone in my office long enough to set up a camera and take all these shots?"

Grobic nodded as intelligently as he knew how. "It does seem strange, Colonel." He pointed respectfully to the top photograph. "Especially when they're so clear and legible."

"Yes. Too clear."

Grobic took a closer look. He held the prints up to the light. "Perhaps a little fuzzy around the—"

"No, no, Grobic. Look again. They're too damn clear to be true, I tell you."

Grobic was struggling. "You mean the . . . the light, Colonel? Or . . ."

"I mean the lines. The folds, the creases. Where are they?"

Grobic took a good long look. "I'm afraid I can't see any folds or creases, Colonel," he said.

"Exactly. But believe me, the copy of Project 107 which I got was folded down the middle, so every page had a damn great crease running from north to south."

Grobic frowned. "You mean . . . this is all a forgery, Colonel?"

"No, it's *not* all a forgery. It's the same report, but Mr. Betty took it into his head to photograph an old copy of it."

"But that's crazy, Colonel." Starin just looked at him. Grobic shuffled the prints, and worried. "If Betty has another copy, why didn't he try and sell us that?"

"Yes. In any case, why fool around with photographs? Why not just run it through a copying machine?"

Grobic snapped his fingers. "Why not?"

Starin snapped his fingers twice. "That's what you're going to find out," he said.

They went to a riverside pub, on the south bank below Tower Bridge. Hale took the drinks out to a wooden balcony which overhung rafts of silent, slab-sided barges, and which looked upriver to an eye-stretching panorama of sparkling Thames and silhouetted bridge and the sunstruck dome of St. Paul's like a blazing mainsail on the horizon. He raised his glass to the view. "All for the price of a pint and a half," he said. "Who said London's expensive?"

"You're very chirpy tonight," Carol said. "Has your merchant bank declared a bonus, or something?"

Hale drank, and thought. "I'm in the middle of a rather exciting deal, actually."

"Tell me about it."

"I'm afraid I can't."

"Well . . . tell me who bit you in the neck, then."

"I got stung."

"Stung in the leg, too? You've been limping."

"Have I? I must've done something to it. Pulled a muscle, I expect."

"No, I don't think so. You probably got stung in the leg, didn't you? When you got stung on the wrist." She touched the plaster on his right wrist, and he spilled his beer. "Sorry. Does it hurt?"

"Bit swollen, that's all. . . . Would you like something to eat or anything?"

" 'He said, desperately' . . . I think I like you with your lip all puffed out like that. It makes you sound like a tough queer.

What have you really been up to, David?"

"If you want to know . . . Flekker Handyside has been in a three-way fight with Schroder Wagg and N. M. Rothschild, Ltd., for the control of Consolidated Prunes. I'm afraid we lost, badly. Can you stand it?"

"Well, I can't stand prunes."

"Steady on. Some of my best friends are prunes."

"Oh, friends. I've had a basinful of them too, lately."

"Just give up the prunes. Prunes are terribly fattening."

"So are friends, sometimes." She looked back at the river. "I knew one man who was horribly fattening."

Hale thought about that and didn't like it. "Why can't you swim?" he asked.

"Because they all expected me to swim, they all assumed that I wanted to and I'd be marvellous at it, like they were. I come from a family of webbed feet. So I decided not to. Why can you swim?"

"School, I suppose. Compulsory. Besides, I was no good at team games. And I just like the water."

She picked an old, weathered beermat off the rail and threw it. They watched it spin away, curling down into the black-brown chop between the barges. "If I fell in, would you dive in and rescue me?" she asked.

"Yes."

"How about *her?*" She nodded at a large and ugly girl who was talking to a small and weedy girl at the other end of the balcony. The large girl cackled.

"No." Hale looked at the river, sucking softly at the sides of the barges. "No, I think she'd qualify for that conveniently placed lifebelt over there."

"Fat girls finish last, then."

Hale shrugged. "You asked, I answered."

"But that means you'd risk your life to save me, simply because I'm not as ugly as she is, doesn't it?"

"Well. . . ." Hale was puzzled. "What's the right answer, then? *Shouldn't* I rescue you?" He looked at her delicate, serious profile, sating himself with it.

"I don't know. The question is really what you're rescuing. Suppose I fell in beautiful and came out ugly. Would it still be worth it?"

"Oh, my God," Hale said.

They stayed until closing time and then drove home. They were crossing Blackfriars Bridge when she said, "Can we go to your place first? I don't want to go back to the flat yet."

"Sure. Fine. No problem."

"Yes, problem. With four girls in one flat there's always a problem. I promised I wouldn't be back before midnight, that's all."

"What's going on? Bingo?"

"Far from it."

"What, then?"

"Can't you guess?"

Hale was silent for a while. "That seems a bit rough on you," he said. "Besides, I thought it was the man's job to arrange all that."

"Bless your sweet old-fashioned heart, David," she said. Affectionately or not? He couldn't decide.

He poured two brandies and took them into the kitchen, where she was making coffee. She lifted his right hand and touched the bruised knuckles with her finger-tips. "You must have knocked out at least a dozen bees this afternoon," she said. "Did you use your uppercut, or your straight left?"

"All right, all right." He put his hands in his pockets. "Listen here," he said. "I don't have a sweet old-fashioned heart, and I still think the set-up in your flat is all wrong. What d'you do: keep a bookings chart pinned to the bedroom wall?"

"Oh no. We arrange things in a much more feminine way. We just leave everything to the very last minute, and then we fight like hell over it."

"Good God. I couldn't live like that."

"Well, I'm not very good at it, either. They take it all so *seriously*. It's like being on a diet, or doing P.T. before breakfast. They have to keep their scores."

"The trouble with sex," Hale said gloomily, "is it takes all the romance out of romance."

He carried the coffee into the next room, and they sat down. He switched on the record player. The disc was an early Stan Getz, and the sax ran with the melody like a boy with a kite. Hale shut his eyes and listened, and remembered Carol's smooth, strong legs and opened his eyes. She was curled up in an arm-chair, almost smiling. "Tell me something, David," she said. "What *would* you fight for?"

"Fight? You mean go to war?"

"Yes, risk your life over."

"That's a funny sort of question, isn't it?"

"Well, you've been doing attle over *some*thing today, haven't you? You didn't get those scraped knuckles from punching bees. And I just can't imagine what you would find worth fighting for, that's all."

"Can't you? There must be a thousand things. Free speech, the right to vote, honest cops, clean government: there's four enormously boring causes, all worth a punch in the nose to someone. England, Ireland, Scotland, Wales: there's four more."

"I thought patriotism was unfashionable."

"So it is. All the same, I like it here, and if anybody tries to spoil the place I'll happily scrape a few more knuckles to stop him."

"Ah, you'd have made a splendid knight, David."

"Why? Because you think I sound old-fashioned? Fashion's got nothing to do with it. I believe in simple solutions to simple problems. I know that's far too complicated for point-one per cent of the population, the freaks who wear fancy dress and talk incoherence and write songs about going back to Cincinnati, Ohio. But then, you see, I've *been* to Cincinnati, and I know what they don't know."

"It's like Huddersfield," she said.

"It used to be. Now they're rebuilding it to look like Middlesbrough."

"Middlesbrough should sue. . . . So you don't like the dotty fringe, then."

"No, no. It's not a question of liking or disliking; what matters is that they're *not* modern, they're *not avant-garde*. They're as ancient as drag. Bohemia. . . . What the hell ever came out of Bohemia, except Bohemians?"

Carol came over and sat on the arm of his chair. "I still think you should have been a knight," she said. "That's one of the reasons why I'm here now."

Hale tried to work it out, and failed. "Why?"

"Because I don't have to do any wrestling. You've no idea how fed up a girl like me gets of wrestling. That's the first reason."

"Is there another?"

"Yes. You remind me of my eldest brother. I was in love with him when I was young. He was the manliest man I ever knew."

"I'm flattered. I'd like to meet him some day."

"Too late. He fell off a mountain when he was twenty-two."

At midnight Hale drove her home. She said he'd better not come up, in the circumstances, but many thanks for a lovely evening. She kissed him, once. He felt dull desire move uneasily in his loins, but by then she had gone.

Divine took a plastic rule from Hubbard's desk and flexed it as if he were thinking of thrashing somebody. "Surely to God, we can find *someone*," he said.

Hubbard stopped looking attentive and started looking worried again. "It does seem a shame, sir," he said.

"Dammit, I've never let the Director down yet," Divine muttered. "It's not a huge job, we *must* have *someone* spare. Where's Payne?"

"Still on holiday, Major."

"Yes, but *where?* Let's get him back."

"He didn't say. That is, he said Frinton-on-Sea, but I'm afraid he's not there."

"Cunning little bastard. . . . We cut short his last leave, didn't we?"

"Yes, sir. And the one before that."

Divine gave the air a good whipping with the plastic rule. "Devious little sod. . . . Clutton's down in Portsmouth, I suppose."

"And just beginning to get results, so he says." Hubbard picked up a list. "There's such a lot *on* at the moment, isn't there, Major? Franklin . . . Eady and Boyle . . . Corby . . . I don't suppose you could move Fletcher?"

Divine thought briefly about moving Fletcher. "Too risky," he grunted. They looked at the dust hanging in the air. "Blast. I hate to miss a trick like this."

Hale came in, bright-eyed and buoyant. "Good morning, sir," he said. "Guess what, sir." He waggled a copy of *The Times*.

"Have you cleared up that Project 107 nonsense yet?" Divine asked sharply. The phone rang. "If that's K5, I'm in the loo."

Hubbard handled the phone delicately, as if it hadn't been well. "I'm afraid he's washing his hands at the moment," he said. They heard a harsh, electronic laugh. Hubbard listened, then hung up. "K3 says his budget is up by ten per cent next year," Hubbard said.

"*Ten per cent?*" Divine flexed the rule violently. It broke into three pieces. "There are times when this place reminds me of a kennel," he said, "full of bitches, all permanently in heat. Oh well. I suppose I'd better tell the Director I can't do it."

Hale said quickly, "I've heard from Starin, Major." He held up his *Times*.

"How nice." Divine waved them out and shut his door.

"We're feeling a little liverish this morning," Hubbard murmured.

"Why? What's wrong?"

"Oh, nothing. I suppose that we were—what shall I say—*on the nest* last night." He handed Hale a typewritten card. It read: *Professor Mervyn James, Peake Research Building, Middlesex.*

"Who—" Hale began; then he realized. "My God, that was fast."

Hubbard shrugged. "Identifying a top nuclear physicist whose initials are M.J. is not a particularly challenging task," he said tartly. He took the card back. "You can remember that, can't you?"

"Yes, I think so." Hale glanced at Divine's door. "I suppose I'd better find out what Starin wants, first."

Hubbard tidied up his desk.

"Unless I check on Professor James first, and do Starin later."

Hubbard put a paper-clip in the paper-clip dish, and issued a small smile. Hale went out. Not all the bitches were in heat, he thought; one, at least, had been doctored.

The message in the *Times'* personal column simply said BETTY PLEASE CALL ME. Hale telephoned the Trade Mission. The number rang, and rang. He found himself thinking about Lavagarde, in Montreal. He had called Lavagarde and tried discreetly to steer him away from any colourful suggestions which Brandon might make; but Brandon had not so far contacted Lavagarde, and it was in any case difficult to be discreetly discouraging about a colleague, so Hale wasn't sure that Lavagarde entirely understood. Perhaps someone ought to . . .

A woman spoke, and told him to wait. Hale realized that he was breathing quite normally, that he wasn't at all nervous. A man came on the line, not Starin, and told him the name of a pub, the Houses of Parliament, in Soho. "The saloon bar at eleven o'clock," he said, deadpan, reading words.

"Yes, but—" Hale began. The line went dead.

The Houses of Parliament was just a regular boozer off Greek Street, with the smell of last night's raucousness still lingering in the stale air. The saloon bar was empty except for an old man with a glass of stout; he sat in a corner looking stolid and impenetrable, as if the management had just taken him out of the broom cupboard and dusted him off and shoved him behind the table in order to take the curse off all that desolate vacancy. Fairy lights curled along the top of the bar.

"Half of bitter," Hale said.

The barman raised only his eyes from the sports pages—his face was too heavy. "You Betty?" he asked.

Instinctively, Hale shook his head; he thought the man was asking about *betting;* then he remembered, and said, "Oh—yes, *me*, I'm Betty, that's right."

"Make your bloody mind up, then."

"No, I'm Betty. I just misheard you, that's all."

"Got any proof?"

"Well . . . No, I—"

The old man in the corner started laughing.

"Haven't you got Betty's driver's licence? Betty's credit cards? Betty's bank-book?" It sounded like a burglary haul.

"No, I'm afraid . . ." The old man cackled some more. Hale took a deep breath and wished down a heart attack from heaven.

"See your neck, then."

"Neck?" He cocked his head.

The barman leaned sideways and looked at the plaster covering the cut from Starin's sharp little finger. He saw Hale's right wrist, also strapped up. "That's proof," he said. The old man guffawed with pleasure. "Got to make sure, you know," the barman said. "Some of the sods we get comin' in here, you wouldn't believe." He gave Hale an envelope.

Hale put it in his pocket and walked away. "Sounds like I've made *your* day, anyway," he said to the old man. "They can't fool me," the old man said. "I been around too long." He winked complacently.

Hale had his hand on the door when the barman said, "Don't you want it, then?" He held up a half of bitter. Hale put money on the nearest table. "You're a gentleman," the barman said.

"Not that I ever doubted it." He took a mouthful.

Hale added more money. "And a pint of hemlock for His Grace the Duke of Dagenham," he said.

The old man half-stood, and pointed an unstraight, unclean finger. "O.B.E." he said.

"My mistake," Hale said. "Sorry."

The old man forgave him with a generous gesture, and Hale walked back into the sunlight.

The envelope said nothing. The paper inside it said: *Jim's Gym, Farley Street, Bermondsey. 12 noon.* Handwritten, probably by the barman. They must have telephoned the pub. Hale leaned against a lamp-post and looked at the blow-ups outside the skin-flick cinema across the road. Then he looked at the sky. Fuzzy blue, eating into the gold haze. Heat coming. From the Russian Trade Mission to the Houses of Parliament (saloon bar) to Jim's Gym: it reminded him of a Young Conservatives' car rally, years before, chasing clues with a vivacious redhead called Sarah who had seemed to be ready to sleep with him until he refused to sign her petition to restore hanging. . . .

It was ten past eleven. Hale decided to walk to Bermondsey. It might be a mistake to get there too early; besides, he could use the time to guess what Starin wanted of him. Presumably something to do with Project 107. If Dr. Lipman was right about using water as nuclear fuel, it was small wonder that Kamarenski had been silenced before he could stammer out the news. On the other hand, what did Starin plan to *do* about it? Presumably he knew who M.J. was and where he worked: Hubbard had traced him overnight, and the Russians had had a week, perhaps longer, to find him. In any case, Starin seemed to have an inside lane to James, otherwise how had he got hold of that research report or summary or whatever the hell it was?

Hale was walking over Blackfriars Bridge when it occurred to him that Starin might ask him to persuade James to defect. He stopped and stared at the river, which sparkled back with pleasure. It was a rich idea. He could protect James for Divine while he pretended to poach him for Starin.

For the first time, Hale relished the kick which comes from honest deceit; and he realized that this was K2's big advantage over Flekker Handyside. Both of them offered challenging and rewarding work, but at K2 a Christian gentleman could deal himself four aces off the bottom and still have a good appetite for dinner; which was curiously satisfying.

Farley Street was a broad, cobbled dead-end with tufts of grass growing in the gutters. The buildings were mainly three-storey warehouses, all locked and barred and packed with old air. The atmosphere was heavy with planners' blight.

Hale walked down the middle of the cobbles. He had a feeling of being watched, and looked up and saw rows of pigeons sitting on the eaves, resting their little pin-brains. He clapped his hands, but they wouldn't move. At that moment a car drove into Farley Street. It carried a driving-school placard on the roof. Hale kept walking and watched it approach. It ground past him at ten miles an hour, turned at the end, and ground back, its driver staring and grinning with tension. The car revved, turned, and vanished. Silence again. Hale stood and looked at the entrance to Jim's Gym. It was twelve o'clock.

The name on the door was painted in a prewar style, black on brown; the paint had lasted better than the style, but not much. Six dirty milk bottles queued forever by the doorstep; maybe they were prewar too. Hale knew now that he should have told K2 where he was going. That was a stupid mistake. Jim's Gym tasted sour already.

He took a step back and worked out how big the place was: two storeys at the front, maybe a hundred feet across. More pigeons on the roof, all giving him the evil eye. On impulse he took a milk bottle and lobbed it up at them; this time they took fright and clattered away. The bottle curled out of sight and clunked onto the roof. Seconds later it rolled off. He dashed forward and just caught it, staggered, and knocked over three of the other bottles. Two smashed. "The hell with this," he said aloud.

The door opened at his touch. All he could see was a flight of wooden stairs. The middle step groaned as he trod on it, then played the groan back as he moved on. The corridor turned right and opened onto a landing with a glass-fronted office. The glass was badly cracked and held together by bandages of brown-paper tape. Bleached fight-posters decorated the pine panelling, some hanging diagonally, some suspended by their feet, a few crumpled on the floor. The sun baked through a skylight and cooked up a soft fug of ancient embrocation, sweat, nicotine, and ballyhoo.

Hale looked down a corridor littered with rubbish. It seemed to dogleg off to the left, but the light was bad at that end. "Anybody home?" he asked. His voice sounded puny. He cleared his throat and called, "Anybody around?" A poster fell off the wall and tobogganed towards him. He picked it up, half-expecting a cryptic clue scrawled on the back. Nothing.

The boards in the corridor creaked like a sound-effects audition. Hale trod noisily past abandoned dressing-rooms, massage-rooms, baths. He paused at the corner and looked into the gloom. Behind him, an invisible man advanced as the floorboards creaked back up into place. Hale felt a tiny bristling of short hairs on the back of his neck. He strode forward, rapping the wooden wall with his knuckles to make more noise. He found himself frowning, and wondered why.

The gloom deepened as he walked towards a pair of high, black double-doors, which opened onto more stairs, with yet another set of doors at the top. Streaks of faded light leaked under the bottom edge and fanned out, searching for his eyes. He went up and pushed open the doors and released a flood of stagnant sunshine. It was the gym.

After those corridors, this place was the Albert Hall. You could have played indoor soccer if you took out the boxing ring which stood in the middle like a bandstand someone had forgotten to return to the municipal park.

Hale walked forward and unconsciously squared his shoulders at the lofty, dusty spaciousness with its remote wallbars and its scattering of elderly apparatus: punchbags, springs, ropes, a vaulting-horse, burst medicine-balls, a rusted rowing-machine squatting in the gauzy sunlight.

He went on, hearing his footsteps strike out sharply and then die in the vastness. A balcony ran around two sides of the gym. He climbed into the ring, partly because it was there to be climbed into, partly to get a better look at the balcony. The balcony was just as empty. He turned around and saw a man watching him.

Hale jumped. "Jesus!" he said. The man said nothing. He was sitting on a folding chair half-way between the ring and wall, arms crossed, his hands cupped under his elbows, legs outstretched. Black shoes, light-grey suit, apple-green tie, neat clean-shaven face, tidy hair, and about six feet four inches of muscle separating the shoes from the hair. He was twenty-five-ish and he looked as if he might decide to live forever.

"Good morning," Hale said. The words went exploring and failed to return. "Or good afternoon, or whatever it is," he added. No response. "I expect you're from the Mission," Hale said helpfully. More silence. "You see, I'm Betty," he explained. From a boxing ring, the name sounded worse than usual. "I could always make it Fred, though," he said.

The big man unfolded his arms and pointed to his left. Against the wall was another folding chair.

For about twenty seconds he sat pointing while Hale stood looking. "I think it's a chair," Hale said. He got down and went over. "Yes, it's a chair, all right," he called. "Would you like me to smash you over the head with it?" The big man had gone back to position one. Hale sat down.

Twenty minutes passed. Hale was beginning to feel drugged by the sunshine and the silence, when a door slammed far away. He stopped breathing and listened to the high, bat-squeak singing of blood in his ears. The remote creak of floorboards sounded; died; returned and approached in a steady march-time. The double-doors banged. Hale stood up. A man who wasn't Starin came in, glanced at him, and went to talk to the big man. Hale sat down. He felt the need to assert himself, and he blew his nose.

The new man came over. "Grobic, from the Russian Trade Mission," he said. They shook hands. Grobic was in his early forties. He was a smiler and a nodder. His damp brown eyes were permanently bagged, suggesting that he worked too hard and too late into the night; but his chunky build was strong and he had a grip like a steeplejack.

"I'm Betty," Hale said. He nodded towards the big man, who was still in his chair. "A colleague?"

"That is Stefan. Stefan talks very little. He is a thinker." Grobic smiled and nodded.

"A thinker? I didn't realize you had room for them."

"Ah, Stefan doesn't think about politics. You know that he boxed for Russia in the Olympics? Yes. A wonderful boxer, Stefan, unbeatable. And then—the accident."

"He had an accident?"

"No, no. His opponent had the accident. I was there that night. One blow to the head—" Grobic snapped his fingers. "The poor fellow died in the ambulance. Stefan has never boxed anyone since."

"That's . . . too bad."

Grobic smiled and nodded. "He asked to be allowed to come today. Just to look, and to think. . . . However, however. I'm sure you are not here to study yet another example of Russian melancholy."

"Well, no. . . ."

Grobic folded his arms and put his head on one side. "Go ahead, Mr. Betty."

Hale blinked. "Mr. Starin isn't—?"

"You can tell me anything. Or better still, everything." Grobic laughed so that his arms shook.

"I think perhaps someone's made a little mistake." Hale

found himself smiling to keep pace with Grobic. "I didn't ask for this meeting."

"You telephoned our Mission?"

"Yes, but only—"

"One moment. Let us both be clear about the situation." Grobic began walking, so Hale went with him. "We paid you a very great deal of money for those photographs. More than they were worth, in fact."

Hale shrugged. "Some people might say they were priceless."

"We are not some people, and we would say that they were counterfeits. Cheap imitations. Not the real thing."

"Counterfeits? But that's ridiculous. Anyway, what d'you mean, 'counterfeits'?"

"That is what *you* should tell *us.*"

"I wish I could. I don't understand what you mean."

"Mr. Betty . . . we wish to be your friend. The goods you sold were not entirely kosher. Now why?"

"God knows." Hale chewed on his lip while he traced events back to Kamarenski. "Mr. Grobic, as far as I was concerned, that was a straight photographic copy. You've got the negatives, you can see for yourself. Why the hell should I want to alter it, anyway? I'm no scientist. All I know about Project 107 is—" He breathed in deeply through his nose and held his breath while he forced his arms down and fluttered his fingers. Grobic smiled and tugged at an ear-lobe and waited. "Is the damn title," Hale said flatly.

Grobic gave a grunt of disappointment. "This kind of thing is very bad for me," he said. He gave the area of his heart a little massage while they walked behind Stefan's chair. Stefan had not moved. "It makes me distressed when, like poor Stefan, I cannot make contact any more." He jabbed two soft holes in the air by way of demonstration. "Well, so that all this shall not be a complete waste, tell me then about your department, Mr. Betty. Are you happy there?"

"I have no department."

Grobic tut-tutted. "Then tell me about the people behind Project 107. You can talk about them, surely." He smiled and nodded.

"You know as much as I do, Mr. Grobic."

"No, no, no. You still haven't told us how you got hold of that report on Project 107. Have you?" Grobic exposed his teeth again. Hale kept his covered.

They walked to the end of the gym, turned and came back. Stefan stood up. He was six-foot-six, not six-foot-four, and his suit was so lightweight that Hale could see the shifting of his shoulders inside it. Grobic spoke to him in Russian, and Stefan replied. Grobic laughed and shook his head. They both looked at Hale.

"Tell me and maybe I'll laugh too," Hale said.

"Unlikely," Grobic said. "Stefan says that this place would be perfect for knocking information out of someone. He points out that it was designed for physical violence."

"Slightly less than hilarious."

"I told you—Stefan takes things too seriously. I explained to him that you really wish to help us. It's just a matter of establishing a mutual dialogue. Then little things like the difficulty over the project report will become perfectly clear." Grobic held his arms wide in a gesture of understanding. "Right?"

Hale copied the gesture and said, "Wrong." Stefan hit him under his outstretched arms with a punch that bent in his ribcage like a plastic bucket. Hale tottered sideways on sparrow's legs and collapsed on his rump. One lung was full of burning, and the taste of seething sickness kept climbing into his head until it reached his eyes and ears and swamped them with yellow fog. He could feel the wooden floor through his palms, very far away, as if on the ends of stilts. Then the stilts dissolved, and he fell flat.

After a few seconds the fog drained out through his ears and made room for the big, hollow room sound. It surged in sluggishly, while his eyes tried to see beyond a screen of hazy smoke. He got up on one elbow. The pain in his ribs felt like a bucket of hot coals.

Stefan had his back to the ring. His arms were outstretched and he was plucking at the lowest rope. Grobic was sitting in Stefan's chair, smiling and nodding.

Hale got to his knees, then to his feet. He felt the blood abandon his face, and he went down on his knees again. He tried to wipe the haze from his eyes. His skin felt cold and damp.

"Stefan, Stefan," Grobic said in the distance. He shook his head. "There was no need to do that, Stefan."

Hale got to his feet, and this time he stayed on them. Something foul came up into his mouth. He spat it out, feebly, and it ran down his chin.

"Mr. Betty was just going to explain," Grobic said cheerfully. "He was going to tell us about the counterfeit copies. Now you've ruined his train of thought."

"You fucking bastard," Hale whispered at Stefan. One of his lungs wasn't working.

"Ah, Mr. Betty has got his breath back!" Grobic clapped his hands. "Splendid. Now we're in for a treat, Stefan!"

"I can't bloody tell you what I don't bloody *know*," Hale whispered harshly.

"Surely you know who you work for?" Grobic said. "Mmm?" He widened his eyes and raised his eyebrows.

"I work for myself," Hale wheezed. Breath was seeping back into that dead lung. He saw Stefan push himself off the ropes and tried to move away from him, but his feet were impossibly heavy.

"In that case you can tell us how you got the film," Grobic suggested. Hale was trying to hobble behind Grobic's chair but Stefan took a long stride and punched him in the middle of the back. The impact jolted Hale's skull and shook his jaws apart, and knocked him flat on the floor.

Grobic suddenly sneezed. He blinked at the sunlight, and

put on a pair of dark glasses. "Stefan is trying to tell us something," he said. "What are you trying to tell us, Stefan?"

Hale crawled behind Grobic's chair and hid. He saw Stefan looming up on the right, and dragged himself desperately around the other side. "The trouble with Stefan is he doesn't understand a word of English," Grobic said. Stefan bent down and pounded Hale's arm on the biceps. "There's absolutely no need for that, Stefan," Grobic said.

Hale tried to crawl around the chair, but Grobic stretched his legs out and he couldn't get by. "You obviously *wanted* us to notice the counterfeiting," Grobic was saying from a long way off. "All we're asking you is *why*. Please tell us." Hale tried to push Grobic's legs out of the way, but he wasn't strong enough. He found that he was crying. Pain bloomed and faded and bloomed again somewhere else. He felt Stefan pick him up by his collar and walk him across the gym. The ring was in front, then Stefan turned him and the ring was behind, propping him up. Hale's head wobbled and his fingers scratched for something to hold. Stefan pulled Hale's jacket open and flipped his tie onto his shoulder. "No, no, Stefan," Grobic's mild voice said. *"Please.* Not the stomach." Hale watched with a kind of remote horror as Stefan, calm and thoughtful as ever, centred his fist just above Hale's belt-buckle and braced himself. Hale wanted to collapse, but his legs no longer obeyed orders. He saw Stefan pull back his fist, he tasted bile in his throat, and he heard a noise like thunder overhead.

The savage crack of the explosion kept circling inside Hale's suffering head after the echoes had battered themselves flat against the gym walls. The next time he looked, Stefan was ten feet away with his hands on his head, and Grobic was getting up and raising his arms. Somewhere a man's voice shouted, "Hustle your ass up that end! Move-move-move! Hands on the head! Face the wall!" Stefan and Grobic walked away.

Hale let his head wobble around to watch them go. It was all extremely odd. That voice was still shouting, but the two Russians were not moving. They stood facing the wall with their hands on their heads. Hale rolled around until his chin was resting on the canvas. More shouting. Louder, if anything. Hale got both hands underneath his willpower and made a supreme effort and looked up.

The shouting was coming from the balcony. A small man was waving a large gun. He was shouting at Hale.

"What?" Hale croaked.

"What? What ya mean, 'what'? Oh, for Chrissake, forget it. You couldn't hold this goddam cannon anyway. Listen, I'm coming down. . . . Shift your fat ass up the other end, kid, away from those bums. . . . *Face that wall, Grobic, ol' Betsy here could knock you right through it.* . . . You keep out of the way, kid. . . ."

Hale stumbled over to a corner and leaned against it. The man on the balcony backed away from the Russians until he was almost opposite Hale. A vaulting-horse stood underneath. He sat astride the balcony rail. "Face that wall!" he shouted. He swung both legs outside. "Hands on heads!" He held the gun in his left hand and reached down with his right to get a grip; then he lowered himself until he was hanging full length. There was a gap of at least a foot. "Face-a-wall!" he shouted. He dropped. One leg of the vaulting-horse folded up under his weight and the whole thing crashed sideways and spilled him. The gun went off and blew a hole in the skylight, and the recoil kicked it out of his hand. Grobic and Stefan raced across the gym. By the time the man had got the horse off his leg and found his own gun they were through the doors and pounding down the corridor. He ran, limping and swearing, to the doors and disappeared. Hale heard four stupendous reverberating shots. Then he limped back into the gym and came over.

"You O.K., kid?" he asked. Bright-red blood trickled out of the corner of his mouth. He tucked the smoking cannon into his waistband and held Hale's chin to steady it. "Take it easy, huh?" He conjured up a hip-flask and put it to Hale's lips. Bourbon scorched over his tongue until he pushed it away.

"Jesus!" he spluttered. He coughed, hard. "Who are you?"

"For want of a better name," he said, "we are the United States Cavalry."

Hale rested his head against the wall and let the bourbon soak down. The American was a small, slightly battered-looking man, with a determined mouth bracketed by deep lines so that they formed a bowed letter H. He had wide-awake grey eyes beneath lids that drooped with the weight of experience. He wore desert boots, grey slacks, a baggy Harris-tweed jacket. Hale watched him bury the enormous gun in an enormous shoulder-holster. "That's some cannon," he said weakly.

"Well, if you're going to shoot a man you might as well blow his head off and be done with it. I'm Gary Fitzgerald."

"George Betty." Hale briefly wondered why he kept pretending, but his brain wasn't accepting heavy loads, so he forgot it. They shook hands. "You're bleeding, you know."

Fitzgerald mopped his jaw, but the trickle continued. "Must have cut open my mouth when I hit the deck," he said.

He took Hale's arm, and they limped towards a basin fixed to the wall. Fitzgerald went away and came back with a fire-bucket full of water. He half-filled the basin, sloshed water inside his mouth, spat, and flushed the red stains away. Then he refilled. Hale washed his face and rinsed his mouth. He began to feel slightly less dreadful.

"Out the back way, George, huh?" Fitzgerald said. Hale nodded, and followed.

They emerged into a delivery yard with a big old Chevrolet Impala parked in it. Fitzgerald opened the door for Hale, and trotted round and got in. His limp had gone now. He drove off at speed.

Sunny, summery London opened up all around. Hale let his head sink back against the warm upholstery, and half-closed his eyes. Seedy, civilized streets, unthreatening, undangerous. Safe in the sunshine. He touched his ribs, and winced. The whole thing was fantastic. "Thank God for the U.S. Cavalry," he said.

"I was about to get bust in two, or something. Thank you very much."

"Any other Methodist minister on vacation would have done the same."

Hale thought about that. "How on earth did you know—?"

"Did I know you were in there; well, don't light too many candles, George, because the truth is I didn't. I been tailing *them*, not you." He glanced across, and gave him the hip-flask. "Have a sip, and bear in mind that this stuff costs me five ninety-five a quart. Unhappily it is not deductible for tax purposes. . . . Where was I?"

"Following Grobic."

"Sure. I know Starin's interested in this Project 107, see, but I don't know exactly how, or why. All I know is the little bastard's started creaming his jeans three times a day with matinees Wednesdays and Saturdays, and that has to be bad news." Fitzgerald swept over Blackfriars Bridge, one hand guiding the power steering.

"Who told you about Project 107?" Hale returned the hip-flask.

"Guy by the name of Kamarenski. Dead now."

Hale looked out of the window and tried to absorb the news. It seemed important but not significant, or possibly it was significant but not important. His head began to ache again. What the hell: Kamarenski was still dead, nothing was changed. "What now?" he asked.

Fitzgerald shrugged. *"Quién sabe?* That's Spanish for 'Do up your fly, big boy, I've been screwed once already.' After today, I might as well cut my losses and go back to selling used cars in Omaha, Nebraska."

"You mean you're giving up?" Hale let some of his surprise and disappointment show. "Why?"

"Well . . ." Fitzgerald stopped at lights and ran his tongue cautiously around his mouth. He took out his handkerchief and spat into it and folded it up. "I can tell you this: blood will never replace booze," he said. "George, that little encounter in the gym was the last thing I needed. They both got a good look at me, they'll know me again. So my cover's blown, right? And all my chances of getting near Project 107 are blown with it."

A blend of gratitude, fatigue, and bourbon worked on Hale's tongue. As the lights changed and Fitzgerald pulled away, he said, "Hell, there must be *some*thing we can do."

Fitzgerald rolled his eyes. "Say on, friend, say on. No contribution is too small."

"Well . . ." Hale eased his aching back. "Look, just for the record, can you show me some kind of identification?"

"Identification? Yeah." Fitzgerald was suddenly annoyed. "Sure I can. Just for the record, friend, what the hell d'you think *this* is?" He held up his handkerchief, stained a dark crimson.

Hale was silent. Fitzgerald worked his way around Trafalgar Square. "Forget it, kid, that was the ulcer talking. Sometimes you can't even see my lips move. Bum joke."

Hale glanced across and saw Fitzgerald's face set with worry and concentration. He wondered whether or not the ulcer was real.

"It's like this," Fitzgerald said. "If you want papers I can show you papers. C.I.A., F.B.I., M.I.5 through 17, French, German, Nicaraguan, you name 'em, I'll get 'em for you in two hours flat, all perfect except they're all fake. But I ask you: where could you get another handkerchief like *this?*"

Hale thought it over, while they came out of Trafalgar Square and turned into Pall Mall. "Is that why you haven't asked me how *I* come into all this?" he said.

Fitzgerald sighed. "O.K., suppose I ask you," he said. "Suppose you tell me. Either it's the truth or it's a heap of crap, right? So now I got to start aggravating myself over *you* as well as over *them*. Too much, man. Too much. The old ulcer can't take it, and I'm not breaking in a new ulcer just to keep you happy. No way."

"Maybe you're right," Hale said. "It just seems like you're taking a hell of a risk. I mean—"

"Listen, George. You gotta learn one thing very rapidly in

this business or you're finished, and that is: the name of the game is the Black Hats versus the White Hats. No matter how complicated and fouled-up things get, just keep asking yourself who is wearing which colour hat, and work on that. Clear?"

"Yes, that's clear."

"This would really be a very straightforward business if people would only stop throwing shit in the fan. You remember those two German civilians who stole a U.S. Army missile and simply mailed it air freight to Moscow?" Fitzgerald shook his head admiringly. "I mean, why have a complicated disaster when for the same price you can have a simple disaster?"

"True," Hale said. "Some people seem to make a meal out of a mystery."

They sat in silence while Fitzgerald eased the Chevrolet past some roadworks. "When I went into that gym," he said, "I remember taking a fast look around and making a quick decision. Which one is the guy in the white hat? It had to be you. The rest was easy. If you wanted to join forces, O.K. If not, well . . ." Fitzgerald shrugged.

"Don't get me wrong," Hale said. "I certainly think we should work together, if that's O.K. by you."

"Any ideas?"

"One. It might pay off, or it might give us nothing more than we have already, but I think it's worth checking out. A chap by the name of Professor Mervyn James is supposed to be linked with Project 107. My information is he works at the Peake Research Building. That's somewhere beyond Twickenham, in Middlesex."

"There should be a road map in that side pocket," Fitzgerald said. "Try and figure out a nice simple route."

Fitzgerald drove slowly past the Peake Research Building and examined it. Rhythm-and-blues twanged quietly from the car's cassette unit until he flicked it off. Five storeys of white brick shone respectfully in the healthy, country sunlight. "Now there's an architect with a mind like an empty Kleenex box," he said.

"The place is probably pretty thoroughly sealed up," Hale said. "I expect they take their security seriously. What do we do, just walk in and ask for him?"

Fitzgerald chewed on his lower lip. "That's the obvious, easy way, isn't it? But somehow instinct says no. I have this feeling we should play this one close to the chest. What d'you think?"

"I think the fewer people know about it, the better."

"Check. So let's go find ourselves a couple of cowboy suits."

Fitzgerald drove to a shopping centre which had a Government Surplus store. They picked out two pairs of ex-Navy boilersuits, two pairs of reconditioned working boots, a pair of gauntlets for Hale, and an old black beret for Fitzgerald. He also chose a well-worn Army pack and a vacuum flask. "Can you pay?" he asked. "This doesn't look the kind of place that takes American Express."

Hale took out his wallet. "You bought the wrong colour hat in any case," he said. "They wouldn't trust you in that." Fitzgerald laughed, and as Hale counted out the notes he felt again the fortifying comfort of teamwork, even if the team was only two.

They drove to a quiet street and got dressed. The clothes felt thick and stiff but they looked convincing and smelled like the back seat in a workman's bus. "Stuff your shoes in your pockets," Fitzgerald said. Hale obeyed, and his mind did a flashback: Kamarenski's feet wobbling under the blanket in a rocking ambulance. . . . He rested against the car and washed his face with his hands. "Hey, you O.K.?" Fitzgerald asked. Hale nodded. Fitzgerald threw some tools into the Army pack: pliers, screwdriver, a wrench, a tire-iron; whatever was lying around in the trunk of the Chevrolet. "Frankly, you look pretty godawful," he said. He coiled a length of tow-rope and put it next to the pack.

"I'm O.K.," Hale said, moving. He got into the car before Fitzgerald could argue.

The Peake Building had a car park down one side and all around the back. Fitzgerald drove slowly to the end and parked. He scanned the building carefully. *"There,"* he said, and pointed to a dark entrance with a small stack of wooden crates beside it. "Place this size, they're not going to take the garbage out through the front door."

Hale carried the pack and the flask; Fitzgerald looped the tow-rope over his shoulder. They tramped across the car park, kicking occasional sparks from their steel-tipped boots. Hale glanced up and saw a man and a woman at a window three storeys above, the man pointing at them, or maybe he was just showing her his new car. Fitzgerald whistled between his teeth. They walked out of the sunlight, past a loading bay, through a set of fire-doors, and into a concrete corridor. Nobody challenged them because nobody saw them. The place was as peaceful as the Athenaeum and far less impregnable.

"Unless they got the corridors mined," Fitzgerald said, "it looks like we're in." They stood for a moment, searching for obstacles. Hale looked at Fitzgerald and shrugged. The pack slipped off his shoulder and crashed to the floor. Still nobody came. "These people ought to be ashamed of theirselves," Fitzgerald said.

They walked to the lift and Fitzgerald pressed the button. Hale saw a wall telephone with a duplicated directory hanging from it. He looked up James, Prof. M. "His number's four-seventeen," he said. "That probably means he's on the fourth floor, doesn't it?"

"Worth trying."

They shared the lift with three men in white coats, who showed no interest in them and did not get out at the fourth floor. They found a men's room and changed back to their normal dress. Fitzgerald folded the boilersuits and stacked everything in a corner. He shook his head sadly. "This is ridiculous," he said. "All this fancy dress. We could've walked in here stark naked, me throwing grenades and you beating a bass drum, for all the notice anyone'd take."

"They do seem remarkably lax," Hale said.

Nobody was in the corridor. They found the room, twenty yards away: James's name was on the door, typed in red capitals on a yellow card. Fitzgerald straightened his tie and checked his fly. "I'll open the bidding, O.K.?" he said quietly. Hale nodded.

Fitzgerald knocked once and went in, just in time to catch the man in the big black executive swivel arm-chair before he'd got his eyes fully open.

"Professor James?" Fitzgerald said.

The man grabbed with both hands and gave himself a good shove and got up. "He's not here," he said, and took a quick look around the room. Hale watched the pouchy eyelids twitching. "He's left," the man said. "What d'you want? Who are you?"

Fitzgerald glanced around. Grey carpet, brown desk, green filing cabinets, black swivel chairs: the room revealed nothing at all. "My name's Fitzgerald," he said. "Garfield Fitzgerald. This is Mr. George Betty. We head up the London office of the magazine *Scientific American,* with which I'm sure you're familiar." He gave the man a card. "You, sir, must be . . . ?"

"Sennet. Gerald Sennet. *Doctor* Gerald Sennet." He held a pair of glasses to his eyes and read the card, turned it over and saw that the back was blank, read the front again, and slid it into a waistcoat pocket.

He was about fifty, with a face which had been trained to command but which now showed restless, worried eyes. His suit of deathless worsted had a button fly, misbuttoned in the middle so that it gaped sideways. "I'm Professor James's special assistant," he said. "If you will be kind enough to explain your business, gentlemen, I will of course render such services as suggest themselves. Please sit down." Sennet was waking up fast. He shot his cuffs: single cuffs, shiny with starch, rimmed with grey.

They sat in the overstuffed black swivel chairs. "It's really pretty straightforward, Doctor," Fitzgerald said. "Our New York office cabled asking for ten thousand words on Professor

James, urgently. We tried to reach him by phone about an hour ago, but I guess everyone was out to lunch, so rather than lose any more time . . ." Fitzgerald smiled a gentle, overworked smile.

"Quite. Of course." Sennet breathed on his glasses and polished them with an old tissue. "Naturally, you would like to see Professor James. Unfortunately, he's staying in the country for a few weeks. No visitors, I'm afraid; none at all. The consultant has ordered total privacy, absolute peace and quiet. Otherwise he could not be allowed to pursue his studies."

"Oh my God." Fitzgerald chewed on a knuckle. "What can I tell New York? They'll want a definite date when Professor James will be available for interview."

Sennet turned down the corners of his mouth. "It could be some months," he said. "It all depends."

Fitzgerald looked at Hale. "That's very disappointing," Hale said. It was as far as he felt able to go.

For a moment they all sat and pooled their disappointment. Then Sennet got up and walked to the window. "Yes, the consultant ordered *absolute* peace and quiet," he said, looking down at the car park.

Fitzgerald nodded sympathetically, and studied Sennet's ageing haircut. "Please forgive me, Doctor," he said, "but one thing puzzles me." Sennet turned. "Professor James is out in the country, resting, while you—his special assistant—are *here*. Surely if you were with him . . . I mean, opening his mail, arranging his meals—"

"Oh, no. Not at all." Sennet clasped his hands behind him, squared his shoulders, lifted his chin. "I can be of more help here. There is a good deal of correspondence to attend to. And I forward various reports and so on to Professor James."

"Ah. So he isn't bedridden?"

"Not entirely, no."

"Good, I hoped he wasn't. Because if you can forward various reports and so on, you can also forward us."

Sennet stood quite still, and searched Fitzgerald's face. "I have already told you," he said. "I thought I had made it clear. An interview is out of the question."

Fitzgerald stood up. "It's really my fault, Doctor," he said. "I have to apologize to you for a slight deception. My colleague and I are not in fact from *Scientific American.*" Hale looked up with interest. "We actually represent the Sun Life Assurance Company of Canada." He gave Sennet another card.

Sennet read it but he didn't like it. Hale noticed that Sennet's nose was pinched, and the skin over his cheekbones was shiny, like waxed paper. There were tiny beads of sweat at the top of his forehead, where the hair began, although it was quite cool in that room. Hale thought Sennet looked ill, but he himself felt too beaten and bruised to worry about other people's health.

Sennet read the front and the back and tucked it away. "If I may say so, without offence," he said, "you don't *sound* like the kind of person one expects from Sun Life Assurance."

"Of *Canada,*" Fitzgerald reminded. Sennet nodded, reluctantly. "The fact is, Doctor, that Professor James recently entered a substantial claim against Sun Life, and when I say substantial I mean *big.* Unhappily there are certain aspects . . . Anyway, the company sent us to investigate."

Already Sennet was shaking his head. "Quite out of the question. That is *exactly* the kind of thing that would upset him and worry him and wear him out. I couldn't possibly consider it."

"That's too bad."

Hale suddenly saw what Fitzgerald was working towards, and how he could help. "It's also too late," he told Sennet. "The claim has been entered. If it's allowed to continue, we shall have no choice but to fight it." Fitzgerald was nodding. Hale said, "Think of the wear and tear involved in a long court case, Doctor."

"Long and *unsavoury,*" Fitzgerald added.

Sennet did a good deal of pacing up and down with his hands clenched behind him. After a while he noticed his misbuttoned fly, and turned away while he adjusted it. When he turned back he was frowning and gesticulating to indicate the difficulty of his situation. "I'm sorry, gentlemen," he said. "I have been given certain instructions. My hands are tied."

For a long moment, Fitzgerald stood with his hands in his pockets and his head bowed. "I see," he said quietly. "I see." He straightened up. "Pardon me, Doctor. I should like to confer with my colleague, if I may." He took Hale to a corner. "This guy is a lush," he whispered. "Don't strike any lights near his mouth. His liver alone would probably burn longer and brighter than the Olympic flame." They went back.

Sennet was sitting behind his desk. "And now, if you will excuse me," he said, "there is a great deal of correspondence to attend to." He took out his fountain-pen and laid it on the blotter, like a staff of office.

Fitzgerald sat down. "Don't misunderstand me, Doctor," he said. The amiable twang had gone; now his voice was harder, harsher. "When we walked in here we had to feel our way. We had to find out if you were a man of experience and intelligence, before we could share with you certain crucial facts. That in turn meant withholding certain information about ourselves. For instance it is not wholly true to say that we represent Sun Life of Canada."

Sennet's mouth was open and his hands were braced against his desk. "What, then?" he asked.

"The organization for which my colleague and I work is Interpol."

Sennet took his hands away and leaned back in his chair and laughed. "Oh, dear me," he said. "Deary deary me. Fancy that, now. . . . Really, you must think me a complete and utter simpleton! First journalists, then insurance men, and now Interpol! Look here: I don't know what your extraordinary game is, and frankly I don't think I care terribly much, but I'm afraid your time is up. Perhaps—"

He stopped, and glanced at the card which Fitzgerald had taken from his wallet, unfolded, and placed on the blotter. Then he leaned forward and studied it. "Most impressive," he said, "but it means nothing to me."

"Then call Interpol Headquarters in Geneva, Switzerland, quote that number, and see what they say."

Sennet thought about the idea, briefly. "Why should I?" he said. "Anyway, I can't spare the time."

"No? Well, I can't spare the time to go back to my office and summon up enough heavy artillery to *make* you spare the time, Doctor, so I'll just place that call myself, if you've no objection?" He dialled 100. "Give me the International operator. Switzerland."

There was a pause while Fitzgerald held the receiver and Sennet watched him, uneasily.

"I'll tell you what," Fitzgerald told him, "just for kicks, how about putting a little pocket money on this? Loser pays for the call. O.K.?"

"No," Sennet said.

"It might be better," Fitzgerald urged. "Then I could tell them it was just a bet. Otherwise they'll think you're not exactly bending over to co-operate. See what I mean?"

"No," Sennet said.

"Hallo, International? I want to call Geneva, Switzerland. My number is—"

Sennet's fingers dropped on the telephone cradle and killed the connection. Now his nose was sweating too. "What the hell do you want?" he demanded.

Fitzgerald laid the receiver on top of Sennet's fingers and went for a short stroll around the room. He ended up with his back to the window. "Take it easy, Doctor," he said. "There's no need to get agitated; we're all on the same side, we all want to do what's best for Professor James. Right? Now, I don't need to tell you that some very wild and dangerous men are kicking around the international scene nowadays. Interpol has gotten wind of a threat to Professor James, so naturally we'd like to go to see him. That's all there is to it."

Sennet wriggled uncomfortably in his chair. "This is most

unfair," he complained. "I have been given certain definite instructions."

"Who by?" Hale asked, just to stay in the circle. Sennet ignored him.

Fitzgerald snapped his fingers. "I've got an idea. Why don't *you* come along with us, Doctor? Then you can satisfy yourself that we're not upsetting the old gentleman. Fair deal?"

"No, no, no. I couldn't do that." Sennet accidentally broke wind: a tiny, sceptical fart which embarrassed him terribly. "The fact is," he hurried on, "Professor James is not at all well, in fact he's very sick. That's why he went into this nursing home. For intensive treatment."

"So right now he's not even working?" Fitzgerald asked.

"A little. Perhaps an hour a day. But . . . no visitors."

"Uh-huh." Fitzgerald digested this; then he came over to the desk and leaned on his knuckles. "Just so you'll realize the seriousness of this situation, Doctor, I'm telling you now—formally, in front of a witness—that we have been drafted from Interpol to assist your Special Branch in this affair, and as such we are entitled to all the assistance which the law expects *you* to give the police."

Sennet refused to look at Fitzgerald. Hale said, "The point is, Doctor, that Professor James needs expert protection. To put it crudely, if somebody else gets to him first we may *all* be out of a job."

Sennet refused to look at Hale, too. He sat hunched in his chair and picked at a ragged edge on his blotter. "Oh, all right," he said. "Save your breath, for God's sake. You're a week too late. Professor James already passed on."

"*Died?*" Hale demanded.

Sennet nodded. "Tuesday evening, ten o'clock."

"Well, for Christ's sake," Fitzgerald said.

"It's not possible," Hale said. "He can't have."

"Sorry if it inconveniences you," Sennet flared.

"Why wasn't his death announced?" Fitzgerald asked.

"Reasons."

"What reasons?"

Sennet stretched his legs and looked at the ceiling. Fitzgerald shrugged at Hale, and turned away. "That seems to be that, then," he said. "Pity you didn't come clean at the start. Let's go, George."

They walked towards the door. "Forgot my gloves," Fitzgerald muttered. He went back, past Sennet's desk, and suddenly turned to a pebbled-glass door leading to the next room, and opened it. "Professor James?" he said.

"Come in." The voice was tired but firm. Fitzgerald stretched an arm in Hale's direction, pointed the thumb upwards, then swung it towards the room. Hale stared open-mouthed for a moment, then hurried across. Sennet shut his eyes as Hale went past.

Professor Mervyn James was like his room: big and comfortable. He sat behind a desk the size of a barn door, except that they don't make barns out of solid mahogany. From one side of the table a gentle arc had been shaved out to accommodate the paunch. His suit was light brown and it sprouted soft white linen at the cuffs and collar like flowers in a forest. He was the uphill side of sixty, with a big, strong head and thick silver hair. He looked up at Fitzgerald and Hale through horn-rim spectacles, low-slung on a buttress of a nose. His wide mouth twitched with a suggestion of satisfaction, as if he had been sucking a nice sweet. He was doing a jigsaw puzzle.

"Good afternoon. I'm glad to see you looking so well, Professor," Fitzgerald said. "You *are* Professor Mervyn James?"

"I am. Who the devil might you be?"

Fitzgerald showed him the inside of his wallet. "I'm Fitzgerald, sir. This is Mr. Betty."

James waved him away. "That . . . gobbledegook is pure gibberish to me, but it matters not. I have nothing to say to you."

Hale said respectfully, "The fact that you're here at all, sir, and apparently in excellent health, is—to say the least—encouraging."

"Why? What did you expect?"

"Dr. Sennet led us to suppose—"

"Indeed!" James laughed so that his elbows bounced. "Sennet told you I was dead, I expect. That's his job, after all: to keep fools and children away. He lacks imagination, though."

Fitzgerald nodded deferentially at the jigsaw puzzle. "How . . . uh . . . how's the work coming along, Professor?"

"What a nasty little villain you are." James took off his glasses and examined Fitzgerald. "What a grubby scoundrel. You mean, of course, why am I not crouched over the Bunsen burners, with a test-tube in each hand and the word 'Eureka' trembling on my lips?"

Fitzgerald looked down at his shoes and exercised his toes.

"I'll tell you why, you squalid prod-nose," James said evenly. "The true scientist carries his laboratory around between his ears. At this very moment I am applying myself to a research problem which would blow every fuse in your tiny brain."

Fitzgerald mumbled, "I'm sure we—"

"You're sure of nothing except what your comic-strip mind actually sees. I do these puzzles as an aid to concentration." He held up the lid of the box to show them the picture. It was a pure white disc. "Concentration with distraction."

"When do you expect to complete Project 107, sir?" Hale asked.

"That is none of your business, and this interview is now closed." James was not angry, not arguing; simply telling them. He turned his powerful head and looked at the door leading to the corridor. They did as they were told and got out. Mervyn James was alive and well and taking no back-answers in Middlesex.

They collected their kit from the men's room and took the lift to the ground floor. There was nobody on duty: no receptionist, no commissionaire, no hall porter. Fitzgerald stood in the middle of the lobby and shouted. "The Russians are coming!" Soft, mid-afternoon echoes drifted away down the corridors and hid themselves.

"They just don't seem to care," Hale said.

"And after all the *trouble* we took," Fitzgerald complained. "I mean, it's so damn discouraging."

They dumped the kit in the trunk of the car and drove away. Hale looked back at the Peake Building: bland, safe, harmless. "I don't know," he said. "Maybe I got the wrong man. I just don't *believe* in that place."

"I do. That's our boy, O.K. Remember what he said when you asked him about finishing the Project?"

"He said it was none of our business."

"Sure. He didn't say, 'Project what?' He didn't say, 'Never heard of it.' He said, 'It's none of your business.' Oh, that's our boy, never fear. . . . Listen, can you get a taxi from here?"

"I expect so. Why?"

"My guess is the boss is going to want me to stick around here for a day or two." Fitzgerald pulled over and stopped. "Until some regular protection gets organized."

"I suppose I'd better get back to town. . . . How can I get in touch with you again?"

"Got a pen? Write this down." He recited a telephone number. "Use that during working hours. They'll tell you it's a funeral home, but you ask for Mr. Spencer. Night-time, call *this* number." He squeezed his eyes shut and, after a moment's concentration, chanted a second set of figures. "You'll get something that sounds like a discotheque, which is what it is. Ask for Jerry Bohm, B-O-H-M. And if you get a big fat emergency, call the American Embassy, extension six-six-one, Colonel Sheridan can help you. How do *I* find *you*?"

"Nothing so complex, I'm afraid." Hale scribbled a number and gave it to him. "Just a plain-and-ordinary answering service. They'll take a message."

Fitzgerald thrust forward his hand, fingers horizontal,

thumb vertical. "Take it easy now, George, you hear me?"

They shook hands, and Hale got out. "Thanks again for the
. . . gymnastic display."

"*Por nada*, chum." Fitzgerald waggled a farewell hand. The
big car surged away, and Hale watched it go until it had lost
itself in the traffic.

It was four p.m. when Hale got back to K2. For once nobody
was waiting in the ante-room. Hubbard sent Hale straight
through.

Divine was working at his desk. Hale was startled to see him
looking so haggard. Divine noticed his reaction, and grinned
sourly. "It's been one of those days," he said. "One of those days
when you've got to keep running like a bastard, in case the
thundering herd catches up and tramples you."

"Yes, of course, sir."

"As you get older, the pace gets hotter. It doesn't seem quite
fair, does it?"

"No, sir, I suppose not."

"Exactly. That's why they do it. It's no good getting a fair
result in this event. That's the last bloody thing we need. It's the
real bastards wot deserves to win, right?" Hale didn't fully understand, so he stood silent. "Anyway, where have you been all
the day?" Divine asked.

Hale told what had happened. While he was talking, Hubbard came in with a bottle of pills: fat red-and-yellow capsules.
Divine swallowed one and kept the bottle. Hubbard went out.

"It sounds to me like a tediously violent day," Divine said.
"Why d'you suppose Starin had you knocked about?"

"Because I wouldn't answer his lousy questions," Hale said
with feeling. Bloody hell, they were *his* bruises.

"Oh, tish. That was mere protocol. You didn't expect them
to pummel you in dead silence, did you?"

"Frankly, sir, I didn't expect them to pummel me at all."

Divine enjoyed that. He seemed to be getting his strength

back; his colour was a little better. "My dear David, you sold them something which they already had. It wasn't even a pig in a poke; it was a *picture* of a pig in a poke! No wonder they were furious." Divine snuffled through his nose.

Hale set his teeth and looked at nothing. He had been going to mention Grobic's questions about the supposed counterfeiting. The hell with it.

Divine got up and walked to the window. "That American sounds very enterprising," he said. "I bet you were glad to see *him.*"

Hale said nothing.

"I must say he sounds *extraordinarily* American, waving six-guns, talking like James Cagney, drinking bourbon, driving around in a—what was it?"

"Chevrolet, sir."

"Mmm. Good car. Too big for London, though. I don't suppose he wore a tartan bow-tie too, did he?"

"Yes, as a matter of fact, he did, sir."

Divine plucked at his Adam's apple. "That's going a bit far, don't you think?" he suggested mildly.

"Not for a dyed-in-the-wool American abroad, sir. Surely the best thing he can do is to go on looking thoroughly American. Hide behind the truth, so to speak."

"And you think he belongs to the C.I.A."

"Well . . . that was obviously the implication. Either the C.I.A. or some similar agency."

Divine grunted. "How does James look?"

"Very fit, sir. According to Fitzgerald, *his* department will probably be guarding him from now on." Hale paused. "Perhaps it wouldn't do any harm if *we* kept an eye on him, too."

"What? No fear. If the Yanks want that particular chore they can have it. I need every man I've got. Don't worry, I'll have a word with somebody over there. You seem to be having some trouble breathing."

"Just the odd twinge, sir." And the odd lick of fire.

"Yes. Well, you look frightful and you smell abominably of

bourbon, so you'd better go home and clean your teeth. And tell Hubbard to come in." He stretched, and braced his arms behind him. The old Divine had been restored.

———————————

Gerald Sennet was unlocking his car when a Chevrolet Impala drifted up and butted its rear end. The impact jolted his car six inches forward, knocked the key out of his hand, and bruised a knuckle. "Bloody idiot!" he cried. "That'll cost you!" Tears of pain and rage prevented him from seeing the driver clearly until he looked through the side window.

"Come on in, I want to talk to you," Fitzgerald said. He leaned across and opened the door.

"And I want to talk to *you!*" Sennet thrust his head and shoulders inside. "Look what you've done to my car!" A little dandruff floated from his head.

"I took a chance," Fitzgerald said. He had a candid smile: warm at the mouth, sad at the eyes. "You looked like a Scotch-whisky man to me, so I took a chance on Scotch. Did I do right?" He reached over to the back seat and pulled a bottle of Dewar's out of a full case. There were seven other cases in the back, all cut open to show the bottles.

Sennet rested a knee on the seat and stretched his neck to get a good look. Only his eyes moved, tracking along the rows of foil-capped tops, checking and counting the mirage.

"Every man to his taste," Fitzgerald said amiably. "Dewar's, Teacher's, Haig, Bell's, Long John, Black and White, Johnny Walker and"—he lifted a bottle to make sure—"yeah, Cutty Sark."

Sennet heaved himself around and sat staring at the dashboard. He twisted and took another look, just a quick glance. "No need to smash my car, was there?" he said.

"Come on, don't be sore. It wasn't even a fender-bender. Just a little bumper-thumper. It didn't shake you up, did it, Dr. Sennet? Have a snort." Fitzgerald offered his flask.

"I can't hang around here." Sennet's shoulders were

slumped, and he was still looking at the dust patterns on the dashboard. "I have an important appointment."

"Oh, relax for a moment. You've had a hard day. You deserve your reward."

"You think you're so bloody clever," Sennet whispered harshly. "Getting in to see James after everything I said."

"Oh, no, no!" Fitzgerald was quite distressed. "No. You utterly convinced me, Doctor. *Utterly*. I was ready to leave when . . . It was a stroke of luck, I heard someone cough in the next room. Otherwise . . . Well, I was on my way home, otherwise."

Sennet grunted.

"Honest," Fitzgerald said. He was still holding out his flask. Sennet took it and drank a quick slug and gave it back.

"No, you had me *completely* fooled," Fitzgerald said. "Besides, it's just as well it worked out the way it did. For *both* of us."

Sennet thought about that. "Us?" he said. He began seeing the cases of whisky again, out of the corner of his eye.

"Sure. You and I can do each other some good. You see, I know about the jigsaw-puzzle man."

Sennet had his hands in his lap, fingers linked. He separated them, but the right hand developed a tremor, so he hid it in his armpit. "You mean Professor James," he said.

"No, I don't think I do." Fitzgerald sniffed the open top of his flask, and smiled dreamily.

Sennet stared, and then turned hastily away. "I really must be going," he said, searching for the door handle; but Fitzgerald held his shoulder.

"Don't leave all that fine Scotch behind, Dr. Sennet. It's yours, you know if . . . Look at it this way: you're only doing your patriotic duty, as a good N.A.T.O. ally, and I'm sure Professor James would endorse that, because my department, Dr. Sennet, sir, is very concerned about Professor James's well-being. *Very* concerned, sir."

Sennet let go of the door handle and sat back. "I was given certain instructions," he said emptily.

"Exactly. And so was I, Dr. Sennet, sir. Believe me, we are hoeing the same row, you and I, we are fighting the same battle, pursuing the same goal!" Now Fitzgerald's face was stiff with urgency. "And if we are to *reach* that holy goal we must, we *must* pool our resources so that we can *redouble* our efforts! You and I *together.*"

"I don't understand," Sennet muttered.

"Let me *tell* you, Dr. Sennet. First, Professor James is urgently in need of protection. Urgently! That we both know. Second, the man in the room next to yours is *not* Professor James. *That* we both know."

Fitzgerald paused, and gestured with his flask. "Dr. Sennet, I wouldn't ask you this unless I was one hundred per cent sure you knew how much it mattered. Where *is* Professor James?"

Sennet reached out blindly and Fitzgerald pushed the flask into his hand. "Paris," he said. He shut his eyes and drank.

———

Hale got home at five and waited until six before he phoned Carol. The number was busy. He watched the end of a western on television, using it as a buffer before he called her again; but again the line was busy. He spooned frozen chili con carne into a saucepan and heated it, while he eased his ribs and thought of other, more accessible girls; girls who could turn one into two, as and when needed. There was a girl called Mary Somebody who had trailed him at a party a couple of months earlier; he could get Mary all right; but could he get rid of her again? He poured the chili into a bowl and looked for crackers. That was the problem. Not the math but the aftermath. Hale ate his meal, one more buffer between calls. He dialled again. The line was still busy. Bloody women.

The flat looked flatter than ever. He looked out of the window. The two homosexuals who lived opposite were cultivating their window boxes and gossiping. One of them saw him and waved a dinner-fork. Hale stiffened. The man made a long face at his partner. Bloody men.

Fitzgerald helped Sennet load the whisky into his car. The exercise stimulated Sennet and gave him a sense of accomplishment. He was quite cordial when the job was done. "Phew!" he said. "I must say I'm glad you were here to help me with *that.*"

"Combined operations, Dr. Sennet."

"Yes, of course," Sennet said vaguely.

"I may be in touch again, Dr. Sennet. Meanwhile, on behalf of myself and my department, thank you for your co-operation."

"Just doing my duty, old chap."

"There's just one other thing." Fitzgerald looked serious. Sennet looked apprehensive. "It's kind of hard to know how to put this, but . . . What impression did you get of my colleague, Mr. Betty?"

Sennet was surprised, and relieved. "Betty? He seemed . . . he seemed . . ." Sennet tried to remember, but there was very little to work on. "Not tremendously forthcoming, was he?"

Fitzgerald nodded, and stood for a moment, swinging his arms. "You spotted it, too, huh? I think I ought to tell you, Doctor: there are two schools of thought about Mr. Betty in the department. I'm inclined to think that you and I both belong to the *second* school."

"Oh dear. That's rather disturbing, isn't it? I mean, considering that he's in such a . . . how shall I say? . . . such a *sensitive* area of operations."

"You've put your finger on it, Doctor. I don't mind telling you, I wish I could put my finger on *him.* Or better yet, my foot."

Sennet and Fitzgerald chuckled, but they were chuckles of caution and concern. "I catch your drift, Mr. Fitzgerald," Sennet said. "In future I shall treat Mr. Betty with the reticence he deserves."

"I'll drink to that," Fitzgerald said.

The evening seemed to become more oppressive as it wore on, as if the dusk were holding down all the spent heat and fatigue of the day. Hale put on a pair of denim shorts and a towelling shirt. His ribs were purple from Stefan's fist, and they burned when he stretched his arms. He made a long, weak whisky and water. The telephone was there, doing nothing, so he called Carol again. This time the number rang.

A girl said, "Yes?"

"Hallo. . . . Could I speak to Carol, please?"

"No, you bloody well couldn't." Slam. Dialling tone. Over and out.

Hale thought about it for a while and then gave up. He flicked through the television channels: comedy, panel game, wildlife film. Maybe he ought to call again and find out what the hell . . . His doorbell rang. Immediately he thought: Grobic, Fitzgerald, maybe Brandon, maybe even Mary Somebody. He deleted Fitzgerald, Brandon and Mary, but Grobic remained in his mind.

He padded out in his bare feet, with his half-drunk whisky, and squinted through the miniature fish-eye spy-hole in the door. It wasn't Grobic. He opened the door. It was Carol Blazey with a suitcase. They stood and looked, like guests waiting to be introduced, and then he said, "Come in."

She put down the suitcase and walked into the middle of the living-dining-sitting room. She was wearing a collarless coat with wide-open sleeves which ended at mid-forearm, and made her look more ripe yet childlike than ever. "I've had the boot," she said. "Can I stay with you?"

Grobic found Starin down in the wine cellars under the Trade Mission building. There was much low, vaulted brickwork and the floor was beaten earth. The air smelled clammy and forgotten. Starin sat on a folding chair with an air rifle across his knees and a big electric lantern on the floor beside him. Its beam was the only light.

"Zeller has telephoned again, Colonel," Grobic said, sounding pleased.

"Not so damn loud, you'll scare the bastards. What's happened?"

"He says Professor James is really in Paris."

There was silence except for the occasional flat smack of distant drops of water, while Starin studied the darkness.

"Paris," he said. "I hope he can explain that."

"It's all written down, Colonel." Grobic gave him a sheet of paper. Starin bent over to read it in the lantern beam.

"In Paris for his health," Starin muttered. "For specialist treatment. A heart specialist. For God's sake, why didn't we find out about this before? How long has he been there?"

Grobic cautiously indicated a further paragraph. "Quite some time, apparently, Colonel."

Starin read it. "So this set-up at the—what's it called?—Peake Research, that's all a blind, is that the idea?"

"It looks that way, Colonel."

Starin folded the paper and stuffed it in a pocket. Grobic stiffened: somewhere in the cellars he heard a racing, scrabbling, scratching sound. "Here they come," Starin said softly. He pointed his air rifle down the beam of light. "Rats as big as dachshunds."

"Surely they won't run into the light, sir?"

"I've got a cat chasing them. She hunts like a tiger." They waited and watched. Nothing happened.

"Zeller was supposed to find out where Betty got that report," Starin said. "That's what I wanted to know. Well, if James is really in Paris, that changes everything. What about Betty?"

"Zeller says he got as much as he could out of Betty, but the question of how and where Betty photographed the report was something he just couldn't bring up without maybe ruining everything. Besides, he felt that James was probably more important. I must say—"

"Shut up." Starin cocked his head and listened. A tiny squeak scratched the back of the blackness. Then silence. "There are too many goddam rats running around. I sent in Zeller to scare a few out. All he's done is find even more."

Starin leaned back just as a panicky scrabbling rushed towards them and two black shapes streaked across the band of light. Starin fired; and like a ricochet came a scream that curled away and died as the body skidded out of sight.

Grobic went and looked. "You've killed the cat," he said.

Starin picked up the lantern and headed for the stairs. Grobic stumbled after him. "Leonid Zeller goes to Paris," Starin said. "You and I are going to the Embassy."

———

Hale made her a drink and freshened up his own. "I've been calling you ever since I got home," he said. "I'd just about given up. I certainly never expected *this.*"

She gave the ghost of a smile, just sideways enough to make him uneasy. He said, "You don't need to look at me like *that.*"

"Like what?"

"As if you were about to be charged rent. You know my stern, old-fashioned principles. Whatever intentions I may have are uniformly honourable."

"Are they? Mine aren't. I'm flat broke, David, and I've nowhere to stay, so my intentions are straight out of the law of the jungle. Can you lend me a fiver?"

"Sure. More, if you need it. Let's get this clear, Carol: I am delighted to see you and you can stay as long as you like."

"D'you think you can stand it?"

"Why not?"

"My dear David, you'll go off pop in a week. And if you don't, I probably shall."

"I don't see why. After all, we're not children."

"That's just the trouble."

"What happened at your flat?"

"Oh, trouble. Fights and arguments. Incompatibility, you might call it."

"Still, they shouldn't have . . . What were the fights about?"

"Money. Rent. Bills." She stirred an ice-cube with her finger; it clinked distantly, like men working underground. "I can't get worked up over money the way they can. That's what makes them really furious."

"You sound tired."

"I'm absolutely shattered. No cab money. The buses were bloody." She sat without moving and watched him tuck his shirt in. "My brother had a shirt like that."

"Big brother?"

"Yes. Dead-mountain brother. I'd like to have it, to wear," she added suddenly. "Can I?"

"Yes. Sure." Hale was surprised. "You mean . . . now?"

"Now, yes, so I can . . ." He got up to go to the bedroom, and she said, "Where are you going? Can't you just take it off?"

"Yes, but . . . Well, my side is in a bit of a mess, you see, and—"

"Show me. What happened to you?"

He showed her. The tender, purpled skin flinched away from her finger-tips. "Good God!" she said. "Who did that?"

"Nobody you know. Just a . . . colleague. You know, a friendly scuffle. He didn't know his own strength."

"He must have hit you with the fourteenth floor, for heaven's sake. Doesn't it hurt?"

"No, no." Hale smiled and inflated his chest, and screwed up his face with pain. "Just a bit, at times." He limped into the bedroom and tried to put on another shirt, but his ribs burned so much when he raised his arms that he gave up and slipped into his jacket instead.

Carol had her arms inside his shirt with the hands poking out of the armholes and cupping her chin. She said, "David, did that really happen at work?"

"Yes, really."

"And all those bee-stings, or wasps, or whatever they were —you got those at work too, didn't you?"

"Right again."

She sipped her drink and watched him thoughtfully. "Are all merchant banks like yours, David?"

"Well, they're . . . I wouldn't say they're . . . Put it this way—"

"You're accident-prone?"

"No, it's just . . . Look, why don't you mind your own business?" She blew a few slow bubbles into her drink, and looked at his bare chest. Hale buttoned his jacket and thought hard about this whole new situation, about how it could become very complicated very rapidly. "You know, I think maybe we'd better agree on a couple of ground rules," he said, trying to make it sound sensible and painless. "No shop, for a start. I don't ask *you* about Pan Am, and you dont' ask *me* about Flekker Handyside. Also, we each come and go as we please, no comments, no questions. If either of us comes home blind drunk at three in the morning with a live pig under one arm and the Crown Jewels under the other—no comment, no questions. O.K.?"

"Can I feed the pig?" Carol asked.

"You can feed it, but you can't question it. . . . Look, are you sure a fiver's enough? You can have some more tomorrow."

"Lovely, lovely." She stretched out and took the banknote. "What's that on your sleeve? It looks like . . . Oh dear. I was going to say—before I remembered the group rules—that it looks like blood, but of course now I wouldn't dream of saying that it looks like blood, although it does look remarkably like . . . blood." She pointed to a string of dark blobs staining the elbow.

"Yes," Hale said, "it does, doesn't it? For once, I'm happy to say, it's not mine." As he spoke he remembered: Fitzgerald in the gym, helping him over to the washbasin; Fitzgerald still dribbling blood from the mouth. "Chap in the office had a nosebleed. Nothing more sinister."

"Of course not! Why, I never imagined . . ." Carol was wide-eyed with fake innocence. "All the same, you ought to soak it now, you know, before it's too late. Give it to me, I'll do it."

Reluctantly, Hale eased off his jacket. "All I do is dress and undress," he complained.

Carol took it into the bathroom. "It's probably too late," she said. "Blood can be awfully hard to get out." She began working on it with a sponge and cold water. Almost immediately the water turned pale pink.

"I've never seen that happen before," she said. "Are you *sure* this is blood?"

"Well, that chap's going to be the talk of Harley Street if it isn't." Hale felt a curious lurch inside him, as if something had come adrift.

She sniffed the stains, which were leaking away fast. "Curiouser and curiouser." She rubbed a finger in the biggest stain, and licked it. "And curiouser still. It's tomato ketchup."

Part of his stomach went over a hump-backed bridge, too fast. "Ketchup," he said. He tested it himself. The smell was faint, but the taste was unmistakable. Gary Fitzgerald had bled tomato ketchup.

Hale's guts came down on the other side of the hump-backed bridge and hit the pit of his stomach.

Before she came, he had been feeling, if not proud of Project 107, at least satisfied with it. Now he knew that something had gone wrong. Probably something had gone very wrong. In fact, the more he thought about it, something must have gone hugely and horribly wrong. He made an effort to get his wits together. "I think we'd better have something to take the taste out of our mouths," he said; as if it could be as easy as that.

"Come in," the Ambassador said. He got up from his desk and waved towards some chairs. Starin entered and sat. Grobic stood on one side, where he could see Starin's face.

"Damned woollen underwear," the Ambassador grumbled.

"It itches like the pox." He scratched one buttock on a corner of his desk and eased his crotch at the same time. "The doctors make me wear it. Otherwise I keep catching colds."

He wandered over to the empty fireplace and stood looking at it, scratching his stomach with both hands. "The trouble with my body," he said, sucking breath through his teeth, "it doesn't know where it's at, any more. Cold feet. Cold hands. And yet the body sweats. And itches. I should never have let them send me here, not after Madrid." His chest jumped with a painful, silent belch; cigarette-ash tumbled down his waistcoat.

Starin watched the Ambassador go back to his desk. He saw that the Ambassador's feet were splayed to support his body, and that his shoulders drooped. The Ambassador was only a year older, yet already he was falling apart. His jowls were puffy and grey, his eyes baggy, his cheeks hollow. He looked like a deflated bulldog.

The Ambassador shoved some papers aside and read his king-size desk diary upside down. "I ought to be in a meeting now," he said. "In fact, in five minutes I ought to be in *two* meetings." He looked up, his back to Starin, and stared at the national flag on the wall behind his desk. He squinted. There was a fly on it. He went up and flapped a hand, trying to hit the fly and not the flag. The fly rose and flew around him and landed on his desk diary. He picked up a newspaper and rolled it and struck out savagely. The fly escaped and flew figures of eight between him and Starin. The Ambassador waited for it to come within range, his tired eyes blinking as they tried to focus on the wandering target, his arm stiffly holding the rolled newspaper. After a while, a different fly came and landed on the raised newspaper. The Ambassador looked at it uncertainly and finally slapped at it with his other hand. The fly cruised away, un-alarmed.

The Ambassador sighed and sat down. "I know that expression of carefully concealed triumph, Colonel," he said. "Tell me whom you have outwitted now."

"Your information department. No great triumph, that.

They couldn't find shit in a sewer."

"Are you saying that you've found that atomic scientist with the initials?"

"Yes, I have. The initials were 'M.J.' The man is Professor Mervyn James. He works at the Peake Research Building in Middlesex."

The Ambassador was writing this down. "They may have some trouble finding Middlesex," Starin said. "It's a little smaller than West Germany and—"

"All right, all right. I suppose you want to know what we have on Professor James?"

"Yes. That's what I always *did* want to know."

The Ambassador picked up his phone and talked to the information department. "They say fifteen or twenty minutes," he told Starin. "I'm sorry I can't offer you a drink, but we've mislaid the keys to the sideboard." He looked at Grobic. "Appalling carelessness, isn't it?"

Hale made conversation while Carol ate a soft-boiled egg and toast. The conversation was fitful; half his mind was struggling to rearrange the facts to fit the new Fitzgerald. But nothing seemed to fit. Fitzgerald was like a figure in a Magritte painting, obviously yet impossibly in two places at once.

They watched an hour's forgettable television before he noticed that she was half-asleep. "You should go to bed now, while you can still walk," he said.

"True, true, true, true, true. I'll sleep in here. Have you got some blankets?"

"No, no, *I'll* sleep in here. Would you like a bath or anything—"

"David, David, listen. I know you're being kind, so please let me have my way and sleep here. Please, if you really want to help."

"O.K." He got up and looked at her, still celebrating his astonishing luck and yet also glad that she was going to bed because now he could really think. "O.K.," he said, and fetched sheets and blankets.

The Ambassador licked his dry lips and put a cigarette between them and lit it and let it burn, squinting to avoid the smoke. He looked at the packet. "They put in all these filters, so that you can't taste anything," he said, "and then they throw in a lot of hairy tobacco to punch up the flavour. Sometimes I think we're all chasing our tails." He put his hands in his pockets, and scratched his left buttock on the corner of the desk.

Starin sat and watched the Ambassador, while Grobic stood and watched them both.

The phone rang and the Ambassador went behind his desk to answer it. He listened, grunted, made notes, listened some more. "Yes, do that," he said, and hung up. "The difficulty this time was not the absence of information but the quantity of it," he said. "Professor James has had an eventful career. Twenty years ago he was even rumoured to be in the running for a Nobel. So were several hundred others, of course."

Starin went across and leaned his knuckles on the desk. "A man like that? Within fifty miles of London? And yesterday your so-called information department couldn't find him?"

"That's right, they couldn't," the Ambassador said, "because you told them he was a nuclear physicist, and he's not a nuclear physicist, he's an organic chemist."

"Balls," Starin said.

"When you ask them to look for apples, you mustn't be surprised if they don't bring you any pears."

"The man's doing research into atomic energy, isn't he?" Starin demanded.

"Perhaps that's what it *looks* like," the Ambassador said, "but then it sometimes looks to me as if you, Colonel, are setting yourself up as a philanthropist, or a numismatist, or maybe even a capitalist."

They looked at each other: the Ambassador resigned, Starin

restless. Starin said, "I'd like to see everything you've got on James."

The Ambassador wrestled with his underwear and gave up. "You're entitled to it, I suppose," he said.

"Good."

"But you're not entitled to do your job at the expense of mine, remember."

"And I might say the same thing. In fact, I *do* say it."

The Ambassador shrugged, or perhaps he only eased his shoulders, as Starin and Grobic went out.

Hale slept badly and woke early. While he shaved he tried to remember everything he had said to Fitzgerald, from the first gunshot in Jim's Gym onwards. By the time he rinsed his face he was fairly sure that he'd given away nothing except the fact of James, which was more than enough. He couldn't remember mentioning K2 or Kamarenski or even Starin; although he'd been groggy enough to say anything and not remember it. Damn and double-damn.

He got dressed, which took him another stage towards actually doing something. Obviously something had to be done. What were the options? Starin, Fitzgerald, Divine, James.

Well, Starin might know something about Fitzgerald, but if he did he wouldn't tell Hale, and if he didn't Hale would be giving Fitzgerald away for nothing, always assuming that Fitzgerald was kosher in the first place. What about Fitzgerald? Hale found the telephone numbers and wondered which to use. It might be too early for a funeral home; on the other hand, it was certainly too late for any discotheque. He called the funeral-home number and got the taxi-rank in Leicester Square, so he called the disco and got the Westminster City Mortuary. Fitzgerald enjoyed a little joke. Hale decided not to call the American Embassy.

Divine? Divine ought to know immediately. He ought to know that Hale had perhaps been conned by the Americans as well as clouted by the Russians. Not an easy thing to admit, especially when it depended on nothing more than a few tomato-ketchup stains which—now that he came to think of it—no longer existed. Bloody hell. Also bugger.

That left James. In a sense, the eminent professor was the only one who really counted. As long as he was safe and well it didn't matter if Fitzgerald went around gargling *sauce Béarnaise*. But then Hale saw the danger.

Fitzgerald now knew where James worked. He might go back and trick James the way he had already tricked Hale. But trick him into what? Only God and Fitzgerald knew, and even God might be guessing.

Carol was still asleep. Hale left her a note and a blank cheque, and went out quietly. He found a coffee stall and ate a stand-up breakfast. The sun was up, the sky was blue, the sparrows darted in and out for his crumbs as if they'd never heard of Project 107. "Gonna be another day like yesterday," the coffee-stall man said happily. "Christ, I hope not," Hale said. The man moved away, offended. Hale got into his car and drove north.

The lobby of the Peake Building was noisy with arriving staff by the time Hale got there. He squeezed into the lift, looking blank. Nobody paid him any attention.

He got out at the fourth floor and looked at a notice board until the corridor emptied. Then he tried some doors. James's room was locked. Sennet's room wasn't. Sennet was by the window, using an electric shaver. The skin on his face seemed to be sliding about like loose wrapping paper.

"Good morning, Dr. Sennet," Hale said. "I hope I haven't called at an inconvenient time."

Sennet switched off the shaver and took his time about unplugging it and winding up the cord. Hale was surprised to find him looking so relaxed; pleasant, even. He put the shaver in its case and put the case in a desk drawer. "Well, well, well," he

said, "if it isn't Mr. Phyllis." He held up his hand, palm outwards, inviting Hale in.

"Betty, actually."

"Why, of course. I was thinking of my wife's sister's name."

"Oh, yes."

"She was a Phyllis, you see. Actually she's dead now." Sennet
patted aftershave lotion onto his cheeks.

"Is that so."

"Oh yes, quite dead. Strictly speaking, of course, she was my
ex-wife's sister, anyway."

"Indeed."

"Yes indeed. No possible doubt about it. One doesn't make
mistakes about that sort of thing, you know."

The door to the next room was open, and Hale could see that
there was nobody behind the desk. He turned to Sennet. Now
that he was nearer, Hale could see faint pink blotches against
the white of his forehead, and he recognized the hectic glitter
in his eyes. Sennet might have other reasons for being so genial,
but the big reason was that he was riding on the crest of a
colossal hangover. Soon, probably, he would slide into the
trough, but right now he was enjoying the view.

"I take it Professor James isn't here yet," Hale said.

"See for yourself."

"Are you expecting him?"

Sennet shrugged. He took a hairbrush from his desk and
began brushing his hair.

"About Mr. Fitzgerald," Hale said. "Have you seen him
since he and I were here yesterday? Did he come back afterwards?"

Sennet arranged the top, which was getting a bit thin, tidied
up the back and sides, which were becoming rather shaggy, and
looked at himself in a small mirror, while he flicked the dandruff
from his shoulders.

"It's a difficult question," he said at last.

"I shouldn't have thought so. Surely the answer is either yes
or no."

"What?" Sennet looked up, and then smiled tolerantly. "Oh, dear me, no. No . . . the problem, d'you see, is whether or not the parting should go *up*, say, half an inch. What d'you think?"

"Me? I've no idea. Can we—"

"Haircut today, you see. Must decide by . . ." He looked at his watch. "Eleven o'clock." He held his arm up so that Hale could see the dial. "Not much time left, I'm afraid."

"Look, Dr. Sennet, can we get down to business? It's very important for me to know—"

"*If . . . you . . . want . . .*" Sennet announced, loudly and slowly, "to know what *your* Mr. Fitzgerald's been up to . . . you just go and ask him."

That was logical. Hale decided to forget Fitzgerald. "Can we go back to yesterday afternoon? You said you had been given certain instructions, Doctor. Who by?"

"I was presented with this silver-backed hairbrush," Sennet said, "by the entire tennis club. You can see where they had it engraved." He showed Hale.

"Very nice. Please, Doctor. This is a matter of urgency."

"Oh yes? Who says? And anyway, who the blazes are you?" Sennet raised his eyebrows.

"Well . . . we went through all that yesterday."

"I don't remember."

"Surely . . . I mean, Fitzgerald offered to call Switzerland, and—"

"Never mind him. What have *you* got to show for yourself?"

"If you mean identification, documents . . . I don't carry that sort of thing."

"Indeed. How odd. Fitzgerald did."

"Yes, but . . . Well, Fitzgerald and I work for slightly separate departments, you see. The systems are different."

"Different, are they? You mean your employers aren't prepared to give you the same backing which he gets?"

"It's not a ques—"

"Who are they, anyway? Get them on the phone, I want to talk to them."

Hale had a mental picture of Sennet challenging Divine, and he mentally shuddered. "I really don't think there's any need for that," he said.

"No, I'm sure you don't," Sennet said forcefully. "I'm *damn* sure you don't."

"But if it were absolutely essential, I can assure you that it could be done." Hale realized that he was on the point of showing his irritation, which would be disastrous: it would turn Sennet off completely. "Look, Doctor, why don't we leave that side of things to Professor James? Let him satisfy himself, and . . ."

"What a peculiar thing to say," Sennet said. "As you well know, Professor James isn't even on the premises."

"Yes, I realize that. Where is he?"

"Ah, where?" Sennet repeated. "Where, indeed? And who wants to know? And why?"

Hale looked into Sennet's quietly truculent eyes, and began to lose hope. Talking to Sennet was like walking through a darkened room full of sharp-cornered furniture: slow, unpredictable, and rough on the mental shins.

Starin stationed himself beside the shaft of sunlight and got a good grip of the Embassy's file on Mervyn James. He watched a bluebottle cruise into the beam, and slammed it right across the room. "He must have a brain as big as a basketball," he said. "I can't even pronounce half the stuff he's discovered." He went over and trod on the buzz.

"So you were right, Colonel," Grobic said loyally. "The Ambassador was wrong."

Starin opened the file and looked at an old newspaper photograph of James: a shaggy, bulky man with half-moon glasses lodged on his forehead. "I wish to hell the Ambassador would stay out of this, but I know damn well he won't," he said.

"He's only *nominally* responsible for the Mission, Colonel. He can't stop you doing what you want, can he?"

"I don't trust the son of a bitch. He's a career diplomat, he didn't get where he is by letting people rock his lovely boat. He's the kind of cunning fart that makes a virtue out of virtue."

"Still, he can't actually *stop* you, Colonel."

Starin shook the curtains, looking for more bluebottles. "Focus the blinding searchlight of your intelligence on Peake Research, Grobic. What do you make of that?"

"Peake? Well, I think Zeller must be right, Colonel, it's a blind or a front, or something. I expect this man James *used* to work there, and when they moved him to Paris they installed someone else just to keep his seat warm and distract attention from—"

"They? Who?"

"The British. One of their departments."

"Why?"

Grobic began to sweat. "Um . . . Zeller says that according to Sennet, James needs specialist medical treatment. Probably the British thought they might as well keep the move secret in order to protect James until he's finished his research."

"Exactly. So how did Zeller sniff all that out?"

"The alcoholic doctor told him, Colonel."

"Yes, yes, yes. But how was it that Zeller knew enough to ask him in the first place, dummy?"

Grobic hadn't thought of that.

"Forget it," Starin said. "Not that you could remember it without tying a knot in your tiny cock." He opened a window to let in more bluebottles. "It looks to me as if the real fairy in the whorehouse is Mr. Betty."

Grobic chuckled; he was on home ground with Betty. "A big powderpuff," he said. "He got right out of his depth. He should have stuck to—"

"When Stefan hit him," Starin said, "what did he say?"

"Nothing. Lost his temper, Colonel, that's all. I think he said he couldn't tell us what he didn't know, something like that."

"Stubborn. Angry. Bad businessman." Starin saw a fly coming and batted it straight back along its path. "A dealer with no deal. Is that it?"

"Well . . . yes, Colonel, but . . . He obviously can't be anyone's agent, so . . ."

"He doesn't fit anywhere, Grobic, that's the whole damn point. He's too ambitious to be an amateur and too clumsy to be a professional."

The phone rang. "Zeller," Starin said at once.

But it was the Ambassador's secretary. "The Ambassador wishes you to know that he will be attending a reception this evening. He says that the Home Secretary will be handing out the cocktails and he feels sure that nobody will want to jog his elbow. The Ambassador is confident of your co-operation."

Starin said nothing, and after ten seconds' silence the Ambassador's secretary hung up.

The call from Zeller came through an hour later. He was still in Paris. "Have you found him?" Starin asked.

"Yes and no. It's kind of hard to explain, you know? I think I may have to stick around here through the week-end to, you know, button it all up."

"What in hell's name does that mean? Either the man is there or he isn't."

"Well, no, it's kind of complicated. You just relax and leave it to me, Colonel. No sweat, huh?"

"You cheating little bastard," Starin said. "You're milking this. You just want a week-end in Paris so that you can get laid, on expenses."

"You are one hard man, Colonel. What can I say to persuade you otherwise?"

"I hope you get seventeen kinds of pox."

"Medical science recognizes only twelve, but I'll do my best." The line went dead, and the operator could not reconnect it.

Hubbard said that Divine had gone to the B.B.C. to see some television film. After that he was driving down to Portsmouth for a naval board of enquiry, something to do with sabotage, and then week-ending at somebody's trout stream in Hampshire. Hale went to the B.B.C.

He found Divine holding a can of film and talking to a disappointed man. "It's such a pity the quality's so good," he was saying. "If it had been fuzzier . . ."

"Well, we teach them to film things so you can see what they are," the B.B.C. man said bitterly.

"Quite, quite. That's just the trouble. Everybody is so tremendously recognizable. It would be an absolute disaster."

"We spent a packet getting that stuff, too. I had three crows working on it at one point. *Three*."

"What a shame. Well, we'll look after it for you and maybe in ten or fifteen years when all our chaps have retired . . . Now, then, how do I get out of here?"

Divine took Hale down to his car and they drove away. "And what's *your* problem?" he asked.

Hale blew his nose. "I thought you ought to know, sir," he said under cover of mopping up with his handkerchief, "I discovered something about that American, Fitzgerald, which suggests that he's not entirely reliable."

"Not reliable?" Divine checked his mirrors and swung through a gap. "Of course he's not reliable. He's a complete fraud."

There was a moment's silence while Hale's brain held the words at arm's length before reluctantly standing aside and letting them in.

"I should have thought that was obvious, laddie," Divine said. He put his foot down hard and beat the lights on the amber. "Friend Fitzgerald was just too bad to be true from the very start."

"So . . . the Americans aren't co-operating with us after all, sir?"

Divine flicked a short, critical glance. "Listen here, you poor, deluded booby," he said. "Do you really imagine that C.I.A. agents drive around in Chevrolets, playing cowboy music and drinking bourbon? Do you?"

"No, sir, unless . . . I mean, it could be done *deliberately*
. . . that is, made to look like that so that—"

"Yes, yes. So you said before."

Hale's voice was thin and jumpy. "I . . . I take it you . . . you
must have . . ."

"Oh yes, I checked with the C.I.A. They were terribly
amused. Terribly."

"So that means . . ."

Divine waited, and then said, "You'd better get it right in
one, my lad, or you'll be joining the ranks of the great unem-
ployed."

Hale cleared his throat. "Fitzgerald must be Starin's man,
sir. The whole business in the gym must have been staged."

"And for what?"

"To . . ." Hale searched miserably for an alternative answer;
there was none. "To locate James, I suppose."

"And you obliged."

"But I thought they knew where James was."

"Evidently you thought wrong."

Hale looked out of the windows. Glittering sunshine, as in-
discriminate as luck and as fickle as success. He had been hungry; now he merely felt empty. "I went back there this morning," he said. "Sennet said James wasn't there."

"Quite correct. Some of my people are taking care of him
now."

"Oh. Really? Ah. That explains it, then. Good." Hale nodded
several times while he laboured over these new facts. "Yes,
well, I'm glad to hear it, sir. I don't know whether you knew,
but security at the Peake Building is virtually nil. Absolutely
anybody can walk in and out, all day long. It's quite absurd."

"It's nothing of the kind, it's perfectly normal."

"Normal, sir? For a research centre?"

"That's what I said: normal. The Peake Building is part of
London University, Hale. It's basically a monumental filing
cabinet full of postgraduate students wondering whether to go
to Australia or I.C.I. If you went to see somebody in the History

Department of London University would you be surprised if you didn't get stopped and searched?"

"No, sir."

"Well then."

So that was that. Hale knocked his knuckles together and tried to think of something that would take the curse off the conversation. "Have you heard, sir? Somebody in the office told me there's a strong rumour that—"

"—that the Home Office is going to et cetera, et cetera. I don't work on rumours, Hale, except when they're *my* rumours." He pulled over and stopped. "You can catch a number five hundred bus from here. Ask Hubbard if there's any spare filing you can do."

Hale walked into his flat and sensed its emptiness. He dropped the newspaper on a chair and stood staring at a squashed cushion. Stupid to feel so let down; all right, then, he was stupid.

He took off his jacket and went into the bathroom. "For God's sake!" he said. She was in the bath, with her hair coiled on top of her head, immersed up to the neck. "If locked doors give you claustrophobia, at least you can *whistle*." He went out.

"Oy!" she called. He came back. "Don't you want to say hallo? Because *I* do."

"Hallo, then." The water was opaque; some kind of bath lotion, probably. He closed the toilet seat and sat on it. "Hallo, hallo, hallo."

"Why are you so angry?"

"Am I? Sorry."

"You're hopping mad. You came through that door as if you were looking for an eye to black. Have you had a rotten day?"

"No, not especially. . . . Well, rotten in parts, I suppose. Agonizing Reappraisal Day, you might say. I thought I had my head screwed on, and then God informed me it was facing the wrong way." He tore off some toilet paper and blew his nose. "Discouraging," he said.

"Perhaps he's wrong."

Hale shook his head. "How was your day?"

"All right. My boss tried to seduce me again."

"Flattering for you."

"Not really. It just means his wife's having her period. I told him you were the jealous, violent sort, and he went off and played squash instead."

Carol lowered her head and blew bubbles. Hale looked at the water and thought of Fitzgerald, rinsing his lying mouth in the dirty washbasin. "You can't see through it," she said. "And anyway, I'm wearing a flannel nightie underneath." Hale looked away and pulled up his socks. "David, say something nice," she ordered. "Go on, just for the sake of it, say something nice. You need the practice."

Hale cleared his throat and frowned.

"On second thoughts, forget it," Carol said. "Are you any good at scrubbing backs?"

"Dunno. Never tried."

She rolled over, briefly exposing a square inch of shining buttock, and rested her chin on her linked hands. "Use the loofah and don't rub too hard, please."

After a while he said, "I don't suppose any of my narrow circle of friends would ever believe that you and I were living here in the most shameless respectability."

"No. Mine certainly wouldn't."

"And they'd probably find it hard to understand the reasons. I find it a bit hard, myself. I expect you've observed that my personality isn't wildly fashionable. If anything, I'm slightly medieval, I suppose. You're my guest, and I treat the obligations of the host pretty seriously. I don't expect rent in any shape or form, you see."

"I understand perfectly, David. Just as long as you're not a virgin, too."

"Oh no. I've been called many things, but not that." He polished a shoulder-blade. "Are you?"

"No, I was lucky. Some brave boy did his duty when I was seventeen."

"Good for him."

"I don't know about that. But it was very good for me. I think that's enough, don't you?" She rolled over. "Thank you. I'd like to take you out to dinner tonight. May I?"

"I thought you were broke."

"Oh, I was." Her smile would have ruffled a bishop at fifty paces. "But it's only a cheap Italian place, and besides, it's really your money."

"Oh. You cashed the cheque, then."

"Mmm. I couldn't decide whether to make it out for five or ten, so in the end I made it twenty-five. So that means we can have wine, too."

The manager recognized Carol as soon as they came in, and welcomed her. As he led them to their table she chatted in Italian; and the waiter who took their order had a short and cheerful conversation too. "All I got from that was 'bella,' " Hale said. "Where did you learn the language?"

"Rome. The airline sent me there for six months, and I got engaged to an Italian count or viscount—he couldn't seem to make up his mind which."

"And what happened?"

"Oh, nothing." She looked down and smoothed a fold in the tablecloth, and when she looked up the smile had faded before it reached her eyes. "Everybody kept telling me he was a fake, he wasn't a count at all. I didn't believe it—there's a lot of nasty gossip in Rome—but a few days after I broke off the engagement he was arrested, and it all came out at the trial. They were right; he wasn't anybody special. Except to me."

"Why was he arrested?"

"Fraud. He got seven years."

Hale whistled softly through his teeth, like a falling bomb. *'Ciao,* and *grazie* for nothing. . . . You had a close call, then."

"Did I?" She raised her eyebrows, and her brow creased and cleared with a gentle flicker of challenge.

"Well . . . didn't you? Unless I've got it all wrong, you could have been married to an Italian jailbird."

"Oh, *David*." She looked completely away, and then looked back. "Sometimes you sound so shudderingly English that I want to stick a little Union Jack behind your ear and tape-record the things you say so that you can hear yourself afterwards."

"Dear me. Then I *have* got it all wrong."

"What happened to him in Rome wasn't why I left him. Fraud . . . what's fraud, anyway? We're all frauds. But he kept treating me like a mindless little doll, someone to be amused and entertained. He was marvellous at that, he could always make me laugh. But he was afraid of going any further."

"I thought that was all Italian men thought of."

"I mean further than that, too."

Hale, momentarily outpaced, won himself time to catch up by ordering a carafe of wine. Then the food began to arrive, and Carol seemed to forget about her bogus ex-fiancé, so Hale concentrated on amusing and entertaiing her. He was surprised how easy it was. She was very good at it.

In the end they got through two carafes, and had brandy with their coffee. Hale was given the bill, and he paid it. "Just as well, really," Carol said. "It simplifies the book-keeping." They left the restaurant in a little flurry of extravagant compliments, and Carol tucked her hand inside his arm as they walked to the car. It was the end of a hazy, sunny evening: one of those rare low-key times when London actually seemed to be on his side.

They were back in the flat, and he was looking at record

sleeves, when Carol said, "See what I bought with your money." She was holding two big tins of paint. Four more stood on the floor.

"All I see is six ordinary tins of paint," he said, "but I expect you're going to perform some kind of trick with them. If it's juggling, I shall watch from the doorway."

"They're for you."

"What a generous fellow I am. Why?"

"To brighten up this place, of course. Look at it—it's like the inside of a big cardboard box. Beige on beige. Ugh. I've got a beautiful blue for that wall, and this is—"

"Just a minute, just a minute. I signed a lease for this place. Furnished. The landlord does the decorating, not me."

"D'you really like it the way it is?"

"Not much, but—"

"Well then, why live with it? Does the landlord have to put up with *your* colour scheme? Come and look at these, and tell me which you prefer. How d'you feel about mustard?"

"Cautious," he said. He took the screwdriver from her and eased the lids off. The paints gleamed like concentrates of voluptuousness, and gave off a faint scent of novelty. "Imagine that sky-blue over there," she said softly, "and maybe that bronzy-looking stuff all over there."

"You'll get me evicted."

"All in a good cause. These walls are a crime."

"We ought to try it on something first, to see what it really looks like."

She dipped a finger in the bronzy stuff, and shivered her shoulders. "Gorgeous. Edibly gorgeous." She wiped her finger on the rim, and looked all around the room, ending up with Hale.

"There's only you. We'll have to try it on you, David."

He snorted. "That'll be the day."

"Why not? Isn't it a wonderful idea? Just *think* of it. Imagine, David! What a perfect way to end the evening!" Her face was alive with discovery. "Can't you see how marvellous it would be?"

Hale hesitated, caught by her enthusiasm and his own secret curiosity. "Why me? Why not you?"

"Why not both of us?"

He looked down at the seductively slick jelly, lightly marked by her finger. "Imagine the *sensation*," she whispered unexpectedly in his ear. He flinched slightly. "Hadn't I better change into something first?" he asked. There was a slight huskiness in his voice.

"Good idea. Shorts would be best, wouldn't they?"

He changed into shorts, and stood with his hands in his pockets while she painted DAVID across his chest and then filled in the gaps to make an oblong. It felt cold and wet, and about as exciting as emulsion paint could be expected to feel. She drew a little ring around his navel, and gave him the brush. "Now me," she said. She pulled her blouse over her head and offered her back.

"You'll be the death of the bra industry," he observed.

"Oh well." She was fumbling with the buttons at the wrists. "A girl's got to show off while she can."

He painted CAROL across her back, and then turned it into an oval. The brush slipped slickly across her lightly tanned skin. Hale found that there was more pleasure in painting than in being painted. It was a most attractive colour. Carol had good taste. "Keep still," he said.

"What are you doing?"

"Painting over the white line from your bikini strap."

"Clever you." She spun round, and the brush left a swerving streak across her breasts.

"My God!" Hale said.

"It's nice of you to say so," she murmured, "but *you* can call me Carol."

"You pinched that joke," he said, looking for somewhere to park the brush. "I can't remember where, but you definitely pinched it."

"Yes, of course I did, dear." She fumbled and then wrestled with the buckle of his shorts, and gave up. Hale threw the brush out of the doorway, unzipped her skirt, unbuckled his shorts, put his arms around her and kissed her. Their clothes slid erratically to the floor. He shoved a couple of paint tins aside with his foot and they lay down; and soon her breasts were smoothing and smudging and sharing the name she had painted on his chest, while her back printed a hazy bronze oval onto the landlord's beige carpet.

"Look what I've found," Carol said during breakfast. She held up a gold-embossed invitation card. "It's my cousin George's wedding this afternoon. I completely forgot. Like to come?"

"I can't. No morning suit."

"Hire one. Then you can take me in your car, then I shan't have to get a taxi, then I can afford to buy tights. Hurray!" She poked him in the ribs. He gasped with pain and doubled up, white-faced. She helped him sit on the couch and squeezed his hand while she cried.

"All right, all right, it doesn't hurt all *that* much," he said. "Why are you crying? It's *my* ribs." Eventually she got up with her hands over her face and went into the bathroom. Five minutes later she was smiling and happy. Hale marvelled.

A rubber-winged newspaper van sidestepped smartly in front of Hale's Cortina and made him stab at the brakes. "Bastard!" he said. He changed down. "Sorry."

"What for?" Carol asked. They followed the van's black and foul-smelling exhaust through Kensington. "Don't you ever feel like driving right into them when they do that?" she said. "Bang crash wallop. Just to teach them a lesson."

"It wouldn't do any good."

"Then what would?"

"Avoiding the whole smelly issue." He turned smartly down a side street. "If you can't beat 'em, don't join 'em."

"That's just cheating. Besides, there are always more newspaper vans." They drove in silence while Hale tried to navigate back to the main road. "Where are we going now?" she asked.

"Same place. Only I'm a tiny bit lost."

"I thought you were. I'm completely lost." They turned a corner and were overtaken by a different newspaper van. Carol pointed.

"Don't speak or I'll bite you in the leg," Hale ordered.

"I was only going to say what a better class of newspaper van you get around here."

The traffic thickened and Hale slowed to a crawl. Carol rested her head against the side window and looked ahead. "How splendid," she said. *"Awnings."* They reached the cause of the jam: limousines unloading outside a large church. A brilliant blue awning covered a path of red carpet from the street across a lawn to the church door. Just as Hale was getting waved on by a policeman Carol said, "Pull in, pull in. Park here. This is it, we're there."

"We can't be. You said it was in Belgravia."

"Never mind old Cousin George, this one's much better. Find somewhere to park."

Hale squeezed into a minimal gap. "Damn good," she said admiringly. "I could never have done that."

He looked across at her. "Whos getting married back there, then? Someone you know?"

"Not yet. Did you see that *carpet*; It looked like the parting of the Red Sea, or something."

"The parting of the Red Sea. Are you sure you've got that right?"

"Oh, stop being so stuffy. Have you ever had the red-carpet treatment?"

"No."

"Well, come and try it. It's like wading through old port."

They walked back to the church and strolled slowly along the red carpet. "Yummy," Carol said. "This stuff costs about five pounds a foot, you know."

"Prepare to enjoy the return trip, then. I think they expect us to have an invitation."

"So they do. That's very proper of them; I approve. Don't you say a word. Just try and smile a tiny bit."

An usher stepped forward and contrived to be respectful while blocking the doorway.

"This is the West German Ambassador's son," Carol told him. "He arrived from Brazil only this morning. His English is very poor, I'm interpreting for him. I believe our invitations are somewhere here?"

"I'm afraid nobody has told me anything about that, miss."

"What a bore. And Sir Charles promised *faithfully*. Has the bishop arrived yet?"

The usher was startled. "I'm afraid I couldn't say."

"Ah well." Carol smiled, dimpling like a three-year-old. "It rather looks as if we're in your hands, doesn't it?" He was looking unhappily over her head: a large party had just got out of two Rolls-Royces and was sorting itself out. "Goody. Here's the bishop now," Carol said easily. "What are we going to do with that German Ambassador's son? Send him back to Brazil, d'you think, or . . ."

"If you could just hang on for a moment—"

"I'm afraid not. The Ambassador's son isn't too keen on hanging about outside churches. I rather think you should either let him in or send him away." The usher washed his hands in worry. Carol shielded her mouth with the back of her gloved hand. "Don't be concerned in case he steals a hymnbook or something," she whispered. "He has *full diplomatic immunity.*"

The party from the Rolls-Royces was advancing slowly and irresistibly. The usher took a deep breath and stood back. Carol led Hale inside. They sat on the bridegroom's side. She looked at the congregation, selected two or three strangers, and smiled at them. *"Lovely* flowers," she said to Hale. "The bride's mum did them. She has a stall in Shepherd's Market, you know."

Hale nodded pleasantly to an admiral across the aisle. He whispered, "The way you bullied that poor chap was absolutely shameless."

"Shame doesn't come into it unless somebody gets hurt. We're not hurting, we're helping."

Jubilantly, the organ played the couple out of the church on waves of trumpetings and thunderings, and the congregation turned to each other with smiles of self-congratulation. "Not bad, I suppose," Hale said.

"Seven out of ten. Too much God, for my taste. . . . Now for the reception?"

"We might as well. Where is it?"

"I think I heard someone say Claridge's. Anyway, *something's* bound to be happening at Claridge's, isn't it?"

As he followed her through the crowd, Hale saw the heads turning to look, and he noticed the way the sunlight brushed the hazy down on her bare arms. He sensed the clean curve of her neck muscles merging into firm and confident shoulders, still freckled under a light tan. She was so *alive,* she made him feel wooden; then she glanced back and smiled, and he felt a giddy emptiness in his guts, as if he had unexpectedly won a coveted prize.

They walked into Claridge's at the same time as a lot of the other guests, including a man who searched his pockets and grunted with relief when he found a gilt-edged card. Hale noticed that several other people had cards.

They trooped along a wide corridor. "We'll never do it this time," Hale muttered. "Religion's one thing, booze is another."

Carol had stopped, and Hale had to go back to her. "Listen," she said. Dance music throbbed somewhere off to their left. He looked at her questioningly, and she widened her eyes with huge and simple pleasure. She found a door and they went down a short corridor to a room in which a woman was washing champagne glasses.

"Oh dear, David," Carol said. "I *told* you that was the wrong door. Now we shall have to do the washing-up."

"That's all right, miss," the woman said maternally. "Tell you what: you just sneak in behind the screens there, and nobody'll know. Don't worry about the waiters, they're all foreign anyway." Carol fluttered her fingers, Hale tipped the woman, and they sneaked in behind the screens to the biggest wedding reception in the Western world.

Sir Douglas Handyside was a man with a whipcord face and a voice like torn cardboard. "I'll tell you what's wrong with this country," he said. "Too much power in the wrong hands, that's what's wrong."

"My goodness, *yes*," Carol said. Hale stopped a waiter and handed around fresh champagne. She flashed him a starlet's smile. "Do go on," she urged.

"Well, everywhere you look there's a lot of jumped-up john-nies shuffling acres of bumf. Personally, I think it's a national scandal, but you mustn't pay any attention to me, my dear, because I've drunk too much champagne."

"What nonsense," Carol said.

"Take my postman. Hair down to here, and he can't even read the addresses. Is it any wonder we didn't win any Olympic medals?"

"Of course not," Carol said. She waved delicately at nobody. "There's Dotty, I must just say hallo, *do* excuse me."

They watched her twinkle away. "Smart girl you've got there, Hale," said Handyside.

"Yes, sir."

"Brains as well as beauty. Not many women see to the heart of things the way she does."

"Mmm," Hale said. "I suppose she has that knack."

"Last thing I expected, bumping into you here. D'you know the deceased?"

"The groom? Not terribly well."

"Neither do I, but I've met the bride once or twice. Frightful woman. They say she can break a man's leg with one blow of her wing."

"Good God. Really?"

"No. Nice idea, though. How are you getting along with Lavagarde?"

"Oh . . . steady progress, sir."

"Good. Pip-pip, then."

Two hours later Carol, skimming along on a cloud of champagne, found Hale being harangued by a woman who was trying to recruit him into the Liberal Party. "He hasn't got a vote," Carol told her. "He's a mad foreign peer out on parole." The woman ground out a smile and went away. "I think we should go to Cousin George's do, now. I really ought to see him, just to say good-bye. It's at the Hilton. We can walk."

They strolled through easy, sleepy sunshine, blinking cheerfully at a London made slightly gauzy with alcohol. The lobby of the Hilton was busy with arriving Americans, and they had to wait a long time before they could get a lift. Someone trod on Hale's toe, and his euphoria steadily evaporated. He felt dry in the mouth and stiff in the legs. His feet were beginning to ache. Suddenly he felt very tired, and tired of people too. He'd had enough for one day.

Somebody made a nonsense of the lift buttons and Hale and Carol missed their floor. They rode to the top, where the lift emptied, came down a couple of floors, and stopped to collect three men in dinner jackets. Two of the men were middle-aged; the third was older, and walked with a stick. All were hot-faced with recent laughter. Hale moved into a corner and stared at his shoes. The lift went down. He raised his head and found the lame man staring. "For God's sake, cheer up!" the man said. "What have you got to be so bloody miserable about?"

The other men grinned. Hale felt the blood pump savagely up to his face, and glowered. He suppressed the hostile messages that rushed from his brain, and looked away. "Christ Almighty," the lame man said, "some people have got a face as long as a double-bass."

Carol turned her stainless radiance towards him. "It's not your fault, of course," she said quietly, "because there's no way you could have known, but . . . my brother's best friend has just been killed in an air crash."

The lame man looked sick. His companions winced. They finished the ride in silence. Hale and Carol got out at their floor and stood looking at the sign announcing Cousin George's reception. She was suddenly quite pale.

"Are you all right?" Hale asked.

She turned to the wall and covered her face and wept. He stood beside her, moving his weight from foot to foot, uncertain whether to touch her, embarrassed in case anyone came along. But she stopped crying after a few seconds and took his handkerchief.

"He deserved it, that rotten man," she said shakily, "I'm not sorry for that. It's just that I started to think . . . how horrible . . . if one's brother *had* just died in an air crash. How really horrible."

Hale swallowed and took a breath and tried to think of something to say, and could not.

Starin was surprised to get a visit from the Ambassador's secretary on Saturday evening; the Embassy staff usually relaxed at week-ends, and it wasn't as if the Ambassador's secretary had anything new or different to say. Starin sat and stared at him as if staring could wear him away.

The young man said, "You see, I'm sure they'd be much happier if only they had a job-title which they could enter it

under. Something to say what it was for. That's the way I read
their minds."

"Bloody accountants." Starin said it like a decision.

The young man smiled encouragingly. "It *was* rather a lot,
Colonel. And in cash. *And* at short notice." He extended the
smile to Grobic. "Both times," he added.

"Listen, you arrogant little matriculated cockroach." Starin
got up fast and talked fast. "You know what you're worth?
You're worth ten grams of gunpowder, and not so very long ago
that's what you'd have got. If I had my way, we'd see one hell
of a lot of pruning and the tree would be stronger for it too,
none of this crawling around on your belly to hear what the
accountants say or the neighbours say or the newspapers. Ten
grams? You're not worth five, you postgraduate pansy, it makes
me puke to think I have to tolerate a yard of piss like you, that's
what's wrong today, all this sickening weakening tolerating going on, tolerating, everybody tolerating everything, it's a god-
damned blight, it's everywhere, I even thought before I got this
posting that some people were beginning to—" He stopped and
glared.

"Yes, Colonel?" Grobic was politely atentive.

Starin's glare kept moving from one to the other. "God rot
the lot of you," he barked. He went out, heels denting the
carpet. Grobic heard the cellar door slam.

"What a bore he is," the young man said.

"It's a very difficult time just now." Grobic was almost whispering. "There's something big coming up."

"Really. How thrilling." The young man stood up and took
his time about looking at Grobic, at his haircut, his tie, his suit,
his shoes. He sighed. "You see, I know how hard it was for
Colonel Starin to get this posting. His peculiar skills aren't in
much demand any more. You have to know your way around
the administration today. You have to be able to manipulate
people. Ten grams of gunpowder. . . . Such an utterly obsolete
way of thinking."

"Kamarenski didn't think so."

The young man grimaced. "Blunder. A crass, clumsy, self-indulgent blunder. If you only knew how angry so many people were over Kamarenski."

"What about all this money?" Grobic said unhappily. "Can't we, you know, camouflage it somehow?"

"For instance."

Grobic worried. "This Trade Reception we're holding. Couldn't we lose it there? Call it a . . . I don't know what, a contingency allowance or something?"

The young man picked up his hat. "I'll suggest it," he said without interest. They heard a muffled crack from the cellar, and he cocked an eyebrow. "He shoots at rats," Grobic explained.

"Vocational training, no doubt. Good-bye."

Sunday breakfast was subdued and thoughtful. Finally Hale picked up his coffee and went for a walk around the room. "Sorry about the melodrama," he said.

"That's all right. After the first fright I didn't really mind."

"I suppose I must have had a nightmare."

"Yes, I think you must. I used to get them all the time when I was small. . . . Dirty trick, isn't it? Creeping up on you while you're asleep."

Hale sipped his coffee and tried to recall the noisy ugliness which had made Carol wake him at half past three in the morning. Nothing came. "I've *never* had nightmares," he said. "Can you have a nightmare and not remember it? Seems pretty pointless. What was I doing?"

"Just swearing."

"Swearing." He topped up his coffee. "That's charming, that is."

Carol walked over to the window and looked at the sun. "I don't believe in all this weather, it's un-English. Who is Starin?"

Hale felt his bowels look over a small cliff. "Who's *who?*" he said.

Carol gave herself a nod of congratulation. "Fancy. Bluebell the Girl Detective strikes again. I guessed from the tone of your voice that Starin was the big bogyman. You gave him effing hell, poor chap."

Hale drained his saucer into his cup. "Let's get this straight," he said. "D'you mean I talked in my sleep?" She nodded. "What did I say?"

"You said a lot of things. You were very angry with a lot of people, and Mr. Starin was one."

"Who else?"

"Someone called Fitz, or it might have been Fritz. You got a bit incoherent, I'm afraid, and I wasn't at my best myself."

"Any more?"

"Oh yes, lots more, but nothing that stuck. Who are they all, anyway?"

"Oh, nobody, nobody."

"What a terrible liar you are, completely incompetent, you go all red, especially around the ears."

"They're just business rivals."

"What awful lies. David you *must* practise more often, you're hopeless. Don't tell me who Starin is, I don't care."

"He's a competitor, they're all—"

"I don't *care*. I don't care if they're all fairies at the bottom of the garden, it doesn't matter in the least."

"No? It does to me." He hesitated, searching for a better way to say it, and found none. "This means we'll have to go back to sleeping in separate beds, Carol."

She stared. "You're not serious. Yes, you are; I can see you are."

"It's the only way. I can't risk it, otherwise."

"Risk what? Don't you trust me with your dreaded nightmares?"

"I just don't want you involved, that's all. It's a messy business and I want to keep you right out of it. These are the ground rules, remember?"

"Oh, poop." She rapped him on the stomach and made him

flinch. He grabbed her hands and held her away.

"You don't know your own strength, my girl," he said sternly. He thought what a fine chest she had for such a slim figure. She looked down at herself. "They're both there," she said. "I counted them this morning."

"I give up," he said. "You see through me like a . . . like a . . ."

"Dirty window. Stop trying to be such a terrible fraud, David. You stand around wearing your decent, noble expression, and all the time you're giving off signals non-stop, like traffic lights. I can feel it pouring out of you like static electricity."

"Static electricity doesn't pour, it's static."

"Well, yours does. Just now I got a wave of it that nearly knocked me on my back."

"I can't think of a better position."

"Neither can I," she said. "So why are we standing around here arguing?"

They walked, hand in hand, into the bedroom. "Besides," he said, "this bed isn't really big enough for two to sleep in comfortably."

"Feeble excuse number twenty-seven," she said. But she smiled as she said it.

They ate a second breakfast at midday, and then decided to paint the flat. "The sweat will compensate for the pleasures of the flesh," Carol said. "And besides, I like painting."

For a couple of hours the paint-rollers thudded and hissed, the radio burbled on top of the stacked-up furniture, the sunshine felt its lazy way across the spread-out newspapers. At half past three Carol came up behind Hale and whistled through her fingers. "The workers are getting ugly," she said. "They demand food. Nothing special—what the boss eats is good enough."

They sat on the window sill, facing each other, bare feet

pressing, and looked down on the street while they ate lop-sided ham sandwiches and drank bottled beer. One of the homosexuals saw them and fetched his partner. Hale could see their disapproval.

"D'you like London?" Carol asked.

"Sometimes. I feel as if I have a stake in the place, so I have to like it. D'you like it?"

"It varies. I don't trust the place. It's like some great big animal. Most of the time it's friendly, but when you're least expecting it, the thing snaps at you. There's too much of it, that's the trouble."

"There's too many people, that's the trouble with the world. You've just got to learn to ignore them, otherwise they wear you down. It used to worry me when I first came here; people everywhere you look. Very exhausting. So I gave up seeing them as people, I just saw them as sort of moving street furniture. Less of a strain, that way."

She was wearing one of his old shirts, hugely rolled up at the sleeves and hanging outside a pair of denim slacks. She stopped eating, and cleaned the crumbs from her lap. "What an awful way to live, though. It's like growing scar-tissue all over. That's what I hate about London: we all go around defending ourselves. It's all take and no give, isn't it? I don't want to spend my life taking all the time. I like to give." She met his gaze for a moment, and then looked down.

"Gee whiz," Hale said. "I must have accidentally pressed the red button, or something."

"Oh, *David*." She pedalled his feet.

Hale waited and watched, but Carol had finished and was pouring more beer. He tried hard to understand her. She was so fresh and young and casually lovely. And obviously so serious. He looked away, at the remote and indifferent sky. No answer up there, either.

Hale stopped painting and turned up the volume. "Listen to this," he said. Carol rested one sleek buttock on the top of the stepladder, and listened.

> " *When love congeals*
> *It soon reveals*
> *The faint aroma of performing seals,*
> *The doublecrossing of a pair of heels—*
> *I wish I were in love again!*"

"Marvellous lyrics," he said. "It's all about love affairs going sour, and yet it's romantic, too. I mean, strictly speaking, that last line should be *"Thank God I'm not in love again!"*

"Should it? I wonder. . . ."

"But of course."

"All the same, and even supposing it's true, wouldn't you rather be in love than not?"

"I'd rather be *happily* in love. No black eyes, no self-deception."

"Would you?" Carol asked. "Self-deception's a good thing sometimes. Otherwise nobody would ever say, 'I love you to the day I die.' Would they?"

"If they meant it, yes. Aren't you being a bit cynical?"

"But if it's a gamble . . . Isn't everything a gamble? Isn't the important thing to make up your mind, and then close your eyes and jump?"

Hale closed one eye and looked up at her along the top edge of his roller. "I'm never quite sure whether you're asking me or telling me," he said.

She pointed her roller at him like a space-gun. "Bang," she said. "You're emulsified."

Grobic said, "Colonel Starin is not available. Who is calling?"

"Betty, for the seventeenth time." Angrily, Hale sorted through his change, looking for more telephone money. "I'm in a call-box and I haven't got much time left, so . . ."

"A message, perhaps."

"All right." Hale switched the phone to his unsweating ear and thought hard. "You remember those photographs?"

"The counterfeits, yes."

"That wasn't my doing."

"But you can explain it."

"No, I can't."

Grobic glanced at Starin, who was listening at an extension. Starin waved him on. Grobic said, "We are agreed that the photographs were faked, therefore you will refund the money."

"No, that doesn't follow at all. Besides, it's irrelevant. Faked or not, they weren't worth the money you paid. They weren't worth fourpence to you."

"Why do you say that?"

'Never mind. Let's forget the pictures, *and* the report. What matters is the man who wrote it, right? I know where he is."

Grobic looked at Starin. Starin pointed to the floor. "When can you come here?" Grobic asked.

"You must be joking," Hale said.

"Not at all. That is the way we do business."

"Suppose *I* say where we meet?"

Starin shook his head. "No," Grobic said.

"Good-bye, Grobic."

"Betty!" Starin said. "Stop playing in the street before you get run over." Hale hung up.

"Sometimes he sounds a bit mad," Grobic suggested hopefully.

"If he comes near me again I'll kill him," Starin said. "And bugger their Home Secretary."

Hale got into the car. "Success?" Carol asked.

"I got through," he told her. "Didn't do much good, though." He rested his hands on the wheel and stared through the spokes.

She reached over and twisted his ear. "Come on, it's only business."

"Sorry. . . . It's a bit worrying, that's all. Did you find anything?"

She had the cinema page from the *Standard*. "*That* one, please."

Hale looked. " '*Outdoor Intercourse*, XX, Swedish-Japanese Lust in the Dust; plus *Four Abreast*, XX, She was insatiable!' "

"Yummy, yummy."

"Are you sure?"

"Yes, yes. Drool, drool. Slaver, slaver."

"O.K. It doesn't seem like you, that's all."

"Like me?" She held him by the ears and tried to look seriously at him. "What sort of person am I like, David?"

"Well, you're . . ." He caught hold of her wrists and tried to get free. "You're like the daughter of . . . of . . ."

"The British Ambassador?"

"Yes. Maybe."

"Not maybe; definitely. Daddy's a diplomat and Mummy's something big in the International Red Cross."

"A fearfully well-bred filly."

"Frightfully." She released him and beeped the horn. "Dirty pictures!" she ordered.

Afterwards, driving home, she said, "I don't know why people say films like that are unhealthy. I've never seen anyone take so much exercise in my life."

Hale made a couple of nightcaps while Carol made her bed. He switched on the radio, and somebody's swinging strings washed around the room.

"D'you dance?" she asked. "With a body like yours, you ought to dance like Nureyev."

"I never really learned."

"Let me teach you." She put down her drink and put herself inside his arms.

It was no good. His back was tense, his hands were too limp

or too tight, his legs moved stiffly. "Sorry," he said. "It's just not my speed."

She put her arms around his neck, and brushed her cheek against his face. "My dear, dear David," she said. She sighed, and her body moved against his. "You're always on guard, always on duty. If only we could share the strain."

He linked his hands behind her, and they stood for a while, silent, in the middle of the room.

"It can't be done," he said. They went to their separate beds.

Thoy heard Zeller's throaty, friendly voice coming along the corridor. "They seem to grow 'em different in Paris, Stefan," he was saying. "They're bigger, and they stick out farther. You can really get a grip of them," he explained as they came through the door. "It's a very exciting experience, I recommend it. Hi, fellas."

"Stefan speaks no English," Grobic said.

"Shoot, that's right, I forgot. I was just telling him about French doorknobs." Stefan went out.

"French doorknobs," Starin said bleakly. "You spent the week-end feeling French doorknobs?"

"Hell, no," Zeller protested. "I've been tracking down this Professor James. It's been *cherchez le James* for little Gary. I scarcely paused to eat, even."

"Speak Russian, Leonid, you lie too easily in English. Where is he and what is he doing?"

"He's where Sennet said he would be," Zeller said in slow Russian, "in an office block near Choisy. That's on the south side of Paris, by Orly Airport. He works on the third floor and lives in the penthouse apartment."

"Did you see him?" Grobic asked.

"Sure. I even gave him his stick once, when he dropped it in the lobby."

Starin showed him the newspaper photograph. "That is

old," Zeller said. "He's balder now. Thinner, too."

"My God," said Starin in disgust, "you speak Russian as if you're chewing nails. Where did you grow up?"

"The Ukraine. Near Kharkov."

"I think I'd sooner hear you murder someone else's language," Starin told him in English. "It seems as if James is not being guarded. Why is he in Paris?"

"He sees a heart specialist twice a week for tests. They're giving him some kind of revolutionary treatment. They may have to operate. And he's *guarded,* all right: by two guys who look like they were carved out of Mount Rushmore."

"Mount Rushmore?" Grobic repeated.

"It's a brand of toilet soap," Zeller said.

"Is James working?" Starin asked.

"Like a madman." Zeller began searching his flight-bag. "Saturday night I got into his studio or whatever the hell it's called and lifted this little lot." He dumped a fat bundle of papers on the floor. "Shazam!"

"So by now the place is full of policemen," Grobic said, "and James is God-knows-where. Masterly."

"These are copies. I went there again Sunday night and put the originals back—so up your ass, Grobic." Zeller thrust his middle finger upwards.

"You did rather well," Starin said. He picked up the papers and riffled them. "Or they did extraordinarily badly."

"It wasn't easy, if that's what you mean. That place is sealed up and tight. *You* might have got inside," he said to Starin, "but *he* wouldn't."

"Zeller loves Zeller," Grobic scoffed.

"Shut up and listen," Starin ordered. "If James is really in Paris, what is this *other* James doing at the Peake Building?"

"Jigsaw puzzles. Seriously, Colonel, that's what he's doing. He's a stand-in. Somebody doesn't want it generally known that James is in Paris, so they hired this guy to sit in his office and breathe in and out."

"Does he look like James?"

"He looks a bit like *this* James." Zeller touched the photograph.

"But you never saw that picture before today," Starin said suspiciously, "so how did you know that Jigsaw James was a stand-in?"

"I sniffed it." Zeller gave a couple of demonstration sniffs. "I scented a false trail. Greasepaint, Colonel. It's unmistakable to an actor, and it made Jigsaw James an actor, which makes sense because he was hired to impersonate. I guess he's in rep somewhere near London, and I guess he never quite gets all the make-up off. Or maybe he even puts a little *on* when he's playing James. I sniffed it the moment I met him." Zeller gave a curtain-call smile.

"Why didn't Betty sniff it, then?" Grobic asked. "He was with you, wasn't he?"

"It takes an actor, laddie, it takes an actor. For six wonderful years I was one of that godlike breed, laddie. I bestrode the stage like a colossus, laddie, all the way from Omaha, Nebraska, to El Paso, Texas. And back again."

Starin stared at Zeller. Zeller smiled back. Starin said, "So James is safe in Paris, alive if not well, working hard on Project 107. I wonder when he'll finish it."

"That I don't know," Zeller said. "And it may be coincidence, but I thought it was worth remembering: there's an international scientific congress opening in Paris next week. Very big deal. And James is on the bill."

Hale spent Monday morning at Flekker Handyside, catching up on his mail. There was a cable from Lavagarde asking for the latest information on Petrolex plans, which made Hale dial Brandon's number; but Brandon was on a business trip to Boston, Mass.: Too close to Montreal for comfort, Hale thought. He tried and failed to telephone Lavagarde, so he sent him a cable, followed by a letter spelling out exactly where Petrolex stood, ran, dodged, or played leap-frog.

Then, to his surprise, Hubbard called and said Divine would like to have lunch with him.

They met at Divine's club, the Army and Navy. Surprisingly again, Divine had little to say during lunch; he made polite enquiries about Hale's social life, marital prospects, plans, ambitions; and said that he would like to meet Carol one day, because she sounded like a fine girl. Coffee came and Hale decided it was time to get down to work. "I'm puzzled about Starin, sir," he said. "Perhaps you can explain . . ."

"Doubt it, David, but try me."

"Two things, really. He had that copy of the report on Project 107, yet he didn't know who wrote it, he didn't know about Professor James."

"Not at first. Neither did we, at first."

"But Hubbard found out, sir, literally overnight. And I checked James in a sort of scientists' *Who's Who,* and he may not be world-famous but he's not a nobody either. They gave him nearly half a column."

"What's your other problem, David?"

"Well, Starin and Grobic keep complaining that the prints I sold them were forged, or faked, or tampered with, which is totally impossible, isn't it?"

"Have they given details?"

"No. They just asked for their money back."

Divine chuckled, and settled down to enjoy his cigar. Hale realized that he was not going to get any explanations. After a while, he said, "I suppose as long as James is safe nothing else matters, but I can't help thinking, sir, that the Home Secretary could make life a lot easier for us by putting Starin at the top of his list."

Divine thought about that as he stared through his cigar smoke. Or perhaps he didn't think about it. Either way, he made no comment.

———————

The Ambassador kept Starin waiting for twenty minutes while he finished his after-lunch nap, and then met him in the library. Both men stood throughout the conversation.

"Let me see now. My accountants—"

"Yes, yes, yes, Mr. Ambassador. Or no, no, no, if you like."

"My dear Colonel, I can't afford to like or dislike any more; I simply make sure the right wheels keep turning. Since you won't tell us what happened to the money—and I'm damned if I'm going to waste *my* time finding out—we shall just have to pass the mystery on to Moscow. Then, presumably, *their* wheels will turn."

"I'm pleased you're pleased."

"I'm not pleased, I'm just relieved. Mind you, I will admit that there's something else." He undid two buttons on his shirt and revealed the gleaming white material beneath. "Silk underwear," he said gratefully. "Always warm but never itchy."

"Congratulations."

"Frankly, I'm surprised that you came to us at all. Six, seven thousand pounds: it's piddling, I know, but then that's what accountants are for. And I thought you had a healthy budget."

"I don't work to a budget, Mr. Ambassador, I work to a *goal*. I have enemies at home, people who want me to fail. They couldn't stop me from getting this posting, but they made damn sure I had no money to spend when I got here. Did they really think that that would stop me? I spend what I need to spend."

"Oh, well, As long as you realize that there's a bottle in the fire, and sooner or later it's bound to go off bang." The ambassador buttoned his shirt. "It doesn't worry me," he said. "I'm insulated."

Hale was drying his hands in the men's room at K2 when the hare-lip came in and ran the water. "A word in thy ear, sweet cousin," he said.

"Well, you know where it is," Hale said. He was getting sick of the oblique approach practised at K2.

"I'm Gibson. You're Hale, I know, and I know what you've been doing lately, because I've been stuck with keeping track of Starin's movements. Bloody boring."

"Too bad. Shouldn't you be out doing it now, though?"

"Oh, he's O.K. for ten minutes. Listen, Hale, could you do me a big favour?"

"No."

"Starin's throwing a reception for his so-called Trade Mission tonight, six-thirty at the Cumberland Hotel, and I ought to be there, but you see I've got tickets for Covent Garden."

"Hard luck."

"*What*? D'you realize how long it took to get those seats?" Gibson shoved the invitation into Hale's hand. "*You* go instead, Hale. Be a pal. It's a free drink, and there's nothing to do. The night shift takes over after the reception. Just enjoy yourself. Thanks a million. It's Wagner, see." Gibson was backing away. "Do the same for you. You know the Cumberland? You'll like it. Chance to meet people. How can I ever . . . ?" He slipped out, urgent to the end.

Hale went back to the bank and worked his way through the rest of the backlog. Towards the bottom he found a report on the political situation in Banzania and skimmed through it. The tone was pessimistic, but then Banzania had never inspired optimism in anyone except the makers of vaccines for tropical diseases. He slid the report under a glass paperweight labelled WORTH ANOTHER LOOK. It was past six; time to set out for the Cumberland.

At six-thirty Hale surrendered his invitation to a man who had never smiled in his life except to show the dentist where it hurt, and went into the Blue Room. He got a drink and looked at the other guests. A middle-aged man in a navy-blue coat came up. "Are you drinking the vodka?" he asked confidentially.

"Gin."

"Ah. It's funny, but their vodka tastes same as ours. I expected different, I don't know why."

"D'you do much business with . . . ?"

"None. I'm in typewriters, you see. Different alphabet. What's your line?"

"Cricket bats."

"Bloody daft, isn't it? Still, it keeps me out the pubs." He moved on.

Hale searched the room for Starin and failed to find him. After a couple of minutes a big American in a suit which seemed to be made of high-grade shiny brown paper came and stood nearby. He had a glass in each hand and drank from either, according to the direction in which he happened to be glaring at the time. A ruthless crew-cut gave him a head like an angry football. He glared at Hale. "You're not drinking," he said accusingly.

Hale showed him his glass, half-full.

"Kill that and get another. We're gonna drink these sonsabitches dry."

"I take it you're not here to trade."

"Trade? I wouldn't give you a pack of cigarettes for their whole goddam country."

"I'm surprised you came, then."

"Get this, feller: I'm a Republican and proud of it, and if I can help combat their lousy stinking insidious Communism then by God I'll do it if they have to carry me out of here feet first."

"Now I'm surprised that they asked you here."

"Wise up, fella. They're aiming to grab my goddam product. Smell that." He held both drinks in his right hand and put the inside of his left wrist underneath Hale's nose. Hale got a whiff of lemons tinged with gin.

"Most refreshing," he said.

"Right. They don't come any refreshinger. Best goddam men's toiletries in the goddam world. Come on, let's hit 'em where it hurts." He raised both drinks. "In the cellar."

Hale saw Starin. "Excuse me," he said. He moved to a better position, and saw Grobic too. Hale watched them talking; they seemed hunched, isolated in the growing crowd. He wondered if they knew anything at all about trade.

A sad African touched his arm. "Are you working for the Trade Mission, sir?"

"No, I'm afraid not."

He sighed. "I can find nobody to talk to. You see, we have a very great deal of cocoa, and they have no cocoa to speak of. We have it, they need it, but nobody is here to discuss."

"It doesn't seem fair, does it?" Hale looked at Starin, then at the African. "You're in luck, you know. The senior Russian cocoa-purchasing agent has just this minute arrived. If I were you . . ." He indicated Starin. The African hurried over. Hale turned away and raised his drink just as a girl in a nearby group did the same. They stared. It was Carol.

For an instant she looked blank. Then she smiled, and that smile was pure reward. She came to him and took his arm. "You won't believe this, I know, but I was just thinking of you, David. What luck!"

"Quite incredible. What on earth are you doing here?"

"Having a free drink, the same as you. My boss couldn't come so I used his invitation. I suppose you're here on business? It's very boring. I was just thinking of going."

"Well, now I can take you home."

"Lovely. Do you know those people? They seem to know you." She was looking past him. He turned and saw Starin staring, Grobic pointing, and the sad African nodding sadly. Hale turned back and shut his eyes.

"Cocoa," he said.

Carol said, "Here comes one." Hale opened his eyes and took a deep breath. It was Grobic, smiling like a head waiter refusing a cheque. "Good evening, Mr. Betty," he said. He bowed to Carol. "Colonel Starin would like a word with you," he told Hale.

Hale smiled at Carol. "Excuse me a minute," he said. The smile fell off, having nothing to hold it on.

Grobic took him to Starin. The African had gone. "I should

have stuffed these fingers in your eyes while I had the chance,"
Starin said. Contempt made his voice dead level, and dragged
his lips back at the corners. "You're turning into the biggest
pain in the ass since Grobic had his piles out."

"Piles, Colonel?" Grobic murmured, mystified. He took out
a pocket English dictionary.

"You run a Trade Mission, and he was a trader," Hale said.
"Why hold a bash like this if you don't want to meet blokes like
him?" He felt safe in this crowd.

"Listen to me. You started out as a crank. Then you became
a joke. Now you're turning into a bloody idiot. Everywhere you
go you leave little piles of shit. I'm sick of wiping my shoes
because of you."

"Really. Well, it's my city, and I'll go where the hell I like
in it."

Grobic shut his dictionary and looked depressed.

"You'll get your head broken open," Starin said. "You've had
a taste of that already. Next time you'll get the full meal." Stefan
came through the crowd and Starin turned away from Hale to
talk to him. Grobic stood by, scratching his head, chasing an
itch. Stefan went away.

"You Russians really are amazing people," Hale said with
feeling. "You think you can bulldoze anything to make it fit the
Party line—economics, history, science, literature, and now you
even want to lick *me* into shape. Why don't you stop kidding
yourselves?"

Surprisingly, Starin was now calm, even smug. "You see, Mr.
Betty, we are history. The revolution succeeds because it is
inevitable. It is inevitable because it succeeds. That is the whole
story."

"Simplified for idiots. You left out the bit where you shoot
everyone who opposes it."

"Destructive criticism invites destruction, wouldn't you
agree? Otherwise nothing would ever be accomplished."

"You pay a pretty sick price for your accomplishments."

Starin scoffed. "Prices, prices! You think like a capitalist. The price is whatever is necessary."

"Oh, balls. Nothing's necessary. You don't have to make your tatty revolution succeed any more, because we all know it's here to stay. You're *obsolete*, mate. There *isn't* a counter-revolution, so stop bloody fighting it. You know as well as I do why you want Project 107. You want to run off home carrying it in your hot and sticky hands, so as to make the West look stupid and you can be a hero. And the revolution can go piss in its fur hat! Right?"

Starin swallowed a yawn. "Shall I tell you your trouble?" he said. "You are what the English call a 'nice boy.' You are rotten with honour."

It was raining, so Hale left Carol with the doorman and fetched his car. While she got in he sat and looked at her legs. She hoisted her skirt up her thighs. "They go all the way up and then meet at the top," she said.

"Listen, why wear skirts if you don't want your legs looked at?" he asked. He wiped the inside of the windscreen.

"It's not the looks, it's the scrutiny," she said. "I feel as if you're trying to decide if I'm good enough to enter in the Smithfield Show." But he was staring past the flick-slap of the wipers.

"I know that damn car," he said.

"Huge. It must be American."

"It's a Chevrolet Impala." He leaned forward to look for the owner. "I'm *sure* it's . . . ?" He saw the Nebraska plates. "It *is*, by God," he muttered. "What a nerve."

"Whose is it?"

He did not reply. Two men were coming out of the Cumberland, sheltering under a single raincoat held over their heads. They reached the Chevrolet. One let go of the coat and opened the door. "Grobic!" Hale said. "I might've—" Then Fitzgerald turned to follow Grobic in, and they saw the enormous gun in his hand, half-shielded from view by the raincoat, but unmistakably pointing at Grobic.

Zeller gently bullied his way across the traffic around Marble Arch and cruised up Edgware Road. "Still there?" he asked.

Grobic held his breath to avoid fogging the rear window. "Slow down, slow down, you're losing him. . . . That's better. There he is, just passing that cab, about three cars back. Black Ford Cortina."

Zeller glanced in his mirror. "O.K., get your head down, I have him. It's going to be a long ride." He plugged a new country-and-western cassette into the dashboard, and punched the button. "God's own music!" he said.

"Well, I saw it," Carol said. "So there's no point in pretending I didn't."

Hale had a short argument with a taxi, and won. "Make sure that door's locked," he said.

"The last time I saw a gun that size, somebody was using it to start a yacht race. Your friends have tremendous style, don't they, David?"

"It doesn't add up," Hale said. "That's Fitzgerald up there, driving the Chevrolet. We know Grobic works for Starin, but I thought *Fitzgerald* worked for Starin too. So what the hell goes on?"

"Dunno, David. The Yard is baffled."

Hale accelerated hard in the wrong gear and stormed past a bus. "As soon as I get the chance I'll drop you. Get ready to jump out and—"

"*Me?* No fear! I'd never get a cab in this weather." Hale set his teeth. "Stop sulking," she said. "You must think I'm pretty dense, David. It's obvious that Starin is Tweedledum so you must be Tweedledee. I read the papers, you know."

"Oh, well."

"And now you're going to have a battle."

"Hell, I hope not."

She looked at a sign. " 'Cricklewood and the North.' Do your friends have friends in Cricklewood?"

Hale said, "Just don't lose sight of that car."

"What's the matter with Starin, anyway?" Zeller asked. "If this idiot child keeps sticking his goddam neck out, why don't we just chop it off?

"It's not that easy," Grobic said. He was lying on the back seat, checking their progress against the A-to-Z. "Slow down a bit, Stefan should be along here somewhere. . . . We can't afford to annoy the British at the moment, and you know how killings upset them. There he is, over there on the left. The limousine."

"I see him." Zeller blinked his lights and picked up speed again. "What about the girl?"

"What about her?"

"Nice piece of tail, huh?"

"She's in for a swift kick up the tail, if she only knew it."

"You could have jumped out then, for Pete's sake," Hale said. "Can't you understand? I don't want you in here."

"Too late, Tweedledee. It was your idea to drive me home, and I'm not going to bail out in the middle of darkest Hendon in a rainstorm at this time of night, not for anyone. I'd ruin my shoes."

"You're a bloody liability. You're a menace."

"Besides, you can't stop now or you might lose them. At this rate we'll soon be out of London, won't we?"

"There may still be traffic lights. If we meet a red light, *you get out*. Never mind your damn shoes. I'll buy you another pair."

"It's been a long trip already," Carol said. "Aren't you afraid they might have noticed you?"

"Nobody remembers Fords, there are millions of them," he said. "Especially black."

"So that's why you drive a black Ford."

"I wish you'd just *go*," Hale pleaded.

The rain grew heavier as they reached the outskirts. The storm was gathering impetus, generating gusts which flung drifting masses of rain across the road. The drops needled the bodywork and pounded themselves to smoke on the tarmac. Hale steered into the tire-tracks of the Chevrolet just as they were fading and dissolving to nothing. Up ahead, the big tail-lights sent a soft-red flame shimmering deep into the surface: twin beacons everlastingly fuelled on water. Like Project 107, Hale thought. He switched on his own sidelights. It was early evening, but the sky was black as ink.

They were far up the A5 now, beyond Edgware, heading for Elstree. The traffic was thinning; Hale dropped back another fifty yards. "I've only got half a tank left," he said. "I hope he's not planning on Scotland."

"I think he's planning on the Motorway. The M1 should be dead ahead." She looked from the map to a road sign and back again. "I make it about two miles to junction four."

"Well, at least it's not Middlesex."

"Why should it be?"

"Nothing. No reason. Forget it. With you in here I can't even talk to myself."

They listened to the rainsoak washing out from the tires, and watched the big blue car speed endlessly while it held endlessly the same position. Then a light pulsed on the Chevrolet and it swung right, following M1 arrows. Hale did the same. A minute later they were on the Motorway, still invisibly linked, still heading north.

"He *must* have seen you by now, mustn't he?" Carol asked.

"Not necessarily. His mirrors can't be a hundred per cent in all this rain, and besides he may not even be looking. And a Ford is still just a Ford."

"Will you really follow him to Scotland, if he goes there?" Hale said nothing. "Golly, I'm hungry," she said. "Haven't you any old biscuits, or anything?"

"Look, if you *won't* damn well get out, at least get yourself well strapped in. That wind's a lot gustier now."

She tightened her belt, and switched on the radio. Woodwinds pirouetted demurely down the scale: it was the middle of the overture to *The Thieving Magpie*. She leaned back and closed her eyes. Something massive smashed against the back of the car and sent it skidding into the next lane. The bash jolted their heads backwards and left Hale grabbing for the wheel with both hands. The sick crunch of metal on metal echoed in his brain, and he heard a tinkle of shattered glass over the shriek of his tires fighting the wet tarmac.

"What in hell was that?" he shouted. Carol braced her legs and hung on with both arms while the car skidded and kicked. Hale finally made it go straight, and as he slowed down she looked behind.

"Someone must have run into us," she said. "There are lights behind, but the window's all rained-up."

"Silly bastard must be blind!" he cried. "I've got my lights on, too. Christ, what a wallop!"

"Aren't you going to stop?"

"I'm going to make sure *he* stops." He set his left-indicator blinking and wound down his window. He put his head into the rain and quickly looked back. It was a big car, a limousine probably, a big black job, forty or fifty yards away. He got his arm out and signalled a slow-down. No response. They were trundling at thirty miles an hour, both on the inside lane.

"This bugger *must* be blind," he said. He blared several blasts on the horn and got his arm wet again. Again no response. "Blind or blind drunk," he said. A couple of cars raced up and flicked spray through his open window and were gone. "I can't *make* the bastard stop," he said. He glanced behind again. The black car was moving up now, gaining fast, growing and filling the lane, expanding with an urgency which suddenly made Hale stop signalling and start accelerating. "Jesus, he's going to do it *again!*" he shouted.

The Ford squirmed as its tires snatched at the drenched roadway, and then took off fast. In his mirror Hale saw the blurred shape behind him seem to magnify itself and fill the frame, and in a panic he swerved into the centre lane without looking to see if it was clear. The big car clouted him on the nearest corner, and again sent him skidding and sliding. This time Carol screamed.

He used up all three lanes before he got the wheels under control. Behind them both, other cars were flashing their head-lights and blaring useless warnings, hanging back, keeping their distance. "Stop, stop, please stop!" Carol pleaded.

"You're damn right I'll stop, before he bloody well kills us." He braked and headed for the shoulder. The rear window disintegrated and at the same time the mirror showed the black car closing up again, one headlight full on. It was a Rolls-Royce. Hale drove too fast onto the shoulder and the Rolls followed, ten feet behind. For ten seconds they racketed along, and then Hale swung back onto the Motorway. "He won't bloody *let* me stop!" he said. "He'll smash into me if I try!" He shoved the accelerator to the floor.

The Rolls breathed down his neck while he built the speed up to sixty. Four or five cars saw their chance and sprinted past. Their horns condemned the combat; white faces stared across; and then they were gone, hiding behind great skirts of spray.

"Why doesn't anyone *help?*" Carol demanded.

"Help? Now? What the hell can anyone do?" He had the accelerator flat on the floor, but the Cortina would not go above sixty. "Something's stuck!" he shouted. They crept alongside a thunderous tractor-trailer, and he felt its bow-wave trying to heave him aside.

Carol pointed to the space immediately in front of its cab. "Get in there, David! He can't touch you in there!"

As soon as his tail was clear, Hale began edging across. The truck-driver blasted at him angrily on a horn so raw that it made Hale clench his teeth. In a few seconds the truck was five feet behind them and the Rolls was not in sight.

"What now?" Hale asked.

"Hang in there and wait for an exit."

For half a mile the truck tried to bawl them out of its way. Then it fell silent and dropped back. Hale eased his aching foot off the accelerator and fell back too. "I wish I knew where that big black bastard is," he said.

Again the truck lost speed in an effort to get rid of this bit of battered obstinacy under its nose, and again Hale fell back. By now they were down to forty miles an hour. "Something's rubbing against a wheel," Hale said. "I can smell the burning." Momentarily he forgot the truck. When he remembered it, the gap between them was fifty feet. He stamped on the brake just as the truck swung into the middle lane and surged forward. The gradient was downhill. The truck came up fast and passed them with a bellow of dismissal.

Hale groaned. Carol had twisted around and was looking behind. She said shakily, "I think he's coming." Hale looked, and he was. Like a statement of intent, the Rolls's single headlight came on. He put his foot to the floor and got the needle up to sixty again. They ran out of a cutting and onto an embankment where the gusting wind flung sheets of rain across the windscreen. The headlight dazzle vanished from his mirror and he sensed a huge shape ghosting up on his right. He risked a glance. The Rolls had a crest on the front. The driver was Stefan.

Stefan came alongside and sideswiped them with the casual confidence of a man who is strapped inside two tons of motor-car. It did the Rolls no good, but it crumpled the Ford and knocked it sideways with a smack that stung Hale's palms and flung Carol against his shoulder.

He stamped on the brakes, but Stefan's brakes worked better and the Rolls drifted behind only to come up on the other side and sideswipe them again, and yet again, deliberately pounding and damaging. A third time Stefan hammered the heavy wing of the Rolls into their side, and this time Hale felt the steering turn to jelly as the car punched sideways until it careered off the crash barrier. Carol screamed again and tried to hide behind her arms.

Hale's foot stabbed from accelerator to brake and back again, searching desperately for an escape. Stefan cruised along the centre lane and matched each move. He clouted selectively, punching the bodywork but not the wheels: damaging the car without destroying it.

Then he missed one. Hale saw him coming and in a fit of madness cut the wheels left to meet him; Stefan misjudged everything, missed Hale, nearly swerved into the crash barrier, fish-tailed away, and dropped three lengths in three seconds. Hale saw his chance and gunned the engine savagely: too savagely, for he completely lost the rear wheels. The car spun twice and ended up drifting along with its nose pointing the wrong way. Carol was sobbing. Hale swore, and tried to bully the gears. Stefan slowed right down: thirty, twenty, ten miles an hour, while he lined up the Rolls. Firmly and deliberately he drove its pillared radiator into the front of the Ford. Carol grabbed Hale's arm as the impact heaved the front wheels off the ground. The blow flung them against their straps, and for a long moment the two cars—now locked together—slid through the rain, the Ford shedding crushed hubcaps and bits of broken glass and torn bodywork. The shock passed and Hale slumped back in his seat, but still they kept moving, grinding backwards, the whole car shuddering and screaming as it gouged out chunks of tarmac. Hale spun the wheel and it came off in his hands. Carol's teeth were bared in a silent cry of terror, her eyes staring at Stefan. Behind the Rolls, a small flood of cars and trucks and buses had come to a halt, waiting and watching in the drenching rain.

Stefan was driving the Rolls as if it were a bulldozer, forcing the broken car off the Motorway. He revved its massive engine and fed bursts of power to its wide wheels. They raced against the slick surface until the smoking rubber burned out a grip and then heaved the wreckage farther, and farther yet. Hale watched helplessly, too stunned to think. Stefan bulldozed them onto the hard shoulder, clouds of spray and smoke rising behind him. Hale thrust his arm out in the rain and threw the steering wheel at Stefan. It bounced off the windscreen and disappeared.

"Can't we get out?" Carol said. Her voice shuddered with the car. Hale tried to undo her seatbelt, and failed. He saw Stefan open his door and jump clear of the Rolls. The two cars were still locked together, and still moving. Then the sky tilted; Stefan was higher than before. The shuddering grind became a jolting slide: the Ford was skidding backwards down the embankment under the weight of the Rolls. Bushes slashed at the sides; Stefan lost all detail and became a tall, strong silhouette. The Ford smashed through a fence and buried its rear wheels in a ditch. Hale looked out at the black ripples surging away. "Jesus Christ," he heard himself saying, over and over, "Jesus Christ, Jesus Christ." At the top of the slope a car appeared and Stefan got in. The shape was familiar: Chevrolet. Hale looked at Carol. She was ashen, trembling, staring. He held her hand, and her other hand sought comfort too. "You hurt?" he asked. She shook her head. He looked up the slope. New figures were silhouetted, pointing and moving; but the Chevrolet had gone.

The bug was small and light-brown, and because one of its front legs was damaged it walked in a long, slow cirlce on the top of the desk. It came to a paper-clip and stumbled. Its back legs slipped on the smooth columns of steel and slewed it around. The bug stopped and waved its tiny antennae. Nothing answered. It rested its throbbing, filigree legs and then went on, curving always to the right. It was going to fall off.

Starin picked up a book and held it flush with the edge. The bug limped onto it and fell over, kicking. Starin rotated the book and waited. The bug got up and walked back onto the desk.

Grobic and Stefan came in. "Well, it was even easier than I expected, Colonel," Grobic said heartily. "Stefan really knocked the daylights out of him."

"Not dead, though?"

"No, no. Alive and gibbering. Mind you, it would have been easy—"

"Oh, I believe you, Grobic. Blunders are always easy." The little bug had lost its way again and was approaching the edge. He used his elongated little fingernail to nudge it back on to its circuit.

"It takes two to make a blunder, Colonel. He may try to blunder back again." Grobic was offended because Starin had not congratulated him.

"Would *you*? If you were what *he* claims to be?"

"No, Colonel." Grobic scratched his nose. "But then, I wouldn't have followed Zeller's car all that way, either."

"It's a matter of budget," Starin said. "I can afford to scare him, I can't afford to kill him. Not yet, anyway. Everything is a matter of budget. All the guts has gone out of the world."

They went away. He sat and watched the little bug limp along its arc. When it got close enough he cut it in half with his nail. It left a thin grey fluid on his finger-tip. He wiped it on his trousers.

The hot bath was one of the unforgettable human experiences of all time. Hale eased his stiff and sticky body into the steaming fluid and felt ten thousand years of cock-ups and corruption dissolve and disappear, shucked off in the prehistoric element. He closed his eyes and let out a soft groan of luxury.

After a while he began to worry about falling asleep. He opened his eyes. Carol was sitting on the edge of the bath, watching him. She wore a pale-yellow cotton night-dress and she had a glass of whisky in each hand.

"For a moment, you actually looked happy," she said.

He thought about that. "I suppose I was. . . . It's been a disaster, but I did everything I could, didn't I?"

"I don't know, David."

"No, I suppose not."

"What are you going to do next?"

"Sleep. Sleep forever."

"And then go to the police?"

"Police? No fear. I've seen enough of them tonight."

"What, then?"

"Nothing."

"You mean, nothing that you'll tell me."

"Is one of those for me?"

She gave him a whisky, and he drank it in three gulps. "Very bad for me, I expect," he said, "but damn good."

She put down her glass, untied the ribbon that held the neck of her night-dress together, and shimmied out of it with a strong shiver of her body. "Move over," she said. She slid into the water and lay on her side, with one arm around his neck and the other hugging his waist, and softly kissed him on the lips.

"I know it's been done in the bath," he said, "but not straight after a bloody great carve-up on the M1."

"I don't want *that*," she whispered. "I just want you. Stop agitating yourself before you make the bath overflow." Hale's eyes closed. He knew it couldn't be forever, but by God it was good while it lasted.

Zeller came in waving the morning paper. "Have you seen *this?*" he asked. Starin turned and smiled. "Yeah, you've seen it, all right," Zeller said. "Colonel, you must be the most relieved man in all London."

"I think it's time you went back to Paris, Zeller. I think it's time we made plans to move James."

"Uh-huh." Zeller looked at the headline, then at Starin. "Now that they're not going to throw you out, you're aiming to kick 'em in the crotch. To me it doesn't add up, but maybe my threes look too much like my eights."

Starin flicked the newspaper. "You think anybody at home *likes* this? Ten of our people expelled? Six Germans, six Czechs, four Poles, eight Hungarians, a couple of Bulgars? All those contacts lost, all those links broken? All that money spent for nothing? It's a small disaster, you know that?" He nodded happily. "What everyone back home is hungry for now is an anti-disaster, a triumph. Just so that it's all worthwhile. Good. I've got James, he's an anti-disaster, and James has got Project 107, and that's going to be the biggest triumph since Sputnik."

Zeller chewed at a hangnail. "You've . . . uh . . . you've got James, Colonel?"

"You should know. He's on ice, isn't he? This morning you get over to Paris and work out how we shift him to East Germany in one easy stage. Him and all his papers. And remember his heart."

"Sure. Talking of his heart, Colonel, will it still be in his work when he realizes that he's in East Germany?"

"That's never yet been a problem. You can't stop real scientists working, Zeller. They get angry when you try. You said there are two guards? Can you remove them?"

"That's never yet been a problem, either."

"I don't want anything or anybody left behind. James is going to vanish. We'll take him out at night and leave a set of bare rooms. With luck the British will blame the C.I.A."

The phone rang. It was the Ambassador. "I expect you're dancing in the aisles," he said. "Frankly it baffles me why the British should expel a respectable bridge-player like that Hungarian cultural attaché, and overlook a known thug like yourself. . . . However, that's not the purpose of my call. Our masters have decided to send you a scientist. I suppose they want to make sure that you're not being sold a pup. He's a man named Kolek, a nuclear physicist."

"I don't want a damn scientist. I don't need one. Tell them to save their airfare."

"Too late, I'm afraid. He landed an hour ago."

"You bastard! You knew he was coming, didn't you?"

"I suspected it, of course. It was a natural thing for them to do, when you were being so secretive. I believe he's very qualified, could be a great help."

"Don't give me that horseshit. He's been sent to spy on me. I'm not having him, he can bloody well go back home, d'you hear?"

"He's on his way to you."

Starin shouted. "Keep him—" But the Ambassador had rung off. "Interfering sons of bitches," Starin said.

"Still want me to go to Paris?" Zeller asked.

"Oh, go to hell," Starin said.

Hale brought in two mugs of black coffee and put one on the bedside table. "No sugar. Brandy instead," he said. Carol slowly sat up and leaned over and sniffed the steam. "Wow," she said. "This must be the stuff they gave Lazarus."

"I think I know how he felt, too," Hale said. He took off his pyjama top and looked at himself in the mirror. He was disappointed to see no fresh bruises. "Extraordinary. We ought to have those seatbelts gold-plated."

"Yes. . . . Mind you, I thought you drove absolutely brilliantly."

"Even backwards?"

"*Especially* backwards."

"I may drive like that permanently from now on. At least it gives you a clear view of the bastard coming at you from behind." Hale drank some coffee. The whole battle on the Motorway seemed curiously remote, as if he had watched it happening to someone else, strangers, people who had been frightened but had survived intact so there was no point in getting too upset. "Anyway, I bet *you* think twice in future before you accept another lift."

"What was it all about, David? Was it really to do with Starin?"

Hale shrugged, and hid behind his coffee.

"You started to explain, last night. Come on, David. Whatever it is, I'm involved too. And maybe I can help. At least I can share the strain, can't I?"

Hale put down his coffee and began sorting out his clothes.

"Oh, for heaven's sake, David, say something! It's too late to count me out. I mean, I could have been killed too, remember."

"Exactly," Hale said. "I should have had more brains. The less you know about all this, the better for you. Just forget it ever happened."

She watched him get dressed. As he put his shoes on, she said, "And I suppose we shall be back in separate beds again tonight?" He brushed his hair. She said, "You don't really approve of any sort of . . . nearness, do you? What am I supposed to do? Pretend Starin and the rest don't exist? Or wait until they all die of old age?"

Hale picked up his keys and scooped up his change. Some coins fell on the floor. He left them there.

"Where are you going?" she said. "Can I ask that?"

"Office," Hale said. He thought of kissing her good-bye, and decided against it.

Hubbard showed in Hale and the hairdresser simultaneously. Divine took off his jacket and sat on an upright chair for the hairdresser to cloak him in a pale-blue sheet. "Say on," he told Hale. "Don't worry about Jenkins, he was my batman for six years, I saved his life several times, or it may have been the other way around, and besides he's stone deaf, aren't you, Jenkins?" The man nodded.

Hale described what had happened at the Cumberland Hotel and on the M1. He didn't say anything about Carol, and he underplayed the demolition of his car.

"More tedious violence," Divine said. "Your life is just one long game of professional football, isn't it? I heard about the Rolls-Royce; the Bolivian Embassy is most upset; apparently they'd just cleaned it, or paid off the H.P., or something. I hope Gibson enjoyed his opera. You seem to have paid rather heavily for his pleasure."

"But what was Starin up to, sir? I mean, I might have been killed."

Divine looked in Jenkins's hand-mirror. "Yes. He probably got fed up with you. Understandable."

"Pity the Home Office hasn't got fed up with *him,*" Hale said bitterly. "I should have thought—"

"No doubt. And another time I should be happy to listen, but not now. You'd better work with Gibson. James is safe enough, but Starin bears watching all the same. And ask Hubbard to get you another car. Thank you, Jenkins." The trim was done, the sheet came off. Hale was dismissed.

Kolek arrived at the Trade Mission in an Embassy car. Grobic met him at the door, and took him to Starin's room.

Kolek was a large, heavy man with a dyspeptic stomach and a moustache like a forkful of hay. He moved restlessly, his belly twisting and shuddering with indigestion, giving the impression that he was looking for something to damage in order to mollify his acid system. He was not impressed with Starin.

"Don't unpack," Starin said. "You're not staying."

"Shut up and read this." Kolek gave him a letter and sat in a chair, disliked it, tried another, and then opened the door and shouted. He told the first person he saw to bring him beer and food and antacid powder. He stretched out on the couch, burping.

"They think they're so bloody clever," Starin muttered. He sat at his desk and picked at the corner of the letter. "All right, you're here and I can't send you back. And I suppose you know why they sent you?"

"I'm a scientist. You've got some kind of research thing about to give birth. I'm here to assist the delivery. Open the beer," he commanded the man who had brought in a loaded tray.

"Cock." Starin got up and took the opener and waved the man away. "You're here to report on me. They don't trust me, only they haven't the guts to say so." Kolek listened impassively, munching radishes like a cart-horse eating apples. "Well, they screwed themselves this time. They've put you on my staff. That makes you my responsibility. I didn't want you, Kolek, but now you're here you can damn well work."

"That's what I came for. Don't give me all this back-stabbing political rubbish, old son. I've heard it all before." He belched resonantly. "Better," he said. "Lousy radishes."

"For a start, you can forget anything anybody told you back home. Have you read my report?"

"Yes." Kolek heaved himself to his feet and wiped his moustache "This fellow Mervyn James. I've met him before."

"That doesn't surprise me. Two atom scientists."

Kolek hauled his belt up over his overflowing belly. Immediately, it began to slip down again. "One atom scientist," he said. "James is an organic chemist. He always has been."

Starin gave him a look of irritation. "Then he must have branched out," he said flatly.

"That's not possible. James is incapable of doing this research."

"Look, do you take me for a fool? Do you think I haven't the elementary intelligence to check my facts? It is beyond dispute that James is a brilliant scientist, *brilliant*. He has more degrees and honorary degrees than you could count." Kolek was shaking his head. "I tell you he's *brilliant*," Starin insisted. "Compared to you he's an absolute genius."

"James is seventy-two years old. He had a stroke when he was sixty-eight. His brain has been slowly running down ever since. Of course he used to be good. But not any more, because the man is burnt out."

"His reputation—"

"His reputation and his ability are two entirely different things."

Starin dragged open a desk drawer and pulled out a document and threw it at Kolek. "Just take a look at that before you start telling me that James is burnt out." He had banged a knuckle on the drawer, and he sucked it while Kolek turned the pages.

"It's impressive," Kolek said at last. "I don't know whether it all hangs together; I'll have to do a lot more work on it—and by the way, you'd better get someone to translate these bits in English; I don't understand anything in that language except 'yes' and 'no' and 'gentlemen.' But I must admit it's certainly impressive. Have you any doubt that James produced it?"

"Not the slightest," Starin said with satisfaction.

"Then the chances are a million to one that it's junk." Kolek and Starin stared at each other for a moment.

"I don't see how you can be so certain," Starin said angrily.

"That stroke he had four years ago," Kolek said. "It paralysed part of his brain."

Hubbard was at his desk, checking somebody's claim for expenses, when Hale came out. With one hand Hubbard pencilled neat, high-tailed ticks against each item, with the other he traced his narrow moustache.

"It needs mulch," Hale said. "Mulch and a top-dressing of permanganate of potash. Wireworm in the roots, that's your trouble."

Hubbard marked his place with his finger, and raised his brows.

"I'm supposed to be working with Gibson," Hale said. "D'you know where he is?"

"Gibson won't report back here again until midday," Hubbard said.

"Oh."

Hale sat on the couch and watched Hubbard sharpen his pencil. He used a very small penknife and fed the shavings into a little glass ashtray. Hale was certain that when he had finished sharpening he would lift the ashtray and blow the desktop clean. Hubbard put the penknife away in a waistcoat pocket, lifted the ashtray, and blew the desktop clean. He emptied the ashtray into a wastebin and dusted his fingers against each other. He took out a handkerchief, unfolded it, wiped his fingers, refolded it so that the used side was innermost, and tucked it away.

Hale took a deep breath and made himself look at something else. At the electric kettle; at the biscuit-tin with the Alpine view on the lid; at the extra hangers for visitors' coats. On a radiator was the hand-towel with Hubbard's nametape sewn on to a corner; on the window sill was his library book to read on the train going home. Hale realized that Hubbard lived most of his life in this room; and that he would continue just like this until he retired. Or died. He was set for life, and set for death. Hale tasted despair. What was happening to him? He was sitting on Hubbard's couch, watching Hubbard go nowhere. *So what are we supposed to do? Wait until they all die of old age?*

He thought gloomily: It would solve everything if Starin suddenly died of old age. Then he was ashamed of the thought; he wasn't solving the problem, he was avoiding it. Starin wouldn't go away to please anybody.

Instantly and effortlessly, Hale had an idea. An outrageously obvious, brilliantly simple idea. It was so good that he opened his mouth to share it, before he remembered that Hubbard would tell Divine; and at this stage Hale did not want Divine to know, certainly not from Hubbard. When Divine got the news it would come from a quietly successful Hale, a competent and effective Hale who had used his imagination and his initiative to bring off a neat counter-stroke which . . .

Hale stood up. "The Major told me to ask you for another

car," he said. "Mine got written off last night."

"Very well. There's one in the pool. I'll call down and tell them to have it ready."

"Good. And also I need a death certificate."

Hubbard unlocked a drawer and took out a slim green directory with a thumb index. " 'Certificates, Death,' " he said. "Yes: room seven-fifteen. That's upstairs. Mr. Forbes will oblige you."

"I should have said a *foreign* death certificate. Sorry."

"Ah. Which country?"

Hale looked at the biscuit-tin. "Switzerland."

" 'Certificates, Death . . . Swiss.' That will be room seven-sixteen. Mr. Lovett."

"And it has to be properly completed. Name, date, signature, and so on."

Hubbard locked his directory away. "I expect you will find Mr. Lovett's work to your satisfaction," he said. "He would not be where he is, otherwise."

Hale smiled his thanks, and went out. Hubbard watched to make sure the pneumatic door-closer did its work, and then returned to his arithmetic.

Sennet came down and met Fitzgerald by the reception desk at the Peake Building. They greeted each other warmly and shook hands. Sennet's hand was slightly off-target but Fitzgerald grasped as much of it as he could. "I know you're tremendously busy, Doctor," he said, "but I hope you can spare me half an hour. My car's outside."

"Ah . . . you brought your car. Excellent. Delightful. Certainly, certainly." Sennet held the door and took the opportunity to check his fly while Fitzgerald went out.

The back of the Chevrolet was empty. "Wonderfully roomy vehicle, this," Sennet said as they drove away. He turned in his seat and looked again. Absolutely bloody empty. Not even a half-filled bottle in one of the pockets. The enthusiasm in his eyes died away, and his mouth slouched to an expression too sulky to be dismay and not angry enough to be resentment. "Where are we going?" he asked. He began to feel shaky. The streets were racing by too fast, although Fitzgerald was simply keeping pace with the traffic. Sennet reached out and felt the edge of the glove compartment to reassure himself. It was only an arm's length away, but it seemed terribly remote. So did his hand. He shut his eyes and wished he was a boy again, or asleep, or among friends.

Fitzgerald drove for a couple of miles and stopped outside a big discount wine-and-spirits store. Its windows were plastered with supermarket-type posters and banners. "The great thing about these places," he said, "is you can wander around and choose just whatever you want." He reached for the door handle, but stopped. "Is it me," he said, "or has the morning turned a little chilly?" Sennet squinted at the sunshine and opened his mouth before he saw Fitzgerald getting the flask out of his jacket pocket, and had to shut his mouth to swallow. They each took a swig of bourbon. "You know, I'm almost *sure* this stuff isn't as good as Scotch," Fitzgerald said. "What do you think, Doctor?" Sennet nodded slightly, anxious not to disturb the golden glow as it sank and spread and gently burned itself out.

Fitzgerald collected a wire trolley by the entrance and they strolled around the store. The liquor was stacked against the walls and dumped in massive islands. "Hey, now, *this* stuff's really *some*thing!" Fitzgerald exclaimed. "Ever tried it? No? Then you gotta have a couple bottles." He put them in the trolley. "It makes molten lava feel like Milk of Magnesia. So tell me, Doctor, who is helping Professor James with Project 107?" He added three bottles of Dewar's.

"Why . . . nobody." Sennet was surprised.

"Ah, come on now, Doctor, I know that's just your loyalty talking, and I admire it, but honestly you've no need to protect the professor; none at all. Isn't science built on teamwork? We're a team, you and me, and so are James and *his* partner." Fitzgerald flashed a smile of encouragement and put in two bottles of Gordon's gin and a bottle of Sandeman's port. "So who's the gifted collaborator? And I don't need to tell you we wouldn't be asking unless it mattered a very great deal." He stacked four bottles of Haig Pinch next to the gin.

"Honestly, all I know is that Professor James went to Paris. Nobody went with him. He works on his own."

"Sorry, negative." A bottle of Smirnoff joined the Haig. "Take it from me, Doctor: James cannot be doing this work alone. He must have another scientist helping him, somewhere, somehow. We depend on you to tell us who that man is. Mixers?" He held up a six-pack of ginger ale.

Sennet shook his head. "I must confess that you've rather taken me aback, Mr. Fitzgerald. I wish I could help, I really do." His voice became husky and he cleared his throat. "A gifted collaborator, you say. Surely it shouldn't be impossible to discover . . ."

"It shouldn't and it mustn't, and, for all our sakes, I hope it won't."

Sennet pushed the trolley and tried to think, but this wasn't the best time of day for his brain: it kept repeating the question and waiting for somebody else to make the effort. He wanted to compel it to work, but somehow his powers of compulsion seemed inadequate, and his thoughts drifted sideways, squeezed out by the pressure, and he pitied himself for always being put under pressure, always being asked for more than was reasonable. . . .

Fitzgerald stopped the trolley and added two bottles of Teacher's. "For *all* our sakes," he repeated.

Sennet felt powerless. "I wish I knew where to start," he said. "That's the trouble. I don't know where to start."

Fitzgerald came to a halt. He stood for a long time, just leaning on the trolley and looking at nothing. Sennet watched nervously. He found that his left eye was watering, and mopped it. Nerves, he thought. In the silence his stomach voiced itself like a faraway drain emptying.

"Isn't that just like me?" Fitzgerald said. "I've gone and

forgot my chequebook." He put the Teacher's on the floor and began unloading the trolley, steadily, carefully.

Sennet stared. His eye was watering again. "What a shame," he said. Out came the Smirnoff, out came the Haig.

"Yes, it really is too bad," Fitzgerald said. He sounded bored with the whole business.

"Maybe—" Sennet began. Fitzgerald looked up. "I was just thinking, maybe there's something in the office." Sennet's voice was pitched higher than usual, and some of his words butted each other in their eagerness. "Couldn't we look? Could we go back now and look? Maybe—"

Fitzgerald was patting his clothes, searching. He found his chequebook in his hip pocket, and gave a little snort of amusement. "Well, did you ever!" he said. They smiled, and Sennet wiped his eye. Fitzgerald began reloading.

After he had finished with Mr. Lovett in room 716, Hale still had half the morning to kill before he could meet Gibson. He used it up on another visit to the Peake Building.

He went there simply because the place was an itch that wanted to be scratched.

There were too many vague dissatisfactions connected with Project 107, too many unanswered questions. Starin had known of the Project before he had known of James: that was odd. Starin insisted that Kamarenski's film contained forgeries: that was odd. Divine had moved James to a safe place yet Starin seemed still to be obsessed with Project 107, and that was odd. Starin had not been expelled, either, which was at least curious.

Yet of all the oddnesses, none had been odder than Dr. Gerald Sennet. The more Hale thought of that twitching, angry, illogical man, the stronger was the urge to isolate that particular itch and scratch good and hard.

He rapped on Sennet's door. Nobody answered, and it was locked. So was James's door, but the lock had a simple-minded spring catch which could scarcely keep the draught out. A group of people were talking at the end of the corridor and drifting towards him. Hale lost all patience with caution. He took out a credit card sealed in plastic and slid it around the catch. The lock clicked, and he walked in.

James's room looked bare, and the surfaces carried several day's dust. Hale went through the connecting door. Sennet's office was not much busier. The desk held nothing of interest, and two of the three filing cabinets held nothing at all. The third was half full of bottles of whisky. Hale wondered what he did with the empties. Smuggled them out in his briefcase, probably.

A wire in-tray contained three big envelopes addressed to Professor James. The labels said they were all from universities; Southampton, Nottingham, Bristol. Hale felt their weight and fingered them. Journals or periodicals, perhaps; proceedings of the institute of codswallop. Should he open one? Pinch the lot? Risky; but who would know? Only Sennet, and what could he do? Hale hesitated; couldn't decide; decided not to decide yet; put the stuff back, and went to search James's room.

It didn't take long. Everything was empty except the big mahogany desk. It had six deep drawers, three on each side. They were stuffed with boxes of jigsaw puzzles, perhaps thirty or forty in all. Hale dragged a couple out: ambitious, expensive productions made for adults with a taste for masochism and the leisure to indulge it. One was a reproduction of a Jackson Pollock painting and about as coherent as a paint-rag; the other showed a close-up photograph of a skyscraper at sunset: ten million windows, a honeycomb of yellow glass. Hale knocked them together. The pieces shuffled and lay still. Thirty, forty jigsaw puzzles, but no sign of work. James had taken his work away with him, of course. So why hadn't he taken his puzzles too? Odd. Odd and uneven.

Hale noticed a slender drawer in the centre, over the knee-hole. It slid open to reveal a block of notepaper, lined. Written on the cover was the single word MAIREWARD! Hale took it out and opened it. *"Have a care, Sir Harry," warned the lean figure with the buccaneering smile and the laughing eyes, "lest I slit thee like a pig for the roasting!" His rapier flashed and flickered in the guttering torchlight.* . . . Hale thumbed ahead; there were another fifteen pages of it, all handwritten. James had been writing an historical novel. Jigsaws and swashbuckling. What a very odd scientist Mervyn James was.

A key chuckled softly in a lock, and someone came into the next room. Hale eased the drawers home and listened. Footsteps shuffled, a voice grunted, the door closed. Two men. Hale walked carefully across the room and looked into the corridor. It was empty. He willed the door to close silently, and walked away.

Sennet sat down at his desk. "How would it be if I wrote down everyone that Professor James knows or corresponds with?" he asked. "I mean, *everyone.*"

"Fine," Fitzgerald said. "For a start, anyway."

Sennet wrote three names and stopped. "Stupid of me," he muttered. "There's a quicker way than this." He went to a filing cabinet and hauled out the bottom drawer. Fitzgerald looked over his shoulder and saw the whisky.

"Still kind of early for that, Doctor," he warned.

"No, no." Sennet reached behind the bottles and took out a notebook, a solid quarto commercial job with a broken chain of drink-rings on the cover. "This is my correspondence book. I keep a record, you see."

Fitzgerald took it from him and flicked through the pages. "My! What it is to have friends, eh? A priceless gift." He handed the book back. "Tell me all about them, Doctor."

Hale found Gibson in a pub about half a mile from the Russian Trade Mission. He bought some beer and sandwiches and sat beside him at a corner table. "I hear you got run out of town last night," Gibson said. "What did you want to go and pick a fight like that for?"

Hale chewed a sandwich and tried to think of an explanation. I picked a fight with the enemy, he thought; but that didn't make a lot of sense. He said, "I certainly didn't get much sympathy out of the Major, that's for sure."

"Of course not." Gibson yawned, crowding his heavy features farther into his overloaded face. Now that he was accustomed to the hare-lip, Hale noticed how strong Gibson's other features were: the jutting jaw, the thick nose, the angry eyes over muscled cheekbones. Gibson's face had more strength than his chunky body could exercise. "You don't expect sympathy from a bloke you hate, do you?" Gibson asked.

"I don't hate Divine."

"You wouldn't push him over a cliff, but you wouldn't burst into tears if he got run down by a lorryload of lavatories, either."

"Maybe not."

"Of course not. Neither would I, neither would anyone. Divine's a right sod, underneath his red braces. He's not a man anyone could honestly like. I'm not even sure he really likes himself. If you let him, he'll make you hate him, and believe me, it's a waste of time hating your boss."

"Christ!" Hale said. "What brought all that on?"

"Listen, I've seen you around these last few days. You look as if you've been sent to sniff out the Holy bloody Grail and you've got asthma. Take my advice, get a grip of yourself. Don't go all noble about doing a job for K2. It's one step up from growing tomatoes on a sewage farm, that's all. Just do it and forget it."

"I'm not going all bloody noble," Hale protested. "I just don't see standing around scratching myself while there's a job to be done. As far as I can see, Starin's getting away with murder, literally and the other thing."

"That's Divine's pigeon. Let it shit on him."

"Thanks a million." Hale glowered over his beer. "It seems to me you owe me a favor after last night."

"Well, you know me. I'll do anything short of self-sacrifice."

"You've been in this business a lot longer than I have. I need a dealer. I need a trader who's accustomed to dealing in classified material with the Communist embassies and so on. He's got to be experienced and reliable. I mean *they've* got to rely on him."

"When d'you want him?"

"Now. This afternoon."

"There's one bloke I know. He might come expensive."

"Can you get hold of him, then? What's his name?"

"Oh, that's *his* affair. All I can do is arrange for you to meet him. I suppose he might even be there now." Gibson took his beer and went out to the telephone. He was back within two minutes. "Lucky. Trafalgar Square, the bottom lion on the left, three o'clock."

"How will I know him?"

"He'll know you. And that'll cost you a pint."

When Hale brought the beer, Gibson said, "Ever been married?"

"No."

"I thought not. You look unmarried. You look as if you need a few months with some real raunchy bird to loosen you up."

"Thanks very much."

"You're welcome. You know, a lot of blokes in K2 seem to think they can't screw the foe *and* their birds. Britannia comes first. It's a lot of cock."

Hale left his beer and walked out. A little of Gibson went much too far for him.

Starin was eating his lunch at his desk when Grobic ushered Zeller in. Zeller showed surprise, and said that he did not want to interrupt the Colonel's meal, especially when he was obviously busy.

"You hypocritical little ponce," Starin said. He turned away and spat a prune-stone at the wastebasket, and missed. "You're peeing yourself because you've made a balls-up, you and your tame alcoholic. Get over here where I can see your dishonest theatrical eyes."

"No, no, I assure you. Nothing has gone wrong, Colonel, nothing." Zeller came forward. Grobic moved to Starin's side. "Everything panned out just fine," Zeller said. "It's just that I thought it might save a little of your time if you got Kolek in on this, too."

Grobic frowned and made small, negative gestures.

"Never mind about time," Starin said. "Just tell me."

"Well . . . It's kind of unusual," Zeller said unhappily. "For a start, it looks as if this Professor James over in Paris actually doesn't know one hell of a lot about atomic energy."

Starin picked his teeth and waited. Grobic's shoulders were hunched as if he were ready to duck.

"He's no fool, mind you," Zeller hurried to say. "It's just that he's always been an organic-chemistry man. *Terrific* on organic chemistry; you couldn't find better. I mean to say—"

"I don't want an organic chemist," Starin said in a voice which made Zeller twitch.

"No, no, of course not. Goddam useless in this case. But . . . well *somebody* has to be doing all that research. After all, Kolek rates it pretty high, right?" Grobic screwed up his face and shook his head. Zeller shrugged and kept going. "So the question is: where the hell is it coming from?"

"Now give me the answer," Starin ordered.

"Sennet forwards a lot of letters and stuff to James. That's really all he does, in fact. He drinks Scotch and readdresses the mail. At least half of that mail comes from a guy in Bristol University. Guy named Henderson. Compared with James, he's just a kid, about twenty or thirty, but he too is no fool. In fact, he knows one hell of a lot about atomic energy."

"And he's been writing to James about it."

"That's the way I read it, yes."

"About Project 107."

"That could be, Colonel, I don't know enough to say." Zeller took a thick envelope from his pocket. "Sennet was all set to forward this."

Starin pulled a bunch of stapled papers from the envelope and looked at the massed ranks of scientific calculations.

"Don't ask me," Zeller said. "The only guy who can read that crap is Kolek. That's why I said . . ." He gave up. Grobic was grimacing again.

"One lousy actor is enough, Grobic," Starin said without looking up. "Keep your face still or I'll get Stefan to immobilize it." He stood up and walked to the window. "Comrade Kolek is having lunch with our noble Ambassador. It's too much to hope that they'll both choke to death on the lentil soup."

"Oh," Zeller said.

"Don't tell him anything about Henderson when he gets back. I want to see what he says about this new stuff first. After that, Kolek can sleep naked with the Ambassador for all I care."

It was a mild and unambitious day in Trafalgar Square. The traffic chased its tail endlessly around the rectangle of tourists, pigeons, fountains, and massive stone lions. Brief gusts of wind pushed the fountain-spray off course and sent children shrieking for safety into the waddling pools of pigeons, who panicked with that perfectly integrated contagion which pigeons do so well, scrambled aloft and massed and circled and rapidly de-panicked and dropped down to a new feeding ground. Then the mild and unambitious day resumed.

Hale wondered what sort of man made his living as a dealer in secrets. The images ranged from a middle-European precision, humourless in rimless glasses, to a mid-Atlantic zip, equally humourless in dark glasses.

Someone was calling his name. He looked around and saw coming towards him, of all people, Jeremy Sanders: the world's foremost expert on exchange currencies. "Shit," Hale muttered. "Hallo, hallo!" Sanders said. They shook hands. "Hope I haven't kept you waiting. Taxis are impossible these days, the tourists seem to live in them. How are you?"

"I'm fine. Are you sure you've got the right man?"

"No mistake. You want a dealer. I'm a dealer."

"But what about Flekker Handyside? What about exchange currencies and everything?"

"What about them? I mean, I might ask you the same sort of question, mightn't I? Look, I suggest we go over to the fountains. The noise muffles conversation."

Hale worried about Sanders until they reached the fountains. "Who put you in touch with me?" he asked.

"Gibson. You're both in K2. Your boss is George Divine. Enough?"

"Yes, enough. Just stop there. O.K. . . . . I take it you've dealt with the Russians before."

"Several times, one way or another. They're . . . not unreasonable people."

"This one is a man called Mikhail Starin."

"Starin?" Sanders's face perked up like a pup hearing the rattle of its dish. "At the Trade Mission?"

"You know him?"

"Oh, yes. We've met."

"Good. I've got a death certificate I know he'll be interested in."

"*Death* certificate? Oh. That doesn't sound terribly promising. Neither classified nor confidential, is it? I don't think I've handled a death certificate before. Is it something special?"

"In a way. It's Swiss."

"The deceased was Swiss?"

"No, no. The deceased was British, but he died in Zurich two days ago. You might as well see it, I suppose."

Sanders unfolded the document. It was slightly larger and squarer than a telegram, densely printed on both sides in French and German, with the details entered in angular, Continental writing and the signatures scribbled in ink of a deep purple. A rubber stamp had been slammed too vigorously on one corner, so that a part of the image was smudged.

Sanders carefully refolded it, using only his finger-tips. All his enthusiasm had gone. "I don't want to invade your preserves," he said, "but I think I must ask what makes you so sure that Starin will want this." The wind blew his fair hair over his eyes, and he pushed it back and held it.

"Certainly," Hale said. "It's quite simple. James was an important scientist. He was the brains in a certain research project which Starin wants. In fact, he wants it so badly that he's being a bloody nuisance about it. When Starin finds out that James is dead, he'll stop coveting him. End of story."

Sanders was watching Hale's eyes, waiting for him to say more. When Hale merely blinked, Sanders looked away. For a long moment he neither moved nor spoke. Hale saw the way he was holding the certificate—by its edges, as if he was afraid the ink might rub off on his fingers—and thought, Blast he's going to turn it down.

"An important British scientist dies in Zurich," Sanders said. "Wouldn't it be in the papers?"

"Normally, yes. The difference here is that James wasn't supposed to *be* in Zurich. Reasons of health, and so on. That's why the news wasn't released."

"But it's bound to come out sooner or later. What about the relatives—"

"James died unexpectedly; he was knocked down by a car. It's not as if he had one of those lingering illnesses where the next of kin gather around the bedside. Tomorrow we're flying the body back here, and in a week or two he'll get knocked down by another car, probably somewhere like . . . well, *here.* And *then* it'll be in the papers."

Sanders looked doubtful. "So you say. But can I tell Starin all that?"

"Better not. But you can tell him to watch out for a discreet casket being taken off the Zurich plane at Heathrow tomorrow or the day after."

Sanders grunted. "And can I tell him why the *original* death certificate is in London, while the body is still in Switzerland?"

Hale sucked his teeth. "I don't see why not. Just tell him that duplicate death certificates are issued by the Swiss authorities, on request."

"Are they?"

"They certainly are."

"Good. Because that's just the sort of thing he might decide to check."

"Look, if you think it's likely to be a problem, why not have the damn thing photocopied, and show him *that*?"

"I'll think about it." Sanders put the death certificate in an inside pocket. "How much should I ask him for it?"

"Why not try five hundred? You never know."

"Yes, I do; I know Starin. I'll try two-fifty and maybe throw in stamps. I suppose you want it done in a hurry?" Hale nodded. Sanders turned and squinted up at the throbbing, spilling fountain. "Well, it'll cost you two thousand."

Hale blinked. *"Two thousand?"* He remembered the money which Starin had paid him; what Hale had earned, Hale could spend. "All right. Two thousand."

"I've met Starin before, remember. In fact, I rather suspect that I've come across James before. Wasn't he responsible for something called Project number one-oh-something? Yes, I can see that he was."

"How in God's name did you know that?" Hale demanded.

"I guessed, but it was a pretty safe bet that the initials 'M.J.' on a scientific report would match up with a scientist called Mervyn James. I sold that report to Starin in the first place. Small world, isn't it?"

Hale worked hard on Sanders to find out who had given him the Project 107 report, but he refused to tell him. "I handled the deal for a third party," he said, "and if I start naming my clients I shan't have any clients. You should know that."

Kolek came in without knocking. "Fancy an omelet?" he said. "I'm going to get the cook to make me one."

"It's only four o'clock," Starin said.

"Yes. I get hungry around this time, especially when I've been working. You can have this back." He put a sheaf of stapled papers on Starin's desk. "I might have some of that ice-cream, too. Ice-cream settles my stomach, I don't know why."

"What did you make of it?"

"Oh, much the same as the other stuff. All very interesting, quite brilliant in a way. You know; well worked out. It's still got several big holes, but nothing that couldn't be filled in by a genius."

"Maybe James is a genius."

"Say it louder, you might persuade yourself. First, it's not his field, and second, he's past it. He couldn't handle a major breakthrough in nuclear physics any more than Beethoven could have invented rock-and-roll. Wrong generation."

"Then how d'you explain all this?" Starin squared off the sheaf of papers.

"Plagiarism, maybe."

"He's too big for that."

"Maybe that stroke sent him ga-ga."

"But if he's ga-ga he couldn't understand work like this."

Kolek shrugged. "How did you get on to him in the first place?"

"Through a dealer. Someone reliable."

"It sounds like a heavy investment." Starin said nothing. "Somebody mentioned twenty thousand roubles."

"Did they? Well, twenty thousand roubles is nothing for a revolutionary new power source."

Kolek laughed. "But a hell of a lot for a bag of nails."

Starin got up and walked around the room, using his feet to smooth out the wrinkles in the carpet. "Suppose I told you that Professor James *isn't* responsible for Project 107," he said. "Suppose I said that a young man doing postgraduate research has really written all this stuff. What would you think of that, Kolek?"

"What's his name?"

"Henderson. We think he used to be a pupil of James's."

"And Henderson's a nuclear physicist?"

"No doubt about that." Starin made a little detour to flatten a new wrinkle.

"That might change things." Kolek took back the stapled papers and sat on the couch while he flipped through them again. "Yes, that might change a lot of things," he said. "This whole project has a young feel about it, a young style. He's always trying to jump fences and take short-cuts. It's not an old man's research, none of it."

"So why send it to James? And why should James put his name on it?"

"Why? I don't know why, but I can guess. Henderson is unknown. He must be, or I'd have heard of him. Now, if he really *has* perfected this thing, his big problem is getting anyone to pay attention to him, take him seriously. They'll tell him to come back when he's built a working model as prototype: that sort of thing. What he needs is about ten million pounds *now*, to fool around with and get a pilot scheme going. Believe me, it's an uphill struggle for a youngster to sell something that big to the scientific world. So he's getting James to do it for him. Everyone listens when James speaks. If James says Project 107 is a winner, everyone will cheer and throw blank cheques. And in due course Henderson will get the credit."

Starin had completed a lap, but there were still wrinkles. "Funny way to carry on," he said.

"No, it's not. Science is like anything else: if you can't get a hearing you might as well shut up. James is Henderson's megaphone, that's all. I wouldn't be surprised if he started booming away during this international congress of whatever-it-is, in Paris. A good platform for a megaphone, that."

"Nobody's going to do any booming, Kolek. Nobody."

"You can't be serious."

Starin's chin jerked in disgust. "What a cheap remark that is. Cheap and superficial. You're a typical scientist, Kolek: you think the world's a laboratory, right? We're all going to end up immunized and sterilized and pacified and standardized and made compulsorily happy, that's what you think, isn't it? Don't you shake your hairy head at me, Kolek, I know what you had for lunch today, you had a dose of the nicely-nicelies from that fat freak at the Embassy, didn't you? Behave nicely, live nicely, sit up nicely, and eat your gruel nicely, and don't play with that foul-mouthed bastard Starin in case you catch his nits."

"Rant away, friend," Kolek said wearily.

"Rant? I'll do more than rant. Whether you like it or not, Kolek, this world is not a laboratory. It's a battlefield. It always has been and it always will be. And Project 107 is a weapon. I'm going to have it. *We're* going to have it."

"No, you're not. That was 1945. Grabbing German jet-engine technicians in Berlin. Get yourself up-to-date, Starin. That style went out of fashion twenty years ago."

"Power is always in fashion." The telephone began to ring, but Starin was too angry to answer it. "What do you know about power? Nothing except that it makes you nervous."

"I know that it can't be got by grabbing it."

"*What?* Look at history! Look at greatness!"

"Look at war, look at ruin. Look at the people who grabbed power and dragged everything down on top of themselves! There are laws—"

"Aaach, laws!" Starin spat on the carpet. "Laws define power. Power creates laws."

"And abducting a scientist is perverting science in the name of common greed."

"James and Henderson are mine. *Ours.* We have fought and bled to make the revolution succeed, and every man will do his part for us or I shall kick his *guts* out!" Starin stood, white-faced and staring with rage. The telephone went on ripping a precise gash in the silence. Grobic was in the doorway.

"A telephone call for you, Colonel," he said nervously. "We know the man. He says it is in connection with Professor James."

Starin picked up the phone. "Yes?" he said.

Hale was standing at the window of his flat, wondering what Starin and Sanders were saying to each other, when Carol came up behind him and placed a kitchen knife against his throat.

"What the hell . . . ?" He looked down and recognized the hand and the weapon.

"This is what happened to me on a flight from Los Angeles to Tokyo," she said. "He was six-foot-two and unhappy because his wife had left him. I had to talk my way out of that." She took the blade away. Hale relaxed.

"I expected you to say he was a highjacker," he said.

"Oh, don't worry; I've met one of those, too. I've also spent a night in a Turkish prison and stopped an attempted suicide from bleeding to death in Jamaica and frustrated a drunken rapist in Snyder, Australia, by rubbing pepper in his eyes. So you see, don't you?"

"See what?"

"That I'm not just a bit of candyfloss."

"I never thought—"

"No, but you never thought I might really be able to help you, either, did you?"

"For Pete's sake, not *that* again. I've told you—"

"No you *haven't*. That's the trouble, David, you haven't told me *any*thing. You just go around carrying a sort of big black invisible umbrella to ward off heaven-knows-what. And you won't even let me *help.*"

Hale took a deep breath and looked at her. Somewhere a window was catching a stream of late-evening sunlight and redirecting it into his flat so that it touched her head and gave her hair a soft and lovely glow. Unfair, he thought, unfair. He went and sat in the farthest chair. "I can't tell you any more. It's just not possible. Perhaps in a few days—"

"No, no, that's no good, David. Tomorrow's no use to me, I can't live on that."

"I'm afraid you'll have to." Hale watched her troubled,

doubting face and made himself think of the job, the job, the job; once the job was done it would all have been worthwhile. "Please," he said, "can't you let it pass? Can't you trust me?"

Her chin came up, her eyes blazed. "Can't *you* trust *me?* Can't you see how guilty you make me feel? We live together and you manufacture worry by the ton and you won't even let me sweep up. It's no good. It's just no good."

My oh my oh my, Hale thought, she does go on. "What you need is a large drink," he said.

She turned away and then looked back. "All right," she said, although it didn't sound all right. "But can we please go somewhere a bit more cheerful?"

"I can't go out yet, I'm afraid. I'm waiting for a phone call."

"Important?"

"Yes."

"You won't tell me why, of course."

"No."

"I should have stayed at the Y.W.C.A.," she said. "At least they have ping-pong."

———

The Ambassador left a meeting in order to see Starin. "I'm glad you came around," he said. "I get annoyed with the telephone sometimes, don't you? It seems to separate people rather than bring them closer."

Starin stared at the pattern on the Ambassador's tie: silver on grey. "I should have thought fat Kolek would have given you a full report on my bowel movements already," he said.

"Would you, now. Well, other movements are possible, and they may affect your health more seriously. Late this afternoon I had an order for your recall. Within the hour it was cancelled. You see how finely balanced the feeling at home must be."

Starin picked up his gloves. "Thank God I don't make my decisions by committee," he said.

"Take my advice and avoid all risks. Let the dust settle. Don't act without authority."

"If Lenin had waited until he had authority in 1917, you would not be sitting here now in your ladies' underpants."

"This is not 1917, and London is not Leningrad." The Ambassador folded back a trouser leg. "Look at that," he said. "Lined with pure silk. My productivity has gone up forty per cent." Starin refused to look.

Carol came out of the bedroom, wearing a bikini and not much of that. "It's a hot evening, isn't it?" she said. "You ought to get out of those heavy clothes."

Hale had been looking at the telephone, wondering about all the things that might have gone wrong. Looking at Carol was more satisfying but less rewarding. "Maybe I will. D'you want a drink? Perhaps there's something on television."

She came up to him and embraced him. "I'm sorry I was such a bore just now," she said.

"Oh, forget it." She felt so lithe and light, she smelled so fresh; he wanted to pick her up and carry her. "I understand how you feel. After last night you're entitled to be a bit worried."

"Can we sit down?" They moved to the couch, and she lay with her head in his lap. "It's much more than last night, David. We *mean* something to each other now, but . . . I really don't see how I can go on being part of your life unless you can be part of mine. Isn't that fair?"

"I suppose so." For the moment, Hale was too absorbed by that small, solemnly ravishing face to think of what he was saying.

"All this business of separate beds . . . and ground rules . . . and me pretending that you go off to work in a bank every morning. . . . " Her eyes were wet. "Yet we're lovers, too. . . . That's what hurts, David. Sometimes I feel as if you think that's all I'm good for, as if I'm not worth the rest of your life, the really important part. . . ."

"That's rubbish. I just don't want you to get hurt, Carol.

That's the beginning and the end of the whole story."

"And what about you? D'you think I can just stop caring? I mean, look what's happened to you in the last week! And still you say nothing. Don't you see, David? We just can't be so close one minute and so far apart the next. We *can't* It's too much to ask."

Hale leaned back and looked at the ceiling. "That almost sounds like an ultimatum," he said. He felt drained and weary. If only the goddam stinking bloody telephone would ring. If only he could get on and get it all over with.

"Call it what you like," she said. "You're the one who made it happen."

———————

Grobic came in carrying a large-scale street map of London. "I told him ten-thirty, so as to avoid the rush-hour," he said. He spread the map on the desk. Starin, Zeller, and Stefan came over to look. "It's right *there,*" he said. They twisted their heads, studying the area.

"Frankly, Colonel, it beats me why you bother with this guy," Zeller said. "I mean, James dead or James alive, who cares? Henderson is the man we want, isn't he?"

"In any case, Zurich," Grobic said. He closed the map. "James is sick in Paris, we know that. Why should he die in Zurich? It's ridiculous, Colonel."

"I know this man," Starin said. "He's a professional. He doesn't do ridiculous things."

"All the same, he's pissing on the wrong lamp-post," Zeller insisted. "Even if James is alive in Phoenix, Arizona, he's dead as far as this job goes. Why bother?"

Starin took his time about replying.

"First you discovered the Jigsaw James," he said. "But he was wrong. Then you discovered the Paris James, but he was wrong too. Now you find Henderson, and by this time tomorrow *he* may be as wrong as both the others. Who do you have in mind for your next candidate, Zeller? Rudolf Nureyev? I expect he knows a little bit of chemistry."

"Physics," Grobic said before he could stop himself.

Starin ignored him. "There must be a reason for this death-certificate thing. Maybe it's just to get us to meet him; maybe he knows other things which he couldn't talk about." He turned to Zeller. "Go to Paris tonight, now, and check that James is still alive. Get back here by eight a.m."

Zeller hurried out. Grobic folded the street map, while Starin sat and cracked his knuckles. The middle knuckle on his left hand wouldn't crack. He looked at it bleakly. Nothing worked properly any more.

"Listen," Hale said firmly. He came out of the kitchen with drinks in his hands and a prepared speech in his mind. "You've been talking a lot of crap. There is absolutely no reason why we can't keep my work separate from our life together, and there's every reason why you shouldn't be mixed up in my work."

"Too late, buster." The tears were gone; she was brisk again. "I'm already in it, and I deserve to know *what* I'm in."

Hale kept his voice calm. "Give me one good reason."

"Reason. . . . You're in love with that word. You are the most reasonable bastard I ever met. D'you know what has happened to me? I have ended up having sexual intercourse with a man who treats me with the utmost possible respect. My God, Mummy never warned me about *that.*"

Hale put down the drinks so that he could throw up his hands. "Suit yourself! If bad temper makes you feel good, go ahead! It doesn't make any sense, but—"

"Sense! I'm living with a Trappist monk who treats me like a mental defective, and you talk about sense!"

"My status seems to vary rapidly. Just now I seem to remember I was the local sex maniac."

"You see? You can't even get properly angry. *That's* what infuriates me. You've got self-control leaking out of your ears."

"Is that such a fault?"

"Yes, it is, because you don't trust yourself, David, that's your bloody trouble. You don't trust yourself one bloody inch beyond what's proper for a decent bloody Englishman to do and feel. That's why you're such a bloody phoney."

"That was a lot of bloodies."

"Not nearly enough. Bloody bloody bloody."

"O.K.! Finished your little tantrum? Because I have news for you. While you've had your mouth so wide open, I've had plenty of chance to count your teeth, and believe me, you're not nearly as grown-up as you think you are. The fact is, you're a spoiled little bitch with a pretty face and a brain the size of an adolescent prune, who's always had her own way and blows her fuse in her greedy little body the moment she's thwarted." His voice had started flat and level but already it was harsh, and getting louder. "Do you think it's easy for me to keep my mouth shut? Why the hell d'you think I do the damn job? It's squalid and boring and too many people get hurt. I do it because I happen to *like* this country and I think it's worth doing a certain amount of dirty work to keep it clean for people like you."

"You'd really like to believe that, wouldn't you?" she said. "There's only one reason why people like you do work like this: because they enjoy it. You're queer for patriotism, David, that's your trouble." She came forward and picked up her drink. "You won't tell me anything, so I'll tell you something. I dreamed about you last night. You were standing in front of me, absolutely naked, and you had the most magnificent erection, only I couldn't actually see it because it was covered over with a doily. And that's exactly what you are, David. A great big hard-on with a lacy doily over it."

Hale reddened and turned his back on her. She looked at his back for a while, and then got up and went into the bedroom. When she came back she was dressed to go out, and carrying her suitcase.

"Good-bye, David." He saw that she was crying a little, and he felt tears trying to sabotage his own self-control. "I hope . . . I don't know what I hope. I just hope something." She dropped a piece of paper on a chair. "Here's your cheque. I didn't need it."

Hale looked at it. She had never even filled in the amount. It made no sense at all. She picked up her suitcase and he found himself opening the door. When he heard the lift go down he closed the door and looked again at the unused cheque. It made no sense.

Twenty minutes later Sanders telephoned. "Well, you were right," he said. He still didn't sound enthusiastic. "He says he's interested, and we're meeting tomorrow morning. Ten-thirty, on neutral ground."

"Where?"

There was a pause. "Look, I don't want *you* there too."

Hale felt a sudden anger; was it for this he had lost Carol? "No? Why not?"

"Because it's not your show. Because it's an extra risk. Because you can't help. Oh . . . a million reasons."

"Really. Well, I can give you two thousand reasons why I *have* to be there."

"What's that supposed to mean?"

"I expect you want to get paid, don't you? Well, I'm going on holiday tomorrow."

"Holiday? In the middle of a job? That's absurd."

"No, it's not. The minute you're finished, the job's finished too, and I'm off."

"How long?"

"Six weeks," Hale said. He was surprised how easy it was to lie, and how pleasurable. "Maybe a couple of months. D'you want to wait that long?"

Sanders sighed. "Well . . . all right. I mean, it isn't all right, but . . . Don't show yourself before eleven o'clock, Hale. Stay well away until eleven at the very earliest."

"O.K.," Hale said easily.

"It's a parking lot. A pretty squalid spot on the wrong side of Earls Court. Tamworth Street. I'll be in a red Rover, EHT six-three-six K."

"Right, got it."

"I just hope that . . . Look: even after eleven o'clock, don't come anywhere near me as long as I've got my sidelights on. Understand?"

"Yes, I understand."

Sanders sniffed. "I wish I'd never called you. In fact I wish . . ."

"What?"

"Never mind." Sanders rang off.

The rain reached London at dawn. It came like a municipal decision, a sudden, heavy downpour which sluiced the billions of footprints off the pavements and washed the gutters unnaturally clean. When Hale woke up it had eased to a steady drizzle. He shaved without really seeing his stiff face, and stood at the window while he drank his coffee. The flat felt colourless and empty; futureless, like a hotel room. He went to get more coffee and saw the blank cheque lying on the arm of a chair. It still made no sense.

The rain gave him an excuse to set out early. He refuelled the middle-aged Saab which Hubbard had provided in place of the Cortina, and trundled slowly over to Earls Court, windscreen wipers stropping themselves on the sprinkled glass. He reached the car park at ten, and backed into a slot where he could watch the entrance.

Within two minutes all the windows had fogged up. He cleared the windscreen and left a quarterlight open, but the humidity was relentless. At twenty past ten Sanders's Rover drove past him and parked about thirty yards away. Its sidelights came on. They were as soft as candlelight through the gently thrumming rain.

At ten-thirty, a Vauxhall Viva came in and drove slowly around. It stopped level with the Rover, then backed and found a vacant slot, five or six cars away. There was a distant, throaty roar from the engine, and then silence. After a moment, three men in hats and raincoats got out. One had an umbrella and might have been Starin; but Hale's windscreen was so thickly pebbled with rain that it was impossible to be sure.

They reached the Rover. The near-side doors opened and they got in. The interior light glowed. Hale cautiously wound down a window but there was nothing else to see: only a diffused yellow glow behind the streaming glass. With four men breathing that steambath atmosphere, the car must have fogged-up solid almost at once. Hale left enough windows open to give him a clear view, and settled down to wait.

After a while he found himself remembering Carol, trying to think of a savage reply which would have hurt her as much as she had hurt him. It was painful even to think of her, yet the pain was worth having if it brought something back. None of the savage replies he invented seemed right; but he remembered, irresistibly, a sunny afternoon, heavy with the smell of fresh paint, and someone singing: *the furtive sigh, the blackened eye, the words "I'll love you till the day I die," the self-deception that believes the lie . . .*

Twenty minutes passed before Hale began to worry. He wound down the window and stared unhappily at the dim glow of the Rover. He looked again at his watch. The sweep hand twitched around the dial and flicked past the vertical and began eating another lap. Twenty-one minutes. Too long.

All he could do was sit tight and keep watch. He wiped the rain from his face, and stared. And worried.

Starin sat beside Sanders. Grobic and Zeller sat in the back. The atmosphere was dense with humidity and discontent.

"One does see what you mean," Sanders said.

"I don't mind a good swindle," Starin said, "but this is so clumsy it's downright insulting."

Sanders smoothed the creases in the death certificate. "It certainly looks as if somebody has miscalculated rather badly, doesn't it?" he said.

"Miscalculated? No. *Blundered.*"

Sanders used his handkerchief to blot his forehead. "I suppose it couldn't be a sort of . . . practical joke?" he suggested.

Starin leaned back, rested his head on the top of the seat, and looked at the roof. When he spoke, it was in Russian; and Grobic and Zeller replied in Russian. Sanders politely looked at his shoes.

"Stimulate your shrunken brains," Starin said.

"The thing that strikes me," said Zeller, "is that it can't be easy to get hold of a fake Swiss death certificate. So whoever supplied this one must be pretty well organized."

"And?" Starin rolled his eyes towards Grobic.

"Well, that rules out a genuine free-lance dealer," Grobic said. "It's got to be somebody working for a department, or an agency."

"Obviously it didn't come from a free lance," Zeller said. "Why should a free lance go to all this trouble just to mislead us? There's no percentage in it."

"So you conclude that some department tried to unload this rubbish," Starin murmured.

"Hell, *that* doesn't add up either," Zeller said.

"Why not?" Grobic asked.

There was a moment's silence while Zeller got his thoughts straightened out. During the pause, Sanders looked up and held out the certificate to Starin. "I'll tell you what: you keep this for nothing," he said, "and I'll chalk up the whole sad affair to experience." Starin ignored him.

Zeller said, "It doesn't add up because any department should know better. They should know that the first thing we'd do is check on James."

"Right," Grobic said. "And another thing: they should know that James doesn't matter. It's the younger man who matters."

"Then why pretend that James is dead?" Starin said. "Why go to all this trouble?"

"I can't tell you how sorry I am about all this," Sanders said in English. The muscles in his thighs were jumping as if he wanted to go to the lavatory.

Zeller said, "It looks as if they chose Zurich completely at random. It might just as well have been, you know, Rotterdam. Or Vancouver."

"Or Paris," Grobic said. "Why wasn't it Paris?"

"The whole stupid idea was bound to fail," Starin said. "That's what annoys me. What do they think I am, a five-year-old?"

"If there's anything I can do to compensate you for your wasted time," Sanders said. "Anything at all . . ."

"Hey!" Zeller said. "No obituaries! The man is supposed to get himself killed two days ago, but nothing gets into the news!"

"Some cover-up," Grobic said.

"It's a fuck-up," Starin said.

"Now that I come to think of it," Sanders said rapidly, "I don't know why I didn't mention it before, silly of me, but never mind; would you be interested in a fairly top-level analysis of last month's N.A.T.O. manœuvres?"

"This whole mess stinks," Zeller said. "I mean, it really stinks."

"The Americans weren't at all happy, you see," Sanders said.

Starin reached across and rested his hand on the top of Sanders's seat. "Something occurs to me," he said, and waggled his thumb. "It is not impossible, is it, that our friend here understands our language." Grobic, who was sitting behind Sanders, craned his neck to look at the back of Sanders's head.

"The whole mess stinks, and he stinks with it," Zeller said. Grobic took an automatic out of one coat pocket and a silencer out of another.

Sanders's hands were desperately squeezing the steering wheel. "I met a man yesterday who as good as promised me the new Dutch air-force codebook," he said. "Brand new. I swear it."

Starin nodded, and took his hand off Sanders's seat. "Well,

this'll give the bastards something to think about, anyway," he said.

"You know, I really must be going," Sanders said. He reached for the key in the ignition. Starin put his hand on top of the gear lever. "No, really," Sanders said.

The Rover's sidelights went out. Hale at first refused to believe it. The three Russians must still be in the car; how could they possibly have left without his noticing it? And the interior light was still on, so obviously Sanders was still there, too.

He dragged on his raincoat, awkwardly, searching for reasons to stay where he was. He got out and buttoned the coat and stood blinking at the car while the rain tapped and pecked at his scalp and hurried down his forehead and into his eyes. Nothing moved, nothing changed. He walked slowly towards the Rover. Its windows were blank with luminous fog.

When he was twenty yards away he heard music. A boys' choir was singing Bach against an organ background. Hale edged forward, and the music grew. The car radio was on. Loud.

He stared at the gleaming, streaming bodywork and listened to those high, pure voices cutting through the hiss and splatter of the rain, until water began to dribble down his neck.

Stepping carefully to avoid puddles and loose stones, he walked to within a few feet of the driver's door. The windows were fogged-up, but he thought there might be a clear patch in a corner of the windscreen. He bent to look, and failed to see a finger wipe a spyhole on the rear side window. An eye came, and went. Hale straightened up and stood looking at the driver's door, unsure of anything except the risk of action and the danger of inaction. Suddenly the window was wiped clean and he saw Sanders's naked body with its bloody head on the steering wheel, and instantly Grobic leaned across with a heavy, clumsy gun coming up fast at Hale's face. Hale fell flat as the window grew a black hole with fuzzy tentacles reaching away from it and he heard the double *chunk* as the bullet went into the next car and out the other side.

By then he was running, hands scrabbling in front to stop himself falling, dodging around the first car he saw and swerving left to put as much steel as possible between himself and Grobic. When he was a dozen cars away he stopped and squatted under cover. His heart was banging against itself and his eyes were trying to look in three directions at once and his brain kept showing flashbacks of Sanders's crimsoned head.

When nobody came out and shot at him, he got up cautiously and dog-legged between the cars until the Rover came into view again, still safely remote. One door was wide open. He was still working out his next move when he saw the Russians' Viva drive off. By standing on somebody's bumper he watched it go all the way out of the car park. It was in no great hurry.

Hale moved carefully over to the Rover, but for all the difference it made he could have played handbells. Sanders was the only thing in the car, and Sanders would never hear anything again. He had a large hole in the back of his head and a small one in the front. They had taken all his clothes.

Hale switched off the interior light and shut the doors. He returned to his own car and ran the engine and tried to make his brain forget Sanders's head and start working on what to do about it. After a while he went back and got into the rear seat of the Rover. He put his hands under Sanders's armpits and hauled him backwards over the driver's seat. Already the body felt cool and the armpits were slippery and clammy. Hale was sweating; Sanders was the wrong way up, he wouldn't bend properly and his legs kept hitting the steering wheel. He wrestled the body around until Sanders was face-down and his buttocks were high on top of the seat. Then he reached over and grabbed the legs.

Sanders slid and tumbled headfirst, and the rest of him fell sideways, the feet hitting the floor with a double thud. Hale pushed an arm down flat; he could still see the impression left by Sanders's wristwatch. He spread his raincoat over the body. The feet showed. He found a road map and covered them. The keys were in the ignition. He locked the car and stood in the rain, wondering whether or not to be sick. Then he drove to K2.

Starin had a wet umbrella in one hand and a damp death certificate in the other, so he kicked open the door of his office. He wouldn't need it again, anyway.

"Where's Kolek? Fetch him," he told Stefan.

"He went to the Embassy, Colonel."

"Yes? Better still. Get him on the phone." He watched Grobic and Zeller cutting and ripping Sanders's clothes to pieces. There was a secret pocket on the inside of the trouser belt, but all it contained was money. Then his call came through.

"You and *I* are going to Paris, Kolek," he said. "Since you are at the seat of power, you can get them to book two seats on the plane."

"When?"

"Now, today. As soon as possible."

"Why Paris? What happened to your young discovery?"

"Henderson? Oh . . ." Starin sniffed noisily. "Henderson turned out to be a dummy, a decoy. He was a false trail, created to lead us away from James. Instead, he led us back."

"Led you back to nowhere, you mean."

"I'm not very interested in your opinions any more, Kolek. I prefer to listen to James; he knows."

"And do you seriously expect me to help you carry out your squalid act of thievery? You amaze me, Starin."

"Remember two things, my fat friend. Remember that you are on my staff. And remember Kamarenski."

Kolek laughed. "I'll book the seats, with pleasure; I'll even come with you to Paris. But that's all I'll do. And believe me, it's all *you'll* do, too."

Both men were smiling as they hung up. Kolek looked at the

Ambassador, who had been listening on the extension. "What an extraordinary man he is," the Ambassador said. "I'll have his recall waiting for him when he lands."

Starin looked at Stefan. "Go out and steal a big new car, nothing conspicuous," he said, "and put new plates on it." Stefan ducked his head and went out.

Half-way through his story Hale stopped talking because he thought Divine was going to have a heart attack. His face had turned a dull red around the eyes and cheekbones, but the jowls were grey and the eyes moved slowly and with difficulty. One corner of his mouth had tightened like a spring and Hale could see a tic working in front of the left ear. Divine's arms were rigid on the top of his desk. Hale sensed the shock which Divine was absorbing and felt sick with anticipation of his rage.

Divine unlocked an arm and got out a handkerchief and wiped his lips. "Get on," he said.

Hale told him the rest. It sounded dreadful.

"Sanders is dead? You left him there?"

"I covered him up. I didn't want to waste any time."

Divine shuddered like some heavy animal waking up. "You bloody clodhopper," he said. He picked up a loaded in-tray and hurled it across the room. It smashed into the wall and fell apart, leaving a trail of papers. "You bloody *cretin*," he roared. He raised his clenched fists and brought them crashing down on the desk.

Hale sat on an upright chair and stared back, fearfully, mutinously, guiltily.

"What in the name of God do you think you've been doing?" Divine shouted.

"I was just trying to make Starin's life a bit more difficult," Hale muttered. Droplets of sweat ran down his ribs. "I thought that if he thought James had died in Zurich he—"

"Died! In Zurich! On the strength of a piece of paper? Where did you get it?"

"Here. Upstairs."

"This was your own idea? You didn't consider it right or proper or necessary to consult *me?*"

Hale looked at his hands. "I can't explain, Major."

"But you must explain. This isn't a deficiency in the petty cash, Hale. A man is dead. *Dead!* Now what in the name of Christ's sweet charity got *into* you?"

"I don't know." Hale sucked in a lungful of air, but it did little to counter his sense of physical weakness. "I suppose I got sick of being kicked around, that's all."

"That's *all!*" Divine picked up another file and sent it skimming across the room. "Well, bully for you, sonny. Bully for you. It looks to me as if you've crowned your brief and unsuccessful career with a monumental cock-up. In fact, there's an outside chance that you may have ruined the whole damned operation." He walked to the windows, and looked at the drizzle. "Oh my *Christ,*" he breathed.

"It's never exactly been a runaway triumph, has it?" Hale said sullenly. He wiped his nose on his handkerchief. The sodden mess disgusted him. He threw it into a wastebasket.

"On the contrary, it was on the verge of complete success. And despite your strenuous sabotage there is still a good chance."

Hale waited. "Go on," he muttered. "Astonish me."

"I think I might." Divine walked back. His face had changed: the shock had gone, some of the confidence had returned. "In fact, I know I shall. I don't know why the Russians killed Sanders, but whatever the reason, it clearly indicates that they never believed for a minute in your death certificate. And that's encouraging."

"It gladdens the heart," Hale said.

Divine turned on him. "Listen and learn," he snapped. "And stop guzzling at that trough of self-pity before you choke yourself." Hale gave up: he was weak with defeat. "Starin knew that Professor James couldn't have died in Zurich, because Starin knows that Professor James is alive and well in Paris. Or, to be scrupulously accurate, alive and frail in Paris. Starin knows all that because you told him, or rather you made it possible for him to find out, and all this happened because I arranged for it to happen, and if I'm not going too fast for your puny brain, this ought to be the point where you ask yourself why I should want to simultaneously conceal *and* reveal the whereabouts of Professor James."

"*Now* astonish me," Hale said.

"I think I shall. I intend to disgrace Starin. I don't want to defeat him, I don't want to frustrate him, I don't even want to kill him. I want him to make a complete and utter bloody fool of himself, in public. The entire point and purpose of this operation has been to persuade Starin to attempt to abduct Professor James in Paris, because when he does that thing, it will be the most sensational abduction of all time. In the block where James lives there are hidden film cameras monitoring every square inch, watching him twenty-four hours a day. This will be the most photographed abduction you ever saw. We shall have thousands of feet of it, *in* colour, *with* sound. Imagine how that will look on a hundred million television screens next day! Little Starin will get the push so fast, his little feet won't even touch the ground."

"I've been conned, then."

"Don't take it to heart, laddie. You're in good company."

Hubbard brought in a pot of coffee and poured for them both. "No calls for a little while, Stanley," Divine said. Hubbard nodded and went out.

"I suppose *he* knew exactly what was going on," Hale said sourly.

"More or less, yes. The broad outline."

"It strikes me that you've been very lucky, Major. It's been a string of flukes: every time the ball bounced, it bounced your way."

"Yes; well, you *would* think that, Hale. Psychologically it's the inevitable reaction. When justice fails, blame luck. You're wrong, of course. I worked this operation out in some detail, several months ago."

"*Before* Kamarenski?"

"My goodness, yes." Divine had a little chuckle at that. "It began last Easter, on Sunningdale golf course. My partner was a Dr. Henriques. You've never met him; he's Director at the Peake Research Building. We had a long wait at the fourteenth, and Henriques mentioned this rather preposterous research project. I asked him what it was about and he said it added up, or boiled down, to extracting nuclear power from common water. Fascinating nonsense, Henriques said."

"That's not what Lipman thought."

Divine waved Lipman aside. "Later, later. There is more, or rather less, to Lipman than meets the eye. The trouble with James, according to Henriques, was his reputation. As a Grand Old Man he claimed more respect than this work of his justified, which made life difficult at times. Anyway, James was moving to Paris quite soon, so Henriques said, and that would ease the pressure."

"Why Paris?"

"For his health, his heart. He's seventy-two. Anyway, the essential ingredients were all present as far as I was concerned. Henriques procured from James a copy of his research report, and I procured young Sanders, God rest his soul, to transmit it to Starin at a suitably exorbitant price."

"So *Sanders* . . . God, what a mess. He must have wondered what the hell was going on: you, me, Starin. . . ."

"Sanders is well accustomed to keeping his mouth shut."

"He is now," Hale said.

Hubbard stood in the doorway. "You said no calls, Major, but I think you ought to speak to Gibson," he said.

Divine picked up the phone. Hale drank his coffee and listened to the Major's appreciative grunts. "Stay with it," he said, and hung up. "Do two things," he told Hubbard. "Alert the Paris crew that Starin is on his way, and get me on a Paris plane as fast as possible." He turned to Hale. "They're off and running," he said.

"Why do you want me to come with you, anyway?" Kolek asked. They were riding up the escalator in the Terminal Building at London Airport. "I'm not going to help you there."

"Oh yes you are. I shall need you to go through James's papers. I don't want to carry off a lot of rubbish."

"You must be losing your wits. I've just told you that I'm not going to help, Starin. You're on your own."

"Oh, no. I have history behind me. And if you refuse to help me, I shall shoot you." They reached the top. "Just as I shot Kamarenski."

Kolek stood aside and looked closely at him. "But I'm not going anywhere near Professor James. I'm going straight to the Embassy."

"Oh no you're not," Starin said, "because I shall shoot you in the arrival lounge at Orly. I think I'll shoot you in the stomach."

Kolek stared, his great body tense. "Amazing," he said.

"Well then, Kamarenski was lucky," Hale said. "You were lucky to find him, and he was incredibly lucky to find anything at all."

Divine was checking the contents of an overnight bag. He looked sideways at Hale. "Oh, no. We'd been grooming Kamarenski for years. Years and years." He got on with the case. "I'll grant you ten per cent luck insofar as he turned up opportunely, but the rest was pure merit."

"Sheer luck," Hale insisted. "You didn't know Kamarenski was going to take those pictures. By rights he should have seen nothing worth photographing and kept his thumb over the lens when he shot it. Kamarenski was as thick as three planks. Those photographs were an absolute miracle."

"They would have been, if he'd taken them," Divine said. He poured himself more coffee. "As he didn't take them, they weren't."

"Who took them, then?" Hale felt a curious unreality, as if he had lost a day somewhere.

"I did." Divine opened a drawer and pulled out a sheet of contact prints. "I'm no expert, but as they were supposed to look a bit amateurish it seemed a waste to call in the professionals. These are pictures which I took of the research report before I gave it to Sanders to sell to Starin. Simple."

Hale looked at the drab little images as if they showed scenes of atrocities. "So Kamarenski's film was blank, then?" he said.

"Every frame."

"And he died for nothing."

"Now you're being maudlin. Kamarenski's death was an irrelevance. If he'd fallen under a bus it would have been the same. His function was to persuade you that Starin had that report on Project 107, and he did it jolly well. In his uncomprehending way, he made sure you were pointing in the right direction."

"And was I?"

"Yes, of course. You went straight to Starin and did a deal over the pictures, which was reassuring because it confirmed that he valued them."

"Good for me. You must have been proud, Major."

"And then, of course, Starin came right back and set up that scenario in Jim's Gym. Almost on cue, you might say. I admit that I enjoyed that."

"I'm glad somebody did."

"It had a satisfying double-edged quality: first you told Grobic nothing, which made him hungry, and then you told Fitzgerald everything, which pleased him enormously. People are always pleased when their little conspiracies work."

Hale was suddenly furious, "And you're so pleased that you're pissing yourself!" he shouted. "You've got us all running around like blue-assed baboons, while you play golf with Henriques and Old Mother Hubbard out there makes the tea! What about Sanders? You've forgotten him already, haven't you?"

"Have I?" Divine closed his case. "Who killed Sanders, Hale? You or me?"

Hubbard was waiting to speak. "There's a flight in about an hour, sir," he said. "I'm afraid it's not B.E.A." He picked up Hale's chair. "And Gibson has just called to say they're at the airport."

Gibson wiped the rain from the lenses of his binoculars and focused on the figures climbing into the Air France jet. Kolek was unmistakable, hauling himself up with both hands on the rails. Starin came behind. He looked impatient with Kolek's slow pace, but clearly it was the only pace that Kolek had.

There was the inevitable fooling and fussing with umbilical cables before the doors were swung shut. The engines coughed smoke, and built from a whine to a scream. Behind them the puddled runway grew deep ripples. At last the aircraft moved, and the pools were blasted into vapour by the howling jets.

Gibson watched the plane prowl away into the mist. It reached the end of the runway and joined a line of waiting aircraft. At that range they were all so small and so alike that even through the binoculars Gibson couldn't be sure which was which. More rain blew into his face. He packed the binoculars away and went to telephone K2.

"Now, Starin's redeeming quality is his total lack of trust," Divine said. "You gave him Professor James on a plate. I knew he wouldn't like that. Far too easy. I knew that Starin wouldn't respect and covet James unless James was both hidden and guarded, so I put a screen around him. It had to be a weak screen, or Starin wouldn't be able to knock it down. On the other hand, it had to fall with a convincing thud."

"You mean Sennet?" Hale said. "But . . . Fitzgerald and I got past Sennet in ten minutes."

"Of course you did. And you found a man doing a jigsaw puzzle. He was part of the screen, too. Fitzgerald went back later and gave the whole lot a hard shove, and it fell over."

"Sennet wouldn't fall over for me," Hale said morosely.

"Yes, well, alcoholics require special handling. You'll probably know better in future."

"I thought you said I hadn't got a future."

"Perhaps as an alcoholic."

"Look, how d'you *know* that's what happened? How d'you *know* Starin's going to Paris to get James? He might—"

"Fitzgerald's been over there already, Hale. We let him snoop around, we showed him a couple of guards, we even let him do a bit of burglary; in fact we filmed that episode as a dress rehearsal. He turned up again last night, probably doing a last-minute check. Oh, it's on, all right."

Hale sat and looked at the grounds in the bottom of his cup. "Hadn't you better go?" he said. "You'll be late for your triumph."

"Plenty of time," Divine said. He was clearing his desk.

Starin waited until there was only one airliner standing in front of them at the end of the runway, and then he called a stewardess. "I demand to be allowed off," he said in English. He spoke evenly and soberly.

"I'm afraid that's impossible, sir," she said. "We'll be in the air very shortly."

"You have no legal right to force me to fly when I don't want to," he said, "so go now and tell the captain what I say. I demand to be allowed off."

"What seems to be the trouble, sir?" she asked.

"No trouble, unless you take off after I have told you I don't wish to fly, in which case I shall sue Air France for a hundred million francs. The law is quite clear." He indicated Kolek. "This man is a witness. I demand to be allowed to get off. Go." "What was all that about?" Kolek asked. "This pilot has never flown to France before," Starin said. "I offered to show him the way."

For another minute the airliner stood in the rain, gently trembling against its brakes. Then it rolled forward, turned sharply, and taxied back towards the Terminal.

Divine was waiting for his car to arrive. "Your function," he said, "was to help to make it difficult for Starin to trace James. Every time Starin advanced another stage and gathered another bit of information, he invested more time and effort in the operation, which made him more and more determined to stick with it to the end. As he has done."

"I could have avoided a lot of grief and pain if you'd explained all this at the start," Hale said bitterly.

"Quite possibly. But you wouldn't have played your part so well. Let's face it, you're a bloody awful actor, Hale. The truth is always more convincing, isn't it? Sennet was the truth, and so were you."

"I've just realized why Starin wasn't on that Home Office list," Hale said. "You kept him off it."

"Obviously."

"I think I agree with Lipman. You people make a meal out of a mystery," he said. "This one's beginning to look like a three-day feast."

"Lipman has a very second-rate brain," Divine said. "That's why I told Hubbard to use him. He was bound to get worked up over Project 107. A mediocre man, really."

The stewardess said, "You may disembark now, sir."

Starin turned to Kolek. "I'm just going forward to have a word with the captain." He followed the stewardess through the tourist-class section, past faces which showed surprise or annoyance or indifference. She pulled open a curtain and they went by the galley, through another curtain, into the first-class section. Up ahead a steward pointed left, where the open door was waiting.

Starin hurried down the flight steps and raced across the tarmac, leaping the puddles. He knew that Kolek couldn't see him, because Kolek was strapped into a right-hand seat: but he ran just the same.

Kolek chewed a toothpick and looked at Starin's empty place with a mixture of relief and concern. He loosened his seatbelt. The pressure was giving him heartburn.

"You know, I wasn't going to tell you this, Hale, but . . . Well, it might make you feel a little better about the whole thing."

"If it's an M.B.E., I don't want one. They take too much dusting."

"An M.B.E.?" Divine gave a paternal chuckle. "No such fame. The point is this. I had to know exactly what you were doing all the time, during these last couple of weeks. I couldn't depend solely on your own reports."

"Let's just forget the whole damn thing, Major. It's gone on too long already."

"No, I've a feeling this may be important to you. You appreciate the situation, Hale: I needed someone to tell me where you went, what you did, who you called and when. So I arranged to have this done, and it should have worked, but it didn't."

Hale stared. Divine's manner was suddenly restrained. "What are you talking about?" he said.

Hubbard opened the door. "Your car, Major," he murmured.

"I decided that the best thing was a girl," Divine said evenly, "preferably one of our own people. I asked Miss Blazey, and she agreed."

214

"You mean Carol?" Hale was staggered. "You mean *Carol* works for you, too?"

Divine picked up his case. "In this instance she wasn't much use. We ran into an Act of God which forced her to withdraw. Miss Blazey fell in love with you, Hale."

Hubbard held the door. Divine waited for Hale to speak, but he had no words.

"Fortunately, I don't think it has affected the outcome of the operation," Divine said. Hubbard saw him out, and closed the door behind him.

Starin rapidly signed every piece of paper the Air France people put in front of him, and ran for the exit. Grobic was standing outside. He saw Starin, waved, and turned to signal a car. Seconds later Zeller drove up. They got in.

"What's this?" Starin asked.

"Volvo one-sixty-four, brand new," Zeller said proudly. "Stefan found it only a hundred yards away. Feel that power!" He made the car surge.

"How far is it?" Starin asked Grobic.

"A hundred-odd miles. But it's nearly all Motorway."

Starin looked out of the window. "Good-bye, Kolek," he said, "I told you it's a battlefield."

Hale sat in Divine's room and looked at Divine's coffee set, from which an occasional, wistful wisp of steam crept out.

Conned from the start.

Deceived and deluded.

Hoodwinked, bamboozled, and spoofed from beginning to end. Nothing and nobody had been completely honest. Kamarenski and Hubbard, Lipman and Fitzgerald, Sennet and James, Sanders and Divine—all, in varying degrees, bogus. He'd been led by the nose all the way. Conned at every turn. Divine had been sitting up here manipulating and manœuvring him like a wind-up toy.

And Carol too. Jesus H. Christ. Our Miss Blazey. Miss Blazey agreed. Unfortunately, it didn't work. However, the operation. This may make you feel better.

Hale reached for the coffee pot and curled his fingers around it and hurled it at the wall. The pot exploded with a gratifying bang and left a tremendous brown stain slowly seeping down the creamy plaster.

Hubbard opened the door. "Good gracious!" he said. Hale flung the hot-milk jug at him. It smashed against the door and left a white wake across the carpet. Hubbard gasped and slammed the door. Hale chucked the sugar bowl after him; it shattered in a rain of cubes. He threw one cup at a lamp standard and another at a clock. That left the saucers. The door opened as he grabbed them, so he slung them at it and one of them clipped Carol Blazey on the side of the head.

For a second he was horrified. Then she shut the door. "It didn't hurt," she said.

"Too bad. Serve you bloody right if it knocked your block off."

She looked at the mess. "Isn't this a bit primitive?"

"Damn right it is, and so am I. I've *had* sophistication, thanks. Now I'll stick to the simpler joys, like breaking people's arms."

"Do you want to start with mine?"

"You deserve it. You behaved like a prize bitch."

"I didn't have much choice, did I? And d'you think I enjoyed it?"

"*What?* You must have lapped it up. You weaselled your way into my life, and then into my flat, and finally into my bed. What technique! I bet Divine gave you two gold stars for that performance."

"And did you hate it all? Were you just being kind to me?"

He moved away and kicked sugar cubes against the skirting

board. "I can be conned," he said. "There's nothing easier than leading old Hale up the garden path. They'll be organizing coach-parties to do it next."

She watched him until he became uncomfortable; but he knew that the look on her pale, serious face would affect him, and he refused to look up.

"You're not the only vulnerable person in the world, David," she said. "Why d'you think I'm here now?"

"You came to collect your bonus, I expect."

"Oh, for God's sake, stop that cheap cynicism, it only soils you." Her sudden anger startled him, and he looked up. Astonishing how much strength that small, slim body contained. She said, "I came here because I couldn't think of anywhere else to go. I lost you last night, and I lost my job this morning."

"Pan Am fired you?"

"No, not really. I suppose I made them fire me. I behaved very . . . primitively."

She half-smiled, but Hale refused to give in. He said, "No doubt Divine will look after you. I expect a girl with your talents is in constant demand. You'll find a bed somewhere."

She was furious again. "You just can't damn well resist it, can you? If you really hate me so much, if you really want to hurt me, why don't you hit me? Why don't you revel in some *real* pain?" She was standing in front of him, grabbing his fist, lifting his arm. "Go on, do it! Get your own back! Stop talking for once and do something! Do *anything*, but don't just stand there admiring your martyrdom!"

He shoved her away, but she came back. "That didn't hurt, it didn't hurt at all. Don't you know how to hit people so that it hurts?" She slapped his face, and the edge of her hand bent his nose and brought tears to his eyes. He lashed out and punched her on the shoulder. She gasped and blinked and came at him again. He dodged, and grabbed her arms. For a long moment they wrestled. He stumbled, and she lost balance and lurched against him. There was an instant when the wrestling exhausted itself and became the desperate hug of an embrace, and at that moment her tears came; and Hale allowed his muscles and his mind slowly and gratefully to relax.

Zeller read a Motorway exit sign and checked it on the map. "Maidenhead," he said. "That leaves about ninety miles to go. Say . . . an hour and a quarter from now." Starin made no reply. "About three-forty-five, give or take nothing," Zeller said.

"Just keep it legal, that's all," Starin told him. "How much petrol have you got?"

"Plenty. More than enough to get us there, anyway."

Starin rested his head and closed his eyes. "You look unhappy, Grobic," he said. "If you are going to be car-sick you had better travel in the boot."

"No, no, Colonel. I feel fine." Grobic wasted a smile. "I was just wondering, Colonel . . . I mean, we have never actually seen this man. . . . It sounds ridiculous, I know, but . . . I suppose there is no doubt that he will be there when we arrive?"

"No doubt. I telephoned him last night, person-to-person. He is expecting us."

"Expecting *us?*" Zeller said.

"Expecting a television crew. The B.B.C. is very interested in his work. He'll be there, all right. Now shut up, both of you."

Gibson crunched through the scattered sugar cubes and sidefooted a piece of bone china into a corner. "Our Stanley tells me that you've taken leave of your senses," he said. "It looks to me like a perfectly normal scene of domestic harmony." He picked up the coffee-pot handle and spun it on his finger.

"Have a drink," Hale said. He and Carol were sitting on Divine's couch. "Since I'm going to be fired anyway, I thought I might as well break into sir's liquor. Help yourself. We're on the sherry. It lends an air of respectability."

"Did you see Mr. Starin off?" Carol asked.

"Yes. He took a kind of hairy balloon along with him. Some sort of technical adviser, I expect." Gibson poured himself Scotch. "No ice?"

"Hubbard refuses to help, I'm afraid," Hale said. "So no ice. I nearly hit him with the sugar bowl," he explained. "I suppose you know that Divine is hot on Starin's trail, and all that? I seem to have been the last one to find out. Mrs. Hubbard knew all about it a week past Thursday. She saw it on television, I think." He finished his sherry and poured another.

"With any luck, we'll *all* see it on television tomorrow," Carol said.

"Much as I loathe Divine's greater gut, I've got to admit it's a hell of a good idea," Gibson said. "A whole troupe of Russian kidnappers caught for all the world to see as they try to put the snatch on a top scientist. Now that's show-biz."

"And that's *all* it is, too," Hale said. "It's a colossal counter-intelligence TV spectacular. It won't actually accomplish anything."

"But that's the name of the game, these days," Gibson said. "Let's face it: we can't beat them and we can't join them, so we have to play a spoiling game. Personally, I think it's rather good." He found a cigar in Divine's desk.

"Why? It's a fake melodrama which isn't going to do the Russians any real harm," Hale said. "It's just a bit of cheap propaganda. Next week you'll be back at work again. Right?"

Gibson opened another drawer, "Ah! Soda," he said. "That's better. . . . It's all a question of getting things in balance, you see. Cheers."

Hubbard opened the door but did not come in. "Telephone, Mr. Gibson," he said. He glanced disapprovingly at the other two.

"Not me, chum," Gibson said. "I came off duty half an hour ago."

"I think you should, Mr. Gibson. You see, it's Paris. They say the plane has landed, but Starin wasn't on it."

Exit 16: Swindon. Another thirty-six or thirty-seven miles to go. The rain had passed, the sun was out, the road was drying fast. Zeller glanced at Starin and saw that his eyes were open. "Half an hour, Colonel, maybe forty minutes. I guess the Ambassador knows by now that you're not in Paris."

Starin grunted. "You've been watching behind?"

"Nobody followed."

Grobic opened his mouth, thought better of it, looked away, changed his mind again, and said, "I suppose the Embassy is sure to have the Trade Mission watched."

"We're not taking him back to the Trade Mission."

"Ah."

Zeller said, "My guess would be a chartered aircraft from some nice quiet airfield."

"Wrong," Starin said. "I'm using a Russian freighter from the Port of London. She sails tonight."

"You know best," Zeller said. "I'd have thought a plane was a lot faster."

"Perhaps. But airfields are the easiest of traps to close. I know; I have done it, often. Furthermore, British charter pilots do not willingly fly to East Germany, which in any case is a distance of eight hundred miles and would require an aircraft of conspicuous size."

"And cost," Grobic added.

Starin gave him a bleak look. "Spare me your penetrating tactical insights, Grobic," he said. He tossed a map of Bristol into Grobic's lap. "Get your brain into high gear and direct Zeller." He closed his eyes again.

Gibson stopped scribbling and hung up the phone. "Air France say they can't tell us any more than we know already. He refused to go, he made the plane turn back, he got off, and when last seen he was streaking for the exit."

Carol said, "What about the car that took him there?"

"That came back empty," Gibson told her. "I know because I followed it."

"That's meaingless anyway, there are thousands of damn cars," Hale pointed out. "And he wouldn't be in a hurry unless he had somewhere urgent to go."

The phone rang. Hubbard answered it. "Major Divine's plane took off fifteen minutes ago," he announced.

"Charming," Gibson muttered.

"So Starin's somewhere in England," Hale said, "going we don't know where and doing we don't know what."

There was a short, unhappy pause.

"Unless he's really conned us all," Carol said, "it's got to be something to do with Project 107. Hasn't it?"

Hale shook his head. "You're just guessing."

"Well, of course I'm guessing." Her voice had a crisp edge. "What are *you* doing?"

Hubbard said worriedly, "I think we all ought to wait until the Major gets back."

"Do you?" Hale said. "I don't. I think we all ought to wring our hands and clutch our brows and throw our aprons over our heads. That should do the trick." Hubbard was offended. He looked at the stain on the wall.

"Let's just think about it from Starin's point of view," Gibson said. "He had transport waiting for him at the airport. So he *knew* he wasn't going to Paris. But he wanted everyone to think that he *had* gone. Why?"

Hubbard had found a small plastic dustpan and brush. They watched him start to sweep up the broken china. "It's a mess, all right," Hale said.

Grobic had his head down, plotting a course on the road map, when he felt the car lose speed. They were leaving the Motorway, freewheeling down towards a traffic circle. Zeller shifted his foot to the brake.

"Hey, what exit is this?" Grobic asked.

"This is Bristol." Zeller waved generously.

"Yes, but what *exit?*"

"Exit, schmexit. Bristol you want, Bristol you got, at the earliest possible opportunity. Now, where's the party?" Zeller eased into the traffic circle and picked up speed. "Point me."

Grobic fumbled with the map. "We have to get to a district called Redland," he said. He began to panic: What the hell had happened to Redland? "It's sort of between the part called Clifton and . . . and somewhere else."

"Fine. Fine," said Zeller. "So point me."

"What road is this?" Grobic asked.

"You have the map, Grobic. I just have the wheel."

"I know I have the map, dammit." Grobic was getting rattled: Starin was watching. "But how do I know where to look? Maybe this bit is *off* the damn map. That's why I asked which exit."

"I didn't notice which exit. You didn't say it mattered."

"I didn't say to leave the Motorway, either!"

"Stay cool, Grobic. Just point me, that's all I ask." They were completing their second lap of the traffic circle.

Miserably, Grobic studied the signs. They told him nothing of value. Starin cleared his throat. "Go that way," Grobic ordered desperately. The signs said Downend, Kingswood, Warmley. Grobic began searching the map. None of these places seemed to be shown. He scanned furiously, whispering the names over to himself. They must be here somewhere; they *must*; the bastards were hiding in this stupid tangle of streets and streams and railways.

Zeller cruised on. He could see a major road junction not far ahead. Maybe Grobic would have worked out something by then.

Grobic looked up, and stared at a Baptist church as if it were a pagoda. "Look, are you absolutely *sure* this is Bristol?" he asked.

"We know something," Carol said. "We know Starin wants 107 and we know Starin's in England. That's a start."

"It's a start in the wrong direction," Hale told her. "107 is James and James is in Paris, as Starin well knows. That's why he got rid of Sanders, because he obviously knew that my Zurich paper was a fake and a swindle."

"Maybe so," Gibson said. "But why kill him?"

"To discourage the others, I suppose. Starin must be getting pretty fed up with people crowding him lately."

"Could be." Gibson didn't sound convinced. "The way it smells to me, I think Starin just suddenly felt like clearing the decks for action."

"But what action?"

"I keep saying it," Carol said. "107. He's after it. He must be."

"Don't be bloody silly," Hale said, irritated.

Carol refused to concede. "What else can it possibly be?" she asked. The combination of beauty and logic destroyed Hale. "Rubbish," he muttered. He knew that his face was turning red.

Gibson yawned. "God, what a day. . . . Come on, we're getting nowhere. Someone suggest something. Anything."

Carol glanced at Hale, but he was stiff and silent. "The Peake Building?" she said.

"For heaven's *sake!*" Hale growled.

Gibson thought about it. "That's where it all began, and that's where a lot of it went wrong," he said.

"I've been all through that place," Hale told him. "I've met everyone and I've seen everything. Several times over."

"When you come right down to it," Carol said to Gibson, "what other lead have we?"

Gibson stood up. "Come on," he said. "If we jump up and down hard enough, something might fall off a shelf." Hale scowled and followed them out, hanging back so that he could see more of Carol's legs.

"This would never have happened if you hadn't taken the wrong exit," Grobic complained. "I had it all worked out for the right exit."

"Stop the car," Starin said. Zeller pulled over and parked at a bus stop. "Give me the map." Grobic hastily passed it back, tearing it against the headrest. "Where are we?"

"Somewhere here, Colonel." Grobic's gesture covered ten or twelve square miles of east Bristol. "We want to go *there*." He moved his finger a long way westward. "There isn't a straight road anywhere."

"What is the name of this street?" Starin asked. Grobic and Zeller looked up and down and found no sign. Starin wound down the window. "Please," he asked distinctly, "where are we?"

Two men were waiting for a bus. They looked at him stolidly, as if he were trying to borrow money. "Redland," he said. "We want Redland." It sounded like an old-fashioned battlecry.

"Ah," said one man: a railwayman, with a face like an abandoned parcel. "Go straight the way you're pointed for . . . ooh . . . a mile. A good mile. Then turn right, by the old cinema, and—"

"No, no," the other man interrupted. "That's no good." He gave the railwayman a pitying smile. "What you talkin' about, turn right by the cinema? That's no good, is it?"

" 'Tis, for Redland," the railwayman insisted.

"Rubbish. They got all diversions up around there now. You can't go through."

"Since when? I never seen none."

"Ages, they been up. Ages." The other man addressed Starin. "Go back the way you come, squire, until you see the second set of lights—"

"What you on about?" The railwayman was indignant. "That's bloody miles out of their way, that is. Bloody *miles*.

Listen 'ere," he told Starin, "see where that bus is turnin'? Go down there, mate. You go down there and keep straight on. You can't miss it."

"Waste of time," the other man said.

"Listen—"

"Know where they'll end up? Half-way through bloody Speedwell! What's the point of sending 'em to bloody Speedwell?"

"Never mind," Starin said. "Just tell me where we are *now*." But they were too busy interrupting each other. Starin looked at Grobic. "Did you get anything from all that?" he asked. "No," Grobic said. A horn blared, deep and vibrant. Starin turned. There was a double-decker bus six inches behind them. "Get out of here," he told Zeller.

The Ambassador tugged at a desk drawer and lifted out a jar of seltzer salts. His secretary took it from him and unscrewed the lid.

"But all that was more than an hour ago," the Ambassador said into the telephone. "Why didn't you call me sooner? When you landed?"

"Mr. Ambassador," Kolek said. He was smiling to hide his pain. "We land at Orly. Nobody meets me. I speak no French. I speak no English. I have no French money. I have no English money to change into French money. I don't know your telephone number. I don't know the address of the Embassy here. The sun is blazing down. And the flying has given me severe heartburn. Now, what was your question, again?" He carried the phone over to the sideboard and cut himself another wedge of Brie.

"All right," the Ambassador said. He took the fizzing glass and drank it down. "All right. Eeuuugh. . . . Have you any idea what he's doing?"

"Yes. I think he is looking for a man called Henderson."

"Henderson. Where?"

"I don't know," Kolek said. "He never told me."

Zeller squeezed the Volvo between a double-parked delivery van and a refuse truck. They were in a busy shopping street which narrowed and twisted unpredictably. "You still reckon this is the main route into town?" he asked.

"Shut up and drive," Grobic snapped. His eyes flickered from the street to the map and back again. The car crossed a short, heavy bridge. "That's the railway," Grobic said. "I've got it now. There's a T-junction coming up, isn't there?"

"Yes," Zeller said.

"Turn right."

"I can't. It's one-way." Zeller turned left.

"Blast," Grobic whispered. He twisted his head and searched the map with a chewed fingernail. "That's all right," he said loudly. "This must be Paragon Avenue. Take the first right into East View."

Zeller turned right. "This is Cumberland Gardens, not East View," he said. He pointed at the name.

"*What?*" Grobic stared. "It can't be." He scrabbled at the map. "There *isn't* any Gardens off Paragon Avenue. None at all."

"That wasn't Paragon Avenue," Starin said from the back seat.

"Oh my God," Grobic muttered.

"And this is a dead-end," Zeller said. He turned the car, with difficulty, and drove back.

"Give me the map," Starin ordered Grobic. "And find a policeman," he told Zeller. "Already you two have wasted an hour. Anger will not solve this problem or I would smash your synthetic heads together."

They drove on, through crooked and unpromising streets, and failed to find a policeman.

"No wonder this country never gets invaded," Grobic said gloomily. "You couldn't find it even if you captured it."

Hale knew the way, so he drove Gibson and Carol to the Peake Building. A tall, stringy man was waiting for them in the lobby. He had hollow cheeks and disapproving eyes, and he kept his right hand firmly in the grip of his left, in case it wanted to shake hands with the wrong people. "Mr. Hubbard telephoned to say that you were coming," he said. "I have nothing to tell you, and I forbid you to disrupt the work of the staff in any way."

"Trust bloody Hubbard," Gibson said wearily.

"You must be Dr. Henriques," Hale said. "I'm Hale, and—"

"There is nothing more to be said. It's all in Divine's hands."

"Divine dropped it," Gibson told him. "He's gone abroad and left us in charge. We want to talk about James."

"I'm afraid that's out of the question," Henriques said. "My schedule is exceedingly full, and besides I know next to nothing of the man."

"Then who does?" Carol asked. Henriques looked down at her, surprised that she too could speak. *"Please,"* she said, with a smile that was rape from the neck up.

Henriques's head twitched, and he bared his old teeth at her. "Yes, well, since you ask me," he said, stretching out the experience, "I suppose I might as well tell you that the answer to that one is . . . is Sennet. Dr. Sennet." He beamed like a dying flashlight.

Hale and Gibson went past him, one on either side, heading for the lift. "I say, there!" Henriques called. "He's not in. He's gone home. Feeling poorly." They came back. "Where does he live?" Gibson asked. Carol squeezed Henriques's arm. "Please take us," she said. *"Please?"*

"Where shall I park?" Zeller asked.

"In the car park, idiot," Starin told him. Zeller drove into a space marked VISITORS, and they walked over to the physics building. It looked like four public libraries stacked on top of each other and tied together with drainpipes.

Starin asked the hall porter for Mr. Henderson. The man asked Starin his name. "Binstock," Starin said. "From the B.B.C." The man spoke to Henderson on the phone and then sent them up.

Henderson was waiting at the door to his room. He was a tall man who had never completely grown into his height: the polo-neck sweater and bottle-green corduroy trousers did little to disguise his scrawny build. His mouth and nose were thin but his eyes were large: large and grey and surprisingly confident. He wore his hair in a fuzzy, lop-sided bush. A slight stoop brought his head down to conversational level, and this attitude emphasized his thoughtful, concerned expression. Henderson looked like a man who made a point of treating every case on its merits, and if it didn't have any obvious merits he'd scout around and borrow some from another case of similar size and weight.

He welcomed them. "You know," he said, "I honestly can't imagine what B.B.C.-TV sees in me. Is it for a quiz show?"

"To tell the truth, Mr. Henderson, that was a slight deception," Starin said. "When I explain, I'm sure you'll appreciate the reason for it. In point of fact, we are not from the B.B.C. We are from the Special Branch."

"Good Lord!" Henderson stared, and laughed. "Special Branch! Well I'm damned. . . . I'll probably look even worse in *your* pictures."

Starin gave a short, tough chuckle. "These are my colleagues: Mr. Fitzgerald and Mr. Meredith, also of the Special Branch."

"*Three* Special Branch men? How extraordinary. How flattering. Or should one feel guilty?"

"Well . . . I'll explain, Mr. Henderson, and then you can decide."

Henderson found chairs for them. They sat in a circle. Starin said, "I believe you've been collaborating with Professor James on Research Project 107."

"You believe correctly. But nobody's supposed to know about all that."

"Quite. Did you know that James is in Paris?"

"Really? No, I didn't, but it doesn't altogether surprise me. I had a feeling he wasn't at the Peake any more. I've tried to call him there once or twice. What's he up to in Paris?"

"You're probably not aware that James's life has been threatened."

"*What?* Who by?"

Starin steepled his fingers and looked at Henderson over the top. "Or that your own life is in considerable danger, too."

"Oh, come off it." Henderson smiled, but nobody else was smiling so he stopped.

"For those two reasons," Starin went on, "we would like you to come to Paris with us, now."

"What—today? That's quite impossible. Out of the question. I'm playing cricket for the department at six o'clock, for one thing. We've got a match against Archaeology and Anthropology. I'm opening bat."

"Nevertheless, we think you should leave now. And bring with you as much of Project 107 as you can."

Henderson tipped his chair back and studied Starin's face. "You're serious, aren't you?" he said. "I'm not going to Paris, for God's sake! Why the hell should I? Who says I'm in any danger? It's absolute nonsense."

"I suppose it must sound strange to you. I assure you it's true. After all, we should know."

Grobic and Zeller sat squarely, and watched Henderson gravely. Starin glanced at his watch and waited for Henderson to reply. The attention began to disconcert Henderson. "The whole thing's unbelievable," he said. "I just don't believe it. . . . How do I know that you're . . . what you say you are, anyway?"

Starin handed him a dark-blue, stiff-bound document, like a

miniature passport. Henderson looked at it and flicked through the pages and read a few words, but his mind was elsewhere. He gave it back.

"Paris," he said. "Damn it all, why Paris?"

"Good question," Starin said crisply. "I should have explained earlier. James went to Paris to get specialist medical treatment." Henderson nodded. "The treatment has been extremely effective, but these threats to his life have made him restless. He says he wants to come back to England. The doctors think that would be dangerous, possibly fatal. Hence the urgent need for you to go to Paris."

"But why? What good would it do?"

"For one thing, it would be a lot easier for us to protect you both. For another, it would reassure James. He has become very nervous about Project 107, and he keeps asking if you are all right. He badly needs to see you."

Henderson folded his arms and let his head sink, while he thought about all this. He surveyed his visitors through half-opened eyes. "I'm sorry," he said at last. "It's just too fantastic. I simply can't accept it."

"Not at all," Starin said mildly. "I didn't really expect you to, Mr. Henderson. Not at first, that is. In your shoes I think I'd require more evidence too. Now, sir, I'm in no position to tell you what to do. I can only suggest, and my suggestion is: call Special Branch headquarters in London. Call them now, and talk to Mr. Lee. He sent us here." Starin gave Henderson a card with a number printed on it. "Ask for extension four-oh-nine. Transferred charge, of course."

For a moment Henderson chewed on a corner of the card. He stoood up, reached for the phone, then stopped. "No," he said. "I think perhaps I'll make the call from another room, if you don't mind."

"Why, certainly," Starin said.

Sennet lived in a semi-detached house with heavily leaded bow windows and concrete gnomes fishing for goldfish in the front garden. Hale parked across the garage entrance at the side and rang the doorbell. Beige chimes pealed deep inside. They stood on the doorstep and breathed the warm, honey-suckle-scented air, and listened to the birds twittering with suburban restraint. Gibson thumped the doorbell again, and squinted through the letterbox. "Bugger it," he said. He got one of the gnomes from the fishpond and smashed a pane of glass in the front door. "Good heavens!" Henriques said. "Is that necessary?"

A woman stopped by the garden gate. "I say," she exclaimed. "What on earth d'you think you're up to?"

"See to her," Gibson muttered. He groped inside the door and released the catch. As they went in they heard Henriques begin, "I can assure you, madam, that under the circumstances . . ."

The living-room was empty. Hale looked into the kitchen and saw Sennet trying to hide behind the end of a Welsh dresser. He was holding a glass of whisky. "Get away!" he said. "Get out of here!"

"What's the matter?" Hale asked. "What's wrong?"

"I certainly wouldn't tell *you*," Sennet said, with a little flare of indignation.

Hale took Sennet's drink away and threw it in the sink. "Yes, you will," he said. He poked him hard on the breastbone. Sennet gasped, his knees folded out, and he sat down with a thud which rattled the cups on the dresser. "Get up," Hale said in disgust, but Sennet toppled sideways, and lay with his knees up to his chest and his eyes closed. Hale prodded him in the rump a couple of times and then tried to drag him to his feet. The best he could do was to sit him against the wall. He took a handful of hair and shook Sennet's head. "What's been going on?" he barked. "What have you been up to with Fitzgerald?" Sennet started crying. Hale kept hold of his hair and slapped him in the face just as Henriques came in.

"I say, is that really necessary?" Henriques protested.

"Not only necessary but surprisingly enjoyable." Hale rapped Sennet's head against the wall.

Gibson said, "I don't think you've seen around the garden, have you?" He took Carol out through the back door. She looked pale, and took his arm.

"Really, I don't know—" Henriques began.

"You don't know anything," Hale said. "So shut up."

————————

The operator on the switchboard at the Trade Mission said yes, she would pay for the call from Bristol. The call came through. "Special Branch," she said.

"Extension four-oh-nine, please," Henderson said. She connected him to Starin's office. A short, stout man of about fifty picked up the phone. "Lee," he said.

"My name is Henderson. I expect you know why I'm calling you."

"Quite," said Lee. "And I'm damned glad you are." He picked up his notes. "I expect Binstock has told you we feel you ought to be in Paris, with James."

"Yes. He seems to think I'm in danger." Henderson glanced about the empty room to make sure nobody could hear him making a fool of himself.

"I agree with him, and I'll tell you why. You're not the first, you see."

Henderson listened for about a minute, until Lee said goodbye. He hung up and went outside. He looked as if he had swallowed a sharp prune-stone and it was still going down.

————————

Hale slapped Sennet again, curling his fingers on the backhand so that the knuckles made damage. Blood now mingled with the tears. Sennet slumped, sobbing. A cigarette lighter slid out of his pocket. Hale took it and lit it. "Oily hair," he said, wiping his hand on Sennet's shoulder. "Should go up a treat."

He touched the flame to Sennet's hair. It frizzled, and he screamed and scrambled to his feet, scrabbling at his head. Hale kicked his legs from under him and put a foot on his chest and reached out with the lighter again.

"Oh God oh God oh God," Sennet shouted. He flung his head from side to side, but the lighter followed his movements and came closer. Suddenly he lay still. "All right," he said. "All right. Don't burn me."

Hale let him get up. "Must have a drink," Sennet mumbled. He pointed at a cupboard. Hale opened it and took out a bottle of whisky. Sennet wiped his mouth, smearing blood across his chin, and put out a hand.

Hale smashed the bottle in the sink. "Talk first," he said.

Sennet gaped, and burst into tears. After a moment Henriques turned away, his head in his hands. Sennet sagged against the dresser and wept, head lolling, nose starting to run. Hale filled a jug with water and drenched him. "Talk first, then drink," he said.

Sennet hid behind his hands. Hale took another bottle from the cupboard and smashed it in the sink. Sennet's head jerked up. He watched, fascinated and horrified, as Hale destroyed three more bottles of whisky and two of gin, and the stench of the wasted spirit made his nostrils twitch. Henriques had retreated to the door. Hale opened another cupboard and dragged out a case of Scotch. He took four bottles, two in each hand, and smashed them against each other. "All right," Sennet croaked. Hale pulled out four more bottles, and Sennet's lips stumbled with haste. "I'll tell you, I'll tell you!" he cried. "His name is Henderson."

Starin turned, smiling, as Henderson came in. "Was he there?" he asked.

"He was there," Henderson said. "And he told me about the . . . the others."

Starin nodded, seriously. "Yes, the others. I'm afraid they

provide the most convincing argument of all." He took out a heavy buff envelope, and from it shook a bunch of glossy prints. The first showed a middle-aged man who had been shot in the face. Henderson looked, and quickly looked away. "That was Jolliffe, a metallurgist at the University of London," Starin said. He moved the picture to the bottom. "Dr. Kellner, biology, Manchester University." Henderson's eyes moved across reluctantly, and blinked with shock. That picture was removed, to reveal another. "I'm afraid this was a woman, Miss Mary Blakison, a very brilliant young mathematician at Cambridge," Starin said. Henderson shut his eyes and swallowed.

"That's enough," he said. "I believe you."

Starin put the pictures back in the envelope. "As I said at the start, Mr. Henderson, this is a very serious affair. The Special Branch does not send three men all the way from London to Bristol unless it is necessary. Indeed, essential."

Henderson looked as if the prune-stone had lodged somewhere and taken root. "I didn't know anything about all those people," he said. "It wasn't in the papers, was it?"

"No," Starin said. "None of it."

Henderson hunched his thin shoulders, and hugged his elbows to his sides. "It's dreadful," he said. "All right. What d'you want me to do?"

Hale found Sennet's telephone, called directory enquiries, and got the number of Henderson's department at Bristol University. That took three minutes. He dialled the number. It rang, and rang. He rested his head against Sennet's floral wallpaper and methodically stripped the leaves from a potted plant on Sennet's wrought-iron telephone table. At last the tone stopped. "Physics," said a woman. Hale asked for Henderson.

Henderson was over by a filing cabinet, sorting papers for Grobic and Zeller to pack, when the phone rang. Starin picked it up. "Extension seven-six-two," he said.

"Mr. Henderson?"

"I'm afraid you have the wrong number." Starin pressed down the buttons and ended the call. "They wanted Hendrickson," he said.

"Oh," Henderson said. "He's over in Botany. I keep getting his calls." He went back to his papers. Starin quietly placed the receiver beside the telephone and covered them both with a newspaper. There was still a slight purr, but it was very faint. "Nearly ready," Henderson said.

"Look, I couldn't mistake that voice," Hale said. "He's there, he's in Bristol, and he's in Henderson's room. So now what the hell do we do?"

"Call back," Carol said.

"I've tried. I think the phone's off the hook."

Gibson said, "Can't we get somebody in the university to . . . to . . ."

"Somebody? Who? In any case, long before we've explained everything and convinced someone, Starin will have left and taken Henderson with him."

"The police?" Henriques suggested.

"With no description, no car number? And not even a crime, yet?" Henriques retired, defeated.

Hale said, "In fact, we might as well assume that they *have* left."

"Wait a minute," Carol said. "Don't rush things. Let's start again. A minute or two ago they were in Henderson's room, which is in the university physics department. Right?"

"Right."

"Well, maybe they haven't left yet. It might look bad if Starin tried to rush Henderson out. And when they *do* go, they'll almost certainly leave by the main entrance, won't they? And who knows, maybe the place has a doorman, or a caretaker, or a janitor or someone. What we have to do now is find him, recruit him, and get him to write down the number of Starin's car."

"Nice work, if you can get it," Hale said. "I suppose it's worth trying." He dialled the physics department again. "Is there a doorman or a caretaker in the physics building, please? Ah! . . . Good. Yes, I would." He looked up. "Hall porter," he whispered.

"Let me," Carol said. He gave her the phone. "Is this the hall porter's office?" she enquired in a well-scrubbed voice. "New Scotland Yard here. . . . Yes . . . New Scotland Yard. Hold the line please, I have a call for you from the Assistant Commissioner." She scratched the mouthpiece with her fingernail. "Your call to Bristol, Sir David."

Hale took the phone. "Good afternoon," he said plummily. "I expect you were rather surprised to hear from us. . . . Yes. . . . No, no, no, of course not; I'm sure you haven't. . . . Actually, this is a matter where *you* can help *us*. . . . On the contrary, I'm perfectly serious. . . . Well, it's something quite simple but extremely important, believe me, and your co-operation could make a crucial difference, d'you see. . . . Yes. . . . Well, I hoped you'd say that. . . . Splendid. . . . Look, I'll tell you what we want you to do. . . ."

Grobic and Zeller loaded the cardboard boxes into the boot of the Volvo, while Starin and Henderson watched. "There's enough for you to work with there?" Starin asked. Henderson nodded. He looked around, at the car park, at the building, at the hall porter sweeping the steps. Everything looked so ordinary. "What about money?" he asked. "What about passports, and clothes, and stuff?"

"All that's been taken care of."

Grobic held the door, and Henderson got in the back. Starin sat beside him. Grobic went in front. Zeller got behind the wheel.

"I still can't quite believe it," Henderson said; but by then the car was moving.

Hale came into Sennet's living-room. Carol and Gibson looked up. "The Bristol police say they're looking out for the car now," he told them. "They'll call us as soon as they find it. Where's Sennet?"

"Henriques is putting him to bed," Gibson said. "Did you have any trouble with the law?"

"Some, at first. Their senior copper didn't want to call Hubbard, so I got Hubbard to call him. After that they warmed up fast."

"But they still won't arrest Starin."

Hale shrugged. "For no crime? Plus full diplomatic immunity? They *can't* arrest him, can they? They can't even follow him. Not that I want them to; he might panic."

Carol put her feet up on the sofa. "So . . . Starin's got Henderson, he's got 107, he's got what he wants."

"He's got it and he's off with it," Gibson said. "He won't want to stick around Bristol."

"So far so bad," Hale said. "Where's the bastard *going*? That's the question."

Carol said, "A hundred to one he's coming back to London."

"That's sheer wishful thinking," Hale said. "He might go anywhere. Why come back here?"

"Because it's his base. And if it comes to that, why should he go anywhere else?"

"To put us off the scent."

"What scent? He doesn't know we're on to him, unless he recognized your voice. And you only said two words, didn't you?"

"Yes."

Gibson was getting excited. "In any case, he must have made his plans *in advance*, right? And if he's driving from Bristol to London he has to come down the Motorway, the M4. He must."

"Why must?" Hale demanded. "To suit your needs? I don't accept that he's bringing Henderson to London, but even if he is I can show you half a dozen other routes—the A4 through Reading, the A40 past Oxford, or the Wantage road, or he could go south and come across Salisbury Plain, or—"

A cushion hit him in the face. "Yes, yes, yes, David," Carol said, "and he could take the Polar route and sneak in the back way, via Leningrad and Southend-on-Sea. But why should he? What possible good can it do him?"

"Sure," Gibson said. "Why trundle along a narrow, twisty old lane with built-in wall-to-wall congestion, when you can do a steady seventy along a brand-new three-lane Motorway? Why take four or five hours when you can get there in two? Why?"

"You've got it all worked out, haven't you?" Hale said angrily. "What are you going to say when it turns out that he's half-way over the Severn Bridge into Wales?"

The telephone rang. Hale strode out to answer it.

Carol retrieved her cushion. "Well, what *are* we going to say?" she asked Gibson. They looked at each other soberly.

"I was afraid you might ask that," he said. "I've been trying not to think of it."

Hale came in and looked at the fireplace. "Silly bugger's coming this way," he said.

"What—on the Motorway?" Gibson asked.

Hale nodded gloomily.

"That's a stroke of luck," Carol said.

"Is it?" Hale asked. "What's your magic plan for intercepting a Volvo on a Motorway at seventy miles an hour? Grappling irons?"

"Who says we have to intercept them?" Gibson said. "All we need do is latch onto them and follow them until they stop. They can't drive to Russia."

"And then what?"

"Dunno. Depends what *they* do, doesn't it?"

"You're assuming we find them in the first place. That's a hell of a long Motorway with a hell of a lot of cars on it, including probably several hundred Volvos, and you seem to—"

"Ah, *but,*" Carol said. "We know when they left, don't we, and we can guess their speed, can't we? I mean, Starin won't risk getting done for speeding, not at this stage in the game. If we leave now we can flash up the Motorway while they're coming down it, work out a spot well ahead of them where there's an interchange, and then just park on the bridge and wait for them to zip underneath." She gave Hale a smile of irresistible encouragement.

"I doubt it," Hale said grudgingly.

"I don't," Gibson said. "Then we nip back onto the Motorway behind them."

Hale sniffed. "You'll need eyes like a flock of hawks."

"Binoculars," Gibson said.

"Anyway, hawks don't flock," Carol added. "They're solitary. Are you coming, hawk?"

Hale grunted. "Might as well, I suppose."

"Pity," Gibson said. "I was getting ready to chat up your bird."

Henderson had been thinking, and not enjoying it. "Those photographs," he said. He shook his head. "I've never seen anything like that. I just can't understand people who could do that sort of thing."

"The mind of an urban guerrilla is twisted in a particularly vicious way," Starin said, "especially when you throw in a dash of anarchism."

"These people have a particular hate for young scientists. Is that right?"

"Yes."

"And James? What have they got against him?"

"He is associated with you."

Henderson stared at the Motorway traffic streaking west on the opposite lanes. "I don't see what they hope to achieve," he said. "It's crazy."

Starin said, "Their only aim is destruction, Mr. Henderson. They don't need to make sense."

Hale rested his elbows on the parapet of the bridge and watched the traffic slide in and out of the slightly overblown image which the binoculars gave. Three long-distance trucks crawled into the picture, so he took a moment to ease his back and rest his eyes. The Motorway sliced through soft green hillside, and the air felt warm and spacious, sweet with cowslips and exhaust.

"I've been thinking about last night," he said to Carol. He put the binoculars to his eyes again.

"Yes . . . last night. Mmmm. Things got rather confused last night, didn't they? I was still trying to do my duty for Divine, but you were being so enormously poker-faced that I'm afraid I just couldn't stand it any more. I mean, all professional interests aside, I was really worried. In fact, I was scared stiff."

Hale grunted and adjusted the focus. "And that Trade Reception at the Cumberland; you were on duty there, too, weren't you? Which was why you wouldn't get out of the car. And I thought you were just being stubborn. I should have guessed."

"Blinded by luv, I expect," Gibson remarked.

"That nightmare . . ." Hale began.

"It didn't happen," Carol said. "I made it up. I needed it for blackmail. Sorry."

"Like the doily?"

"No," she said. "The doily was real. I may be a bitch, but I'm not a complete bitch."

Gibson put his pen away. "If they averaged seventy-five, which is illegal but not impossible, I reckon they would have gone past us seven minutes ago."

"Suppose they averaged seventy," Hale said.

240

"Ah, that's different. They would have gone past us *two* minutes ago."

"Always assuming they're still on the M4."

"You have a point," Gibson agreed. "A pointless point, but still a point."

"How long should we keep this up?" Carol asked. "Maybe we ought to set a time limit."

Gibson said, "If it means going back to Divine, I suggest six months."

"*Got 'em,*" Hale said quietly. Gibson and Carol turned. "It's that dark-green Volvo, just passing the Esso tanker. I think Fitzgerald's driving, and that looks like Grobic beside him."

"Don't let them see you," Carol warned.

Hale took one last look. "No doubt about it," he said. He heard Gibson start the engine.

———

Zeller set the turn-indicator blinking and eased into the slow lane. "Petrol," he said. Starin grunted. The Volvo curved up the entry road and slowed as Zeller studied the set-up of the service station, looking for the best place to stop. He pulled up by a pump on the outside rank and sat waiting for an attendant.

Gibson, driving the Saab, had been a hundred yards behind. He saw the Volvo come to a stop as he came off the Motorway, and he drove around the back of the service station, through the restaurant car park and out towards the exit lane from the service station. He stopped on the far side of a tow-truck.

Hale said, "All we have to do is block the exit. If they can't get back on the Motorway we'll have time to get the police here and cook up some excuse for questioning Starin while we isolate Henderson."

"Sounds primitive," Gibson said, "but I can't think of anything better." He looked at Carol. She shook her head. "I'll call the police," she said. She ran to the restaurant.

"Is this car big enough to block the exit?" Hale asked. "They'll get around it, won't they?"

"Bound to. Let's take that tow-truck, too."

"No keys."

"It's on the slope, it'll roll."

The attendant came over to the Volvo. "Four-star, fill her up," Zeller said. He took out his wallet. The nozzle plunged into the tank, the numerals began whirling. The attendant stood with his brain in neutral. Henderson looked up at him. Brother, he thought, you little know.

Hale got the hand-brake off and felt the tow-truck move. When it was rolling at a steady walking-pace Gibson drove past and got in front to help clear the way. The truck was a reinforced ex-Army fifteen-hundredweight, and it quickly picked up speed. Together they covered about thirty yards down the exit lane. Gibson sounded his horn, pulled over to the left next to an outcrop of rock, and stopped. Hale ran the truck up onto the right-hand kerb until they were side-by-side, tramped on the brakes, left the gears in reverse, and jumped out. While Gibson was locking the car, Hale removed the truck's distributor head.

"Can we get back?" Gibson asked.

Hale peered around the back. "I think so, if we move fast. That car-and-caravan seems to be blocking their view. At least, I can't see the Volvo. Can you?"

"No."

They ran up the hill. They had covered twenty yards when the caravan-owner drove away from the pumps and exposed the Volvo. Starin saw two men running, and recognized Hale. "Go!" he shouted at Zeller.

Zeller turned the key, gunned the engine, and let out the clutch all in one movement, just as the attendant was getting a grip of the nozzle handle. The man staggered, and for a second petrol hosed over the back of the car, while the wheels spun on the oil-soaked concrete. Then the Volvo took off.

Hale and Gibson watched it swerve past them. By now the car-and-caravan had added themselves to the barrier ahead. Zeller drove the Volvo hard up over the kerb and on up the grass-and-rock slope, trying to bypass the block. His tyres raced against the soggy turn and threw up black mud; he had to steer crabwise, forcing the nose uphill; the car bucked and crashed into holes and caromed off boulders. One boulder was too big, and the car slewed sideways with the impact, leaving the nose high and petrol slopping out over the rear wheel. Zeller revved furiously, but the back axle was jammed on a plinth of rock. Sparks flew, and the petrol ignited with a dull boom. Starin kicked open the door and dragged Henderson out. "It's them!" he shouted. "Run!"

Henderson ran for ten yards before he remembered his papers in the boot, and stopped. The car was burning hard now: the whole of the rear end was hidden in rich black smoke with tassels of flame swinging at the bottom. A tire exploded and sprayed chunks of rubber into the air. Starin grabbed his arm but he dragged himself free, appalled by the swift, intense wasting of so much of his life.

Hale and Gibson scrambled across the slope. Starin shouted, and pointed at them. Henderson stared and suddenly realized, and turned to run. Terror confused his feet, and within ten paces he had fallen. Starin hesitated, and then ran on. Hale reached Henderson just as he got to his feet with a hunk of rock in his hand. Henderson was staring with fear and fury, and he swung the rock at Hale's head as if to smash them both. Hale tried to dodge the rock, and deflected its edge with his left arm. Henderson lurched forward and while he was off-balance Hale handed him off, the butt of his palm slamming into his chest. Henderson's heels tripped. He dropped backwards down the steep slope, and his head thudded against the ground.

Hale looked for Gibson, and saw him running towards the Motorway. The other three men were already on the Motorway, dodging cars, heading for the centre-strip. A Jaguar swerved to avoid them, its horn blaring, and Gibson stopped on the hard shoulder, helpless before a rush of traffic. At that instant the Volvo's petrol tank blew up. The blast knocked Hale on his face.

Divine looked up when Hale came in, and Hale noticed how his eyes were fractured with red at the corners. God was getting old.

"They tell me Henderson's still in hospital," Divine said. "But I suppose you know all about that."

"Yes, I know all about it." Hale sat down. "Concussion, or something. Anyway, he can't think straight yet, can't remember what happened to him. Poor bastard got himself thoroughly caught in the middle, didn't he?"

"You feel badly about it."

"Oh . . . yes and no." Hale looked for words to tell Divine how he felt, and gave up. He said, "If Henderson loses his memory . . . that'll be just about the end, that will."

"I don't want you to blame yourself for it."

"No? What do you suggest I blame? Gravity?"

"It wasn't your fault, that's all. In any case, Henderson's amnesia may be only temporary. Forget it."

"Is that supposed to be a joke? No, I can see it isn't. Forget it. . . . I suppose we might as well forget all those papers in the boot, too. They were his, weren't they?"

"Yes, indeed."

"Not much of them left after the fire, and the firemen."

Divine yawned with fatigue. "Well . . . they were of value only to Henderson, anyway."

Hale went hot with anger. "Is that your idea of an epitaph? The man worked like hell and made a tremendous discovery—"

"It was a load of balls," Divine said curtly. "Why d'you think I used it? Why d'you think I used James? I risked them because they were valueless. Project 107 was a scientific daydream."

"Rubbish! Who says so?"

"I told you before: Henriques."

"*Henriques?* That mental pygmy? He counts on his fingers. You mean to say you took *his* word?"

"I did indeed. Henriques is a good man." Divine stretched "A bad golfer, but a good man."

Hale felt his anger go sour. "Now tell me Starin's been given a knighthood," he said.

"Well, he's back in London, we do know that; but not for long, I imagine. Future indefinite, I should say. Rather like you, Hale."

"Me? Oh no, not like me. I quit hours ago. I'm no good at this game. I can't lie, I can't cheat, and I get upset when people I know have their heads blown open. I don't think I'll ever grow up to be a real, warm, genuine, callous, murdering bastard like you, sir."

"You may perhaps have grounds for feeling misused, Hale," Divine said, "but please remember that ill-fortune does not excuse bad manners. Good day."

Hale went out. Carol was waiting in the ante-room. She stood and looked at him. To someone else she might have seemed serious, but Hale knew those wide-awake eyes and that mobile mouth.

"I thought I heard a bit of a crash in there," she said. "It looks as if the doily fell off at last."

"It didn't fall," he said. "It was pushed."